J
FICTION
STEWART

Stewart, Sharon
(Sharon Roberta),
1944-

Raven quest.

DATE		

RAVEN QUEST

RAVEN QUEST

SHARON STEWART

 Carolrhoda Books, Inc. • Minneapolis

This book was inspired by the raven research of Dr. Bernd Heinrich of the University of Vermont. Any factual inaccuracies are the responsibility of the author.

First American edition published in 2005 by Carolrhoda Books, Inc.
Published by arrangement with Scholastic Canada Ltd.

Carolrhoda Books, Inc.
A division of Lerner Publishing Group
241 First Avenue North
Minneapolis, MN 55401 U.S.A.

Website address: www.lernerbooks.com

Library of Congress Cataloging-in-Publication Data

Stewart, Sharon (Sharon Roberta), 1944–
    Raven quest / Sharon Stewart.—1st American ed.
      p.   cm.
    Summary: Tok, the most nimble-winged of the young ravens, is banished for a crime he did not commit, and the only way he can restore his honor and his father's name is to perform a brave and daring deed to benefit all ravenkind.
    ISBN-13: 978–1–57505–894–8 (alk. paper)
    ISBN-10: 1–57505–894–4 (alk. paper)
    [1. Ravens—Fiction. 2. Heroes—Fiction. 3. Adventure and adventurers—Fiction. 4. Wolves—Fiction. 5. Fantasy.] I. Title.
PZ7.S84988Ra 2005
[Fic]—dc22   2005003158

Manufactured in the Unites States of America
1 2 3 4 5 6 – BP – 10 09 08 07 06 05

To Roderick, for all the reasons

Prologue

Two ravens do battle, circling high and higher in the icy winter air. The smaller of the two, weakened by long fasting, fights for nest and mate; the other, younger and stronger, to rob him of both. Croaking, they buffet each other with their wings, and slash with their beaks. Then they seize each other with their claws, flipping over in midair and plummeting toward the dark roof of the forest below. At the last moment they break off, and crash through the tops of the trees, losing each other for a moment among the branches, then burst out into a narrow valley between two ridges. There the challenger gets above the defender, and drives him to the ground. At bay now, the smaller bird turns on his back, grappling with his claws and striking out with his beak. But his enemy is stronger: pinning the defender down, he shatters his breast with a few mighty blows of his beak. Blood stains the snow. Leisurely, contemptuously, the victor pecks out the eyes of his dead rival. Then he beats away into the north wind on heavy wings.

From the eaves of the forest another raven has watched the battle. She launches herself into the air and circles once over the valley, uttering a hoarse cry. Then she follows the victor, leaving the body alone, very small, very black against the field of snow.

Part 1

Tok

Chapter 1

*First Raven was jealous of other birds. "You've given
me no gifts," he croaked to Skyah. "No sweet voice,
no bright feathers."*

*"Try your wings," said the Maker, "and dance
for my pleasure."*
                            —Myths of the Tellers

Tok angled his wings against the wind, feeling its lift, letting it carry him toward the south ridge of Mount Storm.
Though spring had come late after a winter of deep snows,
the rocky crest was already bare. The rays of the strength-
ening sun had heated it, creating a thermal of rising warm
air. Tok soared, letting the currents carry him upward,
higher and higher.

Above him, he could see dozens of other ravens. He
used his long sight, bringing the distant shapes into
sharper focus. As he watched, two of them dipped their
wings and rolled over and over in the air, diving down
toward the trees before righting themselves with easy flaps
of their wings and riding the thermal up again. Others

followed them, and soon the air was full of ravens tumbling like black leaves against the bright blue sky.

The skydance! Catching the excitement, Tok bent his right wing and flipped onto his back for a moment. Then he did a barrel roll and powered into a falling-leaf dive that dropped him steeply earthward. Wind sang through his flight feathers as he tumbled, croaking his delight. At last he pulled himself out of the dive, his flight muscles straining in his breast, and rose quickly, the blood pulsing in his head. Finding the thermal, he rode it up again.

At the top he saw Tarkah, a young raven who had appeared in the roost the previous autumn.

"*Rrrock!* Show-off!" she teased, as Tok came up level with her. At her far wingtip flew Grakk, another newcomer. Ever since he had arrived, the big ravenet had pushed himself forward as the leader of the young ravens. All the other males had humbled themselves before him, except for Tok. Now Grakk stared angrily at him and Tok glared back.

"Come on, you snail-wings, dance!" cried Tarkah, twisting into a barrel roll that challenged them to follow.

Tok copied her movement easily, coming out of his own roll level with Tarkah's near wingtip. Grakk, a bigger bird and heavier in the air, misjudged and came out some way below them. Tarkah winked at Tok with the whitelids at the corners of her eyes. Then the two of them dove straight down, wings angled backward, with Grakk trailing behind. Giddy with delight, they saw the ground rushing up at them. At the last possible moment they pulled out of the power dive. Then with lazy wing-flaps they found the thermal.

As they rode it back up, Grakk edged nearer to Tok and gave him a savage blow with his wing. With a mocking quork, Tok rolled onto his back and flew upside down, waving his claws in pretended helplessness, leveling out again just beyond Grakk's reach.

Grakk shot him a glance of pure hatred. "Fancy dancing, clown. But it takes more than that to make a raven-lord," he croaked. "Bravest at the carcass, strongest against your enemies, that's what wins a lady and a territory."

"Big boasts, Grakk," jeered Tarkah, who had caught up with them again. "You haven't won anything yet."

"But I'm Grakk, son of Barakk, lord of wide lands," Grakk snapped. "I have something to boast about. Not like this no-name. He has no lineage. Why, he's no better than a common crow!"

A *crow!* It was a deadly insult to compare a raven to one of those clumsy flappers.

In fury, Tok launched himself at Grakk, giving him a sharp blow with his claws, then doing an insolent loop over his back. "You should know. A crow must have taught you to fly, numb-wing," he taunted. But anger spoiled the joy of flight for him. Even in the air his lack of a proper name followed him. And there was nothing he could do about it. Nothing!

Tilting his wings, he banked away from the other two, arrowing downward toward the forest far below.

"Oh, for Skyah's sake!" Tarkah called after him. "Do you have to be so touchy?"

Tok paid no heed. How could she understand how he felt? She had an honorable name. In another year or two she would command a mate, and a fine territory. But an outcast like him had no future. In the air he was more than a match for any other ravenet. But on the feeding ground, at the roost, he was nobody. Tok No-Name, the others called him, when they thought to call him anything at all.

He landed on the limb of a large maple tree, still leafless after the long winter. Despite his rage, he was ever hungry, and he scanned the floor of the forest, the fine hairlike feathers over his nostrils quivering. At first he saw nothing. Then, the tiniest movement. At the foot of the tree, a careless deer mouse popped out of its snow tunnel, half-collapsed now by the thaw. On silent wings, Tok dropped down and seized it, crushing it with his powerful beak.

Though his hunger was fierce, a sudden thought kept him from bolting down the food. His mother, Lady Groh, had ignored him and had driven him away when he tried to find out more about his father. But now it was the Moon of Nestlings, and food would always be welcome.

Lifting himself low over the treetops, he headed for the cliff where Lord and Lady Groh had built this season's nest. His mother had chosen a different site from the place where Tok had been raised. Were her memories as bad as his? he wondered, remembering the bitter cold of that time, the gnawing hunger in his unfilled belly, and the shriveled bodies of his brother and sister lying in the bottom of the nest. Smaller and weaker than Tok, they had been unable to survive such hardship. Even his mother had come close to starving when the food supply failed long before snowmelt. He could dimly remember his father, fasted to a shadow of himself, winging in with small mouthfuls of food. And then he came no more.

Soon afterward, his mother had returned to the nest, her crop bulging with food. It had the rank flavor of old carrion when she stuffed it down Tok's throat, but he'd gulped it eagerly. He soon found out where the food came from, for a big male raven named Groh appeared at the nest. He stared at Tok with cold eyes, begrudging every morsel of food Tok's mother shared with him. Frightened of he knew not what, Tok had left the nest as soon as he could fly. After that he flapped awkwardly after his mother—Lady Groh now—trying to learn as best he could how to find food for himself. All too soon she lost interest in him, and spent her time foraging and soaring with her new mate. Both adults drove Tok off when he tried to follow them. And so he was left alone.

At first it was not too bad, for it was the way of young ravens to become independent as soon as they could. Tok had banded with other youngsters of his year, foraging in groups wherever they could sneak into the territories of the lords and ladies, roosting together at night for comfort. But soon rumors spread within the roost, and his companions began to shun him. Because when they challenged him, he had no lineage, no father's name, to give them. His mother had refused to tell him, nor would anyone else.

And so Tok had come to understand that his father had shamed him somehow. When the other young birds dispersed at the end of the summer, flying boldly away to seek new homes and future mates, he had not followed them, though his wings ached to. But how could he go? he asked himself. With no lineage to offer a mate, he would never be able to hold a territory. He would remain an outsider wherever he went. His only hope was that his mother would change her mind and grant him his father's name.

So he had stayed where he was, stealing a living as best he could on the fringes of the lords and ladies' territories. In the Moon of the Falling Leaves, young birds who had dispersed from distant ravenlands began to arrive. For a while he was caught up in the excitement of their fall flights, practicing his skill in the air, and rejoicing in it. He joined the bold groups that invaded the feeding grounds, defying the lords and ladies by their sheer numbers and demanding their share of the food. Then came the Moon of the Hunters, the only time the Two-Legs ventured far into the mountains. Most of them only took a little meat from the moose and deer they killed. So the forest was rich in skinned carcasses—prime pickings for ravens. Tok feasted along with the others.

In the evening roosts he listened eagerly to the adventures of the young strangers, especially the dashing Tarkah. For a time he was allowed to be one of them, for the newcomers knew nothing of his past and accepted him as just another stranger like themselves. But then as winter closed in, solitary adult birds from the near territories began to roost with the young newcomers. *They* all knew about Tok's father and they told the story to the newcomers. When Tok shuffled closer in the roost, trying to hear for himself, everyone would fall silent and stare at him. So once again he was Tok No-Name. And now some called him Tok Stay-at-Home too.

Grakk in particular liked to taunt him. A dominant bird, he swaggered about the feeding grounds with bristling feathers, yielding to no one but the lords and ladies. At night in the roost Tok often heard him boasting about his strength and his family to the others; he also had plenty to say about shame and outcasts and ravenets too cowardly to seek new homes. There were always murmurs and whispers of agreement, and the birds who roosted closest to Tok would move a bit further off along the branches. So in the end he was lonelier than ever.

Of course he never let the others know how he felt. When they snubbed him, he pretended to ignore them. He met every taunt with a jeer, every push with a shove. And in the air he danced circles around them. It was all he could do to show he was *kora* despite his lack of a name.

Carrying the mouse in his beak, Tok now approached Lord and Lady Groh's nest. Groh hated him, he knew, and would drive him away on sight. So he landed first in a tree some distance away. But for once his luck was good, and he could see that his mother was alone. She was standing in the nest with half-open wings, shading her four downy nestlings from the direct rays of the sun. Karah, Lady Groh, was a big bird and she was a beauty. In the sunlight her black feathers shone with iridescent color—green on her cheeks and underparts, with shades of blue and violet on her back and wings and wedge-shaped tail.

Tok ventured closer, landing on a dead tree stub beside the nest.

"It's you," said Lady Groh, staring at him out of cold amber eyes. "Why are you still around to shame me? You have no more *kora* than your father—you should have left with your yearmates. If Groh finds you here, he'll kill you!" But she leaned over and snatched the mouse Tok offered all the same. Tearing strips off it, she pulped them in her beak, then crammed the meat down the gaping throats of her nestlings. The last bit of skin she swallowed herself. When she finished, she stropped her beak on the twigs of the nest. Then she roused her feathers so they stood out stiffly around her body, making her look twice her real size. "Go away," she ordered. "Leave this land, as you should have done last year."

"Then grant me my father's name," begged Tok. "How can I go without that?"

Lady Groh hissed in annoyance. "The Kort declared your father *unkora*. He let us starve, remember? You nearly died like the others."

Condemned by the Kort! It was even worse than Tok had thought, for the Kort was the source of ravenlaw. Its dooms were final, fatal. . . . "B–but maybe he just couldn't find food . . ." he quavered.

Lady Groh cut him off. "Your father betrayed us!" she snapped. "He died for that and his name died with him. We ravens do not speak the names of the dishonored, those who die *unkora*. No ravenlines must ever bear their names. That is your misfortune."

"But Mother—" Tok began. Suddenly a great buffet sent him reeling from his perch. Before he could regain his balance he was struck again and then again. He flapped awkwardly into a spruce tree far below the nest, and faced his attacker, who settled on a branch above.

It was Lord Groh. He roused, shaking his feathers, and stared down at Tok menacingly. "What do you mean by sneaking around my nest, meddling with my family?" he growled.

"I . . . I only brought my mother some food," protested Tok. "For the nestlings."

"Bah." Groh fanned his huge wings. "We need no help from the likes of you, outcast. Off with you before I kill you as I did your no-good father!"

Tok shuddered. It was true, then, what he had half-guessed but feared to believe. "Murderer!" he croaked.

Groh dove at him, slashing with his beak, driving him from his branch. They rocketed out of the trees, the larger bird right on Tok's tail as he dodged wildly this way and that. But Tok's nimble wings saved him, and Groh soon began to fall behind.

"Next time I'll leave you for carrion!" the older bird cried. With a sweep of his powerful wings he wheeled and flew back in the direction of the nest.

Tok flew until he could fly no more, then he plunged into a dense copse of fir trees. Heart pounding, he peered out, scarcely able to believe Groh was not still behind him—Groh, his father's murderer!

He shivered. His mother had accepted Groh soon after her mate's disappearance, granting him the territory and the lordship. She must have known Tok's father would never return. Had she and Groh planned his father's death, then? In misery, Tok buried his head under his wing.

Chapter 2

A raven without lineage is unkora; *he or she
may not take a mate or hold territory.*

—Dooms of the Kort

He awoke in the first grey light of dawn. Rousing his feathers he sleepily began to preen them, running the length of each one through his beak. Then he poked his head out of the surrounding branches, gazing westward toward the tall tree where the young ravens roosted. After his escape from Lord Groh he had decided not to return there for the night, but instead had roosted alone in a small but thick-needled fir not too far away.

As he watched, a group of ravenets lifted away from the roost. They circled above it for a while, calling to others to join them, then headed south. Tok could tell from the way they flew, with strong steady wingbeats, that they knew exactly where they were going. Someone must have found a new feeding ground, he told himself. A good one. At the thought, his hunger sharpened from a dull ache to a demanding pang. Tok hurled himself into the air and flew after the others.

He caught up to them in a valley two ridges over. There, in a glade deep within the forest, the melting snow had revealed the carcass of a deer, dead perhaps of starvation during the long winter. As always, Grakk was there at the head of the band of ravenets. They had all gathered in the snow at a respectful distance from the deer. Tok drifted in on silent wings and perched in a tree nearby.

"Didn't I tell you?" Grakk was croaking. "I found it yesterday and decided to share it with all of you." He raised feathers that stood out like ears on the top of his head, fluffed his shaggy leg feathers, and swaggered to and fro, flashing his whitelids at the others.

"Had to, you mean," scoffed Tarkah, with a disrespectful flip of her wings. "This is the territory of Lord and Lady Korak, as you know very well. Do you think they'd let you help yourself without the rest of us to back you up?" The other ravens cawed and quorked their agreement.

"Still we owe thanks to Grakk." Laka, the smallest female in the group, spoke up quickly. "He has sharp eyes indeed." As she spoke, she bowed toward Grakk, fluffing her head feathers and quivering her wings.

Tarkah glared at her. "Let him prove it's safe before we thank him," she said. "Are you waiting for moss to grow on you, Grakk?" she added. Yet they all knew very well why he hesitated. Even the most innocent-seeming food might be dangerous. It might still be alive, capable of giving a kick that could crush wing or breast. Or it might be rigged with a trap or some other evil device of the Two-Legs. There was no end to their trickery.

Grakk settled his feathers, smoothing them around his

body, and turned back toward the carcass of the deer. It might be perfectly safe, and he would gain great *kora* by being the first to dare to approach it. But if it wasn't safe . . . "I found it," he countered. "Why should I take the risk?"

"What a hero!" jeered Tarkah. "Shall I do it for you?"

Tok saw his chance. Gliding down, he landed between Grakk and the carcass, took a hop toward it, then stopped.

"What, another timid fellow?" trilled Tarkah. The other ravens karked and quorked. "Oh, go on, Tok," she urged. "If we wait for Grakk to do it, we'll still be here at sundown."

He'd show her! He'd show them all! Screwing up his courage, Tok hopped toward the carcass. But Grakk bounded into the air and landed in front of him, cutting him off. Both ravens roused, puffed up their throat hackles and raised their feathery ears. Standing tall, beaks upraised, each tried to stare the other down.

"For Skyah's sake, Grakk. Let him get on with it. I'm hungry!" cried Tarkah.

Grakk gave his wings an angry flap, and turned away. "Go ahead, No-Name," he muttered. "No loss if something happens to *you*."

Tok hopped closer and closer to the carcass. Twice, when gusts of wind ruffled the deer's fur, the sudden movements made him jump back, beak agape in panic. But he made himself move forward again. At last he jabbed at the carcass with his heavy beak. Though he jumped back again nervously, he knew that the deer was safely dead. Its hide, softened by freezing and thawing, had yielded easily under his beak. He gave a quork of triumph.

An answering chorus rose from the other ravenets. They would be able to feed! For on a fresh or frozen kill, their beaks were too blunt to part the hide and reach the meat inside. Many and many a time they had had to go hungry with food right there before them. With another croak Tok flapped up onto the deer's back, the position of honor.

In a rage, Grakk launched himself at him, and a blow from his wing tumbled Tok onto his back in the snow. "My find," growled Grakk, raising his feather ears and gaping his beak menacingly. "You feed last—as your rank deserves."

"Not fair!" cried Tarkah. "Tok took the risk. The *kora* is his."

Tok's eyes glowed, and he fluffed his feathers. She thought well of him after all!

The ravenets moved in on the carcass, and in a moment it was surrounded by the eager band. Stripping away pieces of the rotted hide, they plunged their beaks into the rich meat below.

Tok watched bitterly as Grakk took the place of honor and began to feed. Why should he have the *kora* when it was he, Tok, who had risked himself? Furious, he flew at the bigger bird, beak agape, and tried to drive him from his perch. The two of them struck and clawed at each other, rolling over and over in the wet snow. Then a shadow of wings passed overhead, and harsh quorks challenged the ravenets. Lord and Lady Korak had arrived to defend what was theirs.

Tok and Grakk broke apart, glaring at each other. "You've interfered with me for the last time," hissed Grakk, spreading his wings menacingly. "I'll settle with you."

But just then the lord and lady dived at the ravenets, trying to drive them off. Grakk had to duck and ended up with a beakful of snow. With a gleeful quork, Tok tweaked his enemy's tail feathers, flapping out of reach when he tried to strike back. This brought a loud croak of laughter from Tarkah.

Too hungry to give up their prize, the young ravens held their ground in spite of the air attacks. Then the older birds landed and tried to drive them away by combat, the lord against the young male ravens, and the lady against the females. But the ravenets only jeered and danced out of reach, snatching mouthfuls from the carcass the moment the others' backs were turned.

Meanwhile, Grakk set up a furious yelling. Soon other young ravens arrived to reinforce them. Outnumbered, the lord and lady at last gave up their attack and settled in to feed with the rest. But Lord Korak took care to knock Grakk off the top of the carcass, taking the position of honor for himself.

By the time they were all full-fed, the wind had shifted, and flakes of snow were falling thickly around them. One by one, Grakk and the rest of the ravenets straggled back toward the roost, leaving the lord and lady perched on the carcass. Tok trailed behind the others. First they circled high above the roost, tumbling and calling to attract others, then they gathered in groups in trees some distance away. At last, in twos and threes and then in larger and larger numbers, they landed in the old spruce, working their way deep among its sheltering branches.

Inside, there was much shoving and complaining as birds chose a favorite branch or sought to save space for a roost mate. The air was full of croaks and whistles as newcomers arrived, boasting of the day's adventures. Outside the sheltering boughs, a blizzard raged now, but inside it was dark and comfortable. The roost was more crowded than usual that night, as the storm had brought in many birds who would otherwise have roosted alone or in their own territories.

Tok locked his scaly toes around a branch and rode its rocking movement easily. As usual he was at the edge of things, away from the higher-status birds who clustered in choice positions near the trunk of the tree. He could hear Tarkah's bell-like voice there, in the midst of a crowd of young females. What did she really think of him? Tok thought wistfully. Then he remembered how she had spoken up for him that day, and his heart warmed a little. Despite all her teasing, she did like him. If only things were different. If only . . .

He could hear Grakk's hoarse voice too. Telling everyone what to think. Then he heard his own name mentioned, and there was a shifting and rattling of claws among the branches. What malice was Grakk spreading now? Turning his back, Tok began to preen his feathers. Sometimes he wondered why he even bothered to challenge Grakk. Without a name, he could never lead the ravenets himself, never be a ravenlord. But Grakk was a bully, though Tok sensed that he was a coward at heart. Somebody had to stand up to him.

"May I?" croaked a deep voice. A latecomer pushed his way through the outer branches, bringing a flurry of snowflakes with him. Shaking more snow from his wings, he settled near Tok in the darkness. From the way he spoke, Tok could tell the newcomer was of noble lineage. He had asked the question only out of courtesy, not because he felt any doubt about his right to a place.

"The honor is ours, my lord," muttered Tok, shifting over a little.

"Your name, youngster?" the stranger asked.

"Tok, my lord."

The stranger chuckled. "You can drop the title," he said. "I have no mate now and don't hold a territory. My days of glory are done. Just call me Pruk."

Tok peered at him through the darkness. It did happen. A lord or lady who lost a mate sometimes chose not to take another, and so gave up claim to hold a territory. Not like his own mother, he thought bitterly. Had she even waited till his father was dead to find a replacement?

"Tok," the stranger mused. "Not a name I know. And you didn't speak your lineage."

Shame burned in Tok's breast, and for a moment he didn't answer. "I have none," he muttered at last. "My father died and my mother denies me his name. She has a new lord now."

There was a rustle as Pruk lifted his feathers in surprise and settled them again. "A most headstrong lady," he murmured. "May I know her name?"

"She is Karah, Lady Groh . . . now," answered Tok.

There was a long silence, broken only by the whining of the wind outside the roost. Then, "I see," said Pruk. After a moment he added, "I knew your father, young Tok."

Tok felt every one of his feathers stiffen. "You did?" he gasped. For no other raven had ever admitted to that. It was as if Tok's father had never existed among them. Scarcely daring to ask so great a thing, he added in a low voice, "Could . . . would you tell me his name?"

Pruk made a sound deep in his throat, a sound that might have been a sigh or a growl. "I can't do that," he said. "It's forbidden, as well you know. Only your lady mother can grant you his name."

Tok hung his head. Pruk was right. It was the way of ravenkind. He should never have asked. Now Pruk would want no more to do with him—and he had just begun to enjoy having someone to talk to.

But the old raven went on, "I will tell you this, though. Your father was a noble lord. I don't believe he deserved death and the banning of his name. But last winter was the hardest in raven memory. Many of us died, for the snow lay deep over all the feeding grounds. Only those who had cached plenty of food in the autumn—or who stole from others' caches—survived."

"Stole! But isn't that *unkora?*"

Pruk gave a harsh quork of laughter. "*Unkora* to steal? Not at all! We ravens are a freebooting lot. I'm surprised you don't know that already. We take what we want when we can. It's our way. Only duty to mate and nestlings is sacred. In any case, nobody saw what became of your father. There was no trace of him. There was only Groh's word for what your father had done. Yet the crime was so black that the Kort had to act. And so your father's name was banned, and his lineage disallowed. And that, young Tok, is why you have no name."

A crime so black! Tok trembled. "My mother said he betrayed us, but . . ."

"In that time of hardship your father let his mate and nestlings starve while he himself had food," said Pruk gravely. "So said Groh."

"He lied!" cried Tok. A sleepy chorus of croaks from neighboring birds made him lower his voice. "My father didn't have food," he went on more quietly. "He was starving too. I know. I was old enough to see how thin he was, how dull his feathers looked. Didn't my mother tell that to the Kort?"

"She chose to keep silent, as was her right," replied Pruk. "Out of shame, it was said at the time."

Shame? wondered Tok. Or was it guilt? "I know Groh killed my father," he said in a small voice. "He told me so himself."

"Yes. But when the Kort heard Groh's account, they deemed your father's death *kora*. They didn't punish Groh for it." Pruk hesitated, then he went on. "There's more. It's ugly, but you should know it. Though his killing of your father was allowed, the Kort still censured Groh, for he broke ravenlaw. When your father was dead Groh pecked out his eyes."

Pecked out his eyes! Tok shuddered. That was what

was done to dead food animals, to carrion. No raven ever did that to another raven, even in the fiercest fight. Now he understood why the others despised him, why their eyes slid away as they avoided him. It was worse, far worse, than being Tok No-Name. He was Tok, son of an eyeless father, no more than carrion! Shame as well as guilt flowed in his veins with his father's tainted blood. Surely in all his life he could never gain enough *kora* to change that. Bowing his head, he said no more to Pruk that night. But he stayed awake listening to the moan and whistle of the wind until the storm blew itself out before morning.

Chapter 3

A foolish raven once fell in love with the moon.
He thought it was a shining pearl, and flew to
snatch it. But it was too heavy to carry. When the
moon is full you can see him there, still trying.
                                    —Myths of the Tellers

The next morning Tok fled the roost before dawn. Avoiding the new feeding ground, he foraged alone on the fringe of Lord Groh's territory. Near a pond he made a small meal of a half-frozen toad that had emerged from its winter slumber in the mud, only to be caught by yesterday's blizzard. It was not enough—not nearly enough. Trying to fill the ache inside him, he stuffed himself with dried berries that still clung to bushes around the pond. They didn't satisfy him either. Still hungry, he moped about the pond for a while, then he flew on with powerful swishes of his wings.

He made for Mount Storm and soared over its three-sided rocky summit. The Raven Mountains fell away below him, their peaks and rolling forest ridges freshly mantled in snow. Tok knew that in all that wide land he would always be last among ravens. Last in *kora* on the feeding grounds, allowed no more than the furthermost branch of any roost. The others would never accept him. He would never have a mate or hold territory or raise a family of his own.

Even if he flew somewhere else, he would still be alone. Raven lineages were known far and wide, so he couldn't just make up a name or claim to belong to a family not rightfully his own. If only his mother would give him his father's name! Then he could fly far, far away, and hope to find a place where the tale of his father's shame hadn't spread. But his mother would never tell him—he knew she wouldn't. And under ravenlaw she was the only one who could.

Tilting his wings he banked steeply over a ridge and landed on a tall tree stub. Beyond Mount Storm the clouds were lifting, rolling back to leave a sky of brightest blue. With the returning sun his keen ears picked up the *drip-drip-drip* of the thaw in the forest below. In the distance he saw other ravens rising to the skydance. Tarkah would be there, perhaps. He watched their joyous flight, but made no move to join them. His heart was too heavy.

If only he could prove himself somehow! *Kora* was everything, for ravenkind admired bravery and daring above all. In the winter roosts, he had heard Tellers recite tales of raven heroes and their adventures. But what could he do except dance? And that wasn't enough.

At the roost that night he sought out Pruk again. The older raven seemed glad enough to see him and listened patiently as Tok poured out his despair. Then he scratched the back of his head with one claw.

"It's true that a brave deed could gain you much *kora*, Tok," he said after a moment. "But it couldn't be just any deed. It would have to be something remarkable, something to benefit all of ravenkind." He gave his feathers a shake. "There are no deeds like that outside of old tales, I think. No, better to forget dreams of glory. Leave here and try your luck elsewhere. Even without a name, life will be better for you where everyone doesn't know about your father."

Tok knew Pruk was right. Yet his yearning for his father's name still tied him to the Raven Mountains like an invisible bond.

Around them, the other ravens settled in for the night. There was much talk of food or the lack of it. Grakk had once more led the ravenets to the new feeding ground. But a black bear, newly emerged from his winter den and very very hungry, had discovered the carcass of the deer too. Determined to have it to himself, he had sprawled on top of it, clawing fiercely at the angry ravenets. All they had been able to do was snatch a few mouthfuls as best they could. Disappointed, they were wondering now where their next meal would come from. It would be many days yet before the snow was gone and they could catch enough small game to fill their stomachs.

"Nothing but bugs and frogs and berries," one of them complained. "We eat no better than crows."

"Count yourself lucky if you can find enough of even that," counseled an older bird. "This winter has been almost as bad as the last one. Already some nestlings are dying as they did then."

Tok felt their sly glances seek him out in the darkness. As long as ravens went hungry his father's shame would never be forgotten. Never. It would be told and retold to teach youngsters the meaning of *kora*.

Now Laka chimed in. "Why must we ravenfolk go hungry?" she whined. "Crows and jays have their food. Why didn't Skyah provide for us as much as for them?"

So her toadying to Grakk hadn't gotten her any more food than the rest of them, thought Tok, feeling pleased.

"Stop complaining," croaked another. "Have you no *kora?*"

"Indeed. And it is *unkora* to question the wisdom of the Maker," an older female added. "Once things were very different for us ravens. Once we had the Grey Lords."

At once a chorus of voices rose up in the dark.

"Grey Lords? What Grey Lords?"

"Is a Teller among us? Is it a Telling?"

"Tell! Tell!"

Others shouted for quiet. When the clamor died down, the Teller shook her feathers and settled herself more comfortably on her perch. "Once, when the old world was younger," she began, "things were different among ravenkind. For one thing, in those days Two-Legs had no firesticks."

There was a rustle of surprise among the ravenets. Even fledglings knew about the deadly firesticks the Two-Legs used for hunting deer and moose. Every raven mother warned her children that the firesticks were often used to shoot ravens too.

"In those days," the Teller went on, "there were other creatures among us. One race of these was the Grey Lords. No other creatures were so fleet, so tireless in the hunt as they. And with them ravenkind had a special bond. Skyah made us two parts of one whole: we to find prey and lead the Grey Lords to it, they to kill and open the prey so that we as well as they might feed. In winter, when bears slumbered and lesser birds flew south, ravenkind and the Grey Lords ruled the north. And both lived well, each aiding the other as Skyah intended."

The ravenets hung on the Teller's words. A creature to hunt with them, to kill and open the bodies of prey for them? Young as they were, this first winter of their lives had already taught them the meaning of grinding, endless hunger, of food deep-buried in snow, or covered in frozen hide so beak and claw couldn't pierce it. And yet Tellers never lied. So the wonder must be true.

"What . . . what kind of creatures were the Grey Lords?" one ravenet blurted out.

"None of us knows for sure what manner of creature they were," replied the Teller. "They have been gone for years beyond the reckoning of any raven. Our tales tell us only that they were swift and grey. And that they were great singers. So they must have been birds."

"Birds? How big? Bigger than eagles?" cried a ravenet, and a babble of discussion followed.

When they quieted down a little, Tok asked, "What happened to the Grey Lords, Teller?"

"The Two-Legs killed them all." The Teller's voice was cold. "Because the Two-Legs came here to farm with their silly tame animals, so stupid, so easy to catch. How could we know it was forbidden to eat them? The Two-Legs had firesticks by then, and they shot us and the Grey Lords with them. They set traps and put out poisoned bait to make us all sicken and die. At last we ravens fled to these mountains where few Two-Legs ever came. The Grey Lords followed, but they couldn't hide themselves so easily. One by one they were hunted down. And then there were none."

A groan went up among the branches as the ravens thought of what had been lost.

"A curse on all Two-Legs," muttered one very hungry young bird.

"Never fear, Skyah punished the Two-Legs for their wickedness." The Teller's voice held a harsh note of triumph. "Rocks and stones, the very bones of the Earth, rose up through the soil. Their fields failed, and their wives and children grew thin and sickened. In the end the Two-Legs gave up their farms and moved south, leaving the wilds to us. But it was too late. There were no more Grey Lords."

She fell silent. The Telling was ended.

Chapter 4

Cache first, feast later.

—Raven proverb

By the middle of the next day, the true thaw had come and most of the snow from the blizzard was gone. Tok foraged alone again, and had some luck. Returning to the pond at the edge of Groh's territory, he turned over small stones along the edge with beak and claw. In this way he managed to find and eat some snails and crayfish, which only whetted his appetite. Then he caught and killed a hapless frog just emerged from its winter sleep and still too drowsy to escape. Tok could have bolted it down, easily, but decided to cache it instead for another day when foraging might not be so good. He flew with it into the fringes of the forest and hid it in a hole on the mossy side of a dead tree stub.

Just as he tucked it away, he heard the rattle of claws on bark, as though some other large bird were nearby, but when he looked around he could see nothing. Returning to the pond, he found a muskrat den dug into the side of a muddy bank. He knew that food scraps were often to be found outside such dens. Sure enough, the muskrat, full-fed on minnows it had caught in the fast-warming shallows of the pond, had left several fish outside the den. Tok swooped down and devoured them. There were some open mussel shells too, with bits of meat still clinging to them, and he pecked these clean before the muskrat emerged, hissing with rage, and drove him away.

After feeding he dozed for a while, then he climbed into the sky to dance his thanks to Skyah. He tumbled and spun in the air, swooping and diving in a salute to the Maker of All. After a while, hungry again, he circled back down to earth. The sun was still high, leaving him plenty of time to forage. But as he flew low over the forest, he could hear a great outcry. Many deep raven voices were croaking, but he was too far away to make sense of the sounds. Other ravenets were flying toward the roosting tree from all directions. Curious, he followed them. When he got close he saw Tarkah perched in a tree near the roost and dropped down to join her.

"What is it?" he demanded. "What's going on?"

"I don't know," admitted Tarkah. "The ravenlords have gone mad all of a sudden. I was foraging with some others near Black Ridge when some lords arrived and ordered us back to the roost at once. They kept swooping right over us until we went." She roused her feathers and settled them again. "They were very rude."

As she spoke a ravenlord drifted close overhead on silent wings, staring arrogantly down at them. The two ravenets ducked automatically. "You two—get to the roost at once!" he growled. "All you vagrants are under suspicion. Wait until you're called." Uttering a harsh cry, he wheeled away.

"That was Lord Korak," said Tok, as they dived for the roost. "I know we took meat from the deer on his territory, but why should he say we're suspects?"

"Well, I wasn't going to ask him, and I notice you didn't either," said Tarkah, as they plunged among the sheltering branches.

The roost seethed with indignant ravenets. It seemed that lords and ladies had suddenly set upon them wherever they were, ordering them back to the roost and driving them there by force if they refused to obey.

"Who do they think they are?" muttered Laka, preening her ruffled feathers. She had been set upon and roughed up by a ravenlady who caught her trying to hide in the woods.

Tarkah rattled her own feathers. "Don't be foolish," she snapped. "They know exactly who they are. They're the law. This land is theirs. To them we're nothing but poachers until we're old enough to take territories."

"Well, how long do we have to stay here then?" someone else muttered.

"As long as it takes for the Kort to gather," replied another.

A Kort! Tok shivered with excitement. Korts only assembled rarely, for raven lords and ladies normally lived alone on their large territories. What could have happened to make them turn on the ravenets and call a Kort?

A while later, Grakk dashed in with some other laggards, all looking fearfully behind them. A buzz of questions greeted them, but none of them could solve the mystery either.

A long time passed. The ravenets sat listening to a growing chorus of angry voices in the distance. Nobles must be gathering from all over the Raven Mountains.

At last Pruk appeared. "The lords and ladies have sent me to summon you to the Kort," he announced.

"But can't you tell us—" Tok began.

Grakk shouted him down. "Silence, No-Name," he yelled. "Let your betters speak." He turned to Pruk. "Haven't we the right to know what's wrong?" he demanded. "Why have the nobles turned against us?"

A mutter of assent rose from the ravenets.

Pruk ruffled his feathers. "The nest of Lord and Lady Groh has been destroyed," he said gravely. "Their nestlings have perished. The nobles believe some of you have committed this crime."

There was a moment of shocked silence, then shouts of protest followed.

"Who would dare to destroy a noble's nest? That's *unkora!*"

"Why suspect us—what do we have to do with it?"

"How dare they condemn us with no proof?"

Pruk clattered his beak loudly to bring them to order. "Nobody is condemned—as yet. But you are all summoned to the Kort, and go you must." Hopping to the end of the branch, he flew out of the roost.

Grudgingly, the mob of ravenets followed. Pruk led them many wingbeats to a glade near the foot of Mount Storm. At the north end of the open space stood the Kort

Tree, a tall silver maple that was still not in leaf. Its branches were black with the brooding shapes of the nobles. The rest of the ravenhorde, those who did not have the *kora* of holding territory, perched in evergreens along the sides of the glade. From the air, Tok stared down at the scene in awe. Never had he seen so many ravens in one place before!

Pruk landed in the middle of the clearing, the ravenets touching down around him in an angry black mob. "You must sit here quietly," he commanded, over their clamor. "Respect the Kort. Answer truthfully any questions put to you, or it will be the worse for you." Then he flew up into a fir tree at the side of the glade.

For long moments nothing was said. The assembled nobles stared fiercely down at the ravenets. The air crackled with their anger, and even the boldest young ravens were cowed, falling silent one by one. Tok listened to the wind sighing gently in the branches. Overhead, puffs of cloud raced across a pale blue sky. A day for dancing—but there would be no more of that for now.

At last the nobles stirred, rattling their feathers and flapping their wings as they muttered among themselves. Then Lady Korak flew to the Speaker's Branch directly above the assembled ravenets.

"As a senior noble and mother of nestlings, I have been chosen Speaker," she said, glaring down at them. "Pruk has told you the crime you are accused of."

"Nest-breakers! Murderers!" someone shrieked wildly, and Tok recognized his mother's voice. He scanned the Kort tree for her, and found her at last, perched high above

Lady Korak. Lord Groh and another noble were crowded close against her, supporting her on her perch.

"Karah, Lady Groh, please keep silent," said the Speaker gently. "The Kort recognizes your sorrow. Never fear—the guilty will be punished." Turning back to the ravenets she went on, "Whether it was one of you or many we don't know. But we're sure the nest-breaker was a ravenet, for such a thing has never happened in this land before."

Despite their awe of the Kort, there was a yell of protest from the ravenets.

"Does she mean we have no *kora?* Our lineages are honorable!"

"Why should they suspect us just because we're new-comers?"

"How do you know it was any kind of raven?" someone yelled. "It could have been an eagle or jay. Or a rac-coon . . . "

The Speaker shook her head. "The Grohs' nest was high on a rocky ledge," she replied. "No raccoon could reach it. The attacker came from the air. As to a jay or an eagle . . . " She spread her shoulders. "No jay could break a raven's nest. And they are cowardly birds—they would not dare even if they could. Nor do eagles often harm us, even when we nest on the same cliffs. Stupid they may be, but they have their own *kora.*"

"But why would any of us do something so wicked, my lady?" asked Tok.

Lady Korak stared down at him. "To spoil a nesting, perhaps. Fewer nestlings to feed mean more food is available for you ravenets. And you might hope to contest the territory—perhaps snatch a piece of it for yourselves."

The ravenets croaked their anger.

"No, never!"

"We're innocent!"

"Where's the proof?"

The Speaker waited for the shouting to die down. "We have no proof," she said. "But one or more among you must have seen something. You young ones are often in sight of each other, sneaking about our territories. We let you live at our expense. But nest-breaking we will not tolerate. So the Kort would have me say this to you: find the guilty ones among you and hand them over. If you do not . . . " she paused for emphasis, "the Kort will drive you from this land. All of you."

For a moment there was dead silence among the mob of ravenets. Then there was a babble of questions.

"I didn't see anything!"

"Nor I!"

"Where was the nest, anyway? I didn't see any nests."

Laka's voice rose above the others. "What are we going to do?" she wailed. "They'll chase us, kill us, if we don't tell them who did it!"

"But how can we when we don't know ourselves?" demanded Tarkah. She gave her head a shake. "Oh, please stop squealing!"

Tok felt numb. Unless the guilty ones came forward they were all lost. The justice of the Kort would be merciless. But who would give himself up willingly for certain death?

Then Grakk hopped forward out of the mob of ravenets. Keeping his feathers tight against his body, he bowed his head in submission before the Kort.

"My lady, I am Grakk, son of Barakk," he said. "Most of my companions know nothing about this. Only one of us is to blame. And it cannot be justice for all to suffer for the crime of one."

A gasp went up from the ravenets.

"Whaaa?" muttered Tok. Was Grakk going to save them by taking the blame? It didn't seem like him, somehow. He and Tarkah exchanged puzzled glances.

The Kort stirred on their perches, fixing their fierce eyes on Grakk.

"Go on," rasped the Speaker.

"My lady, I and many others foraged far from Lord Groh's territory today. But on my way back, I did see a ravenet on the Grohs' territory, near the pond, and flew down to investigate." He paused, then went on. "That raven was flying with something in his beak. He flew into the edge of the woods and I followed to see what he was doing. He was carrying a dead raven nestling. I saw him cache it in a tree."

Gasps of horror rose from the Kort and the ravenets.

"Caching a raven body!" someone exclaimed.

"Cannibal!" muttered another.

The Speaker drew herself up to her full height. "And the name of this killer?" she demanded.

"My lady, it was Tok," said Grakk, casting down his eyes and covering them with his whitelids.

Chapter 5

A lie is blacker than any raven's feather.
—Wisdom of the Tellers

"Liar!"

Tok heard Tarkah's angry shout from behind him, yet for a moment he was too numb to speak himself. Of course he'd cached something—the frog. And he'd thought he heard another bird nearby. Someone *had* been watching him, and that someone was Grakk—Grakk, who hated him. Now he had found a way to destroy him!

He took an angry hop toward the big ravenet. "Tarkah's right!" he shouted. "You're lying!"

"Grakk accuses you," the Speaker said coldly. "Defend yourself—if you can."

"I *was* near the pond, but it was a frog I was carrying, my lady," cried Tok. "Only a frog! I did cache it—in a hollow tree near the edge of the South Woods." Rousing his feathers, he took another threatening hop toward his enemy.

Grakk jumped backward. "I saw what I saw," he insisted.

Tok hissed in rage, but before he could attack, Lord Groh hurtled down from the Kort Tree like a thunderbolt. He landed face to face with Tok, closing his wings with a snap. He raised his ears and hackles, puffing his belly feathers until he looked twice his real size. "The nest-breaker is *mine*, Grakk," he growled. "Leave him to me!"

"Y–yes, my lord," muttered the big ravenet, edging away.

Groh turned and stared up at the Speaker. "Lady Korak," he said, "I believe what Grakk says. Tok the outcast knows exactly where our nest is. I caught him hanging about there two days ago. He hates me and would be glad to do me an injury, even though my lady is his mother."

"I only went to the nest to see her," protested Tok. "I brought food for the nestlings. Ask her," he added, gazing up at his mother in the tree above him.

"It's—" began Lady Groh, but Lord Groh cut her off.

"Say nothing, my lady!" he shouted. Leaping into the air, he flapped up beside her on the branch. "Don't try to defend the outcast," he went on. "You have suffered enough. And he is his father's son, remember!" He turned and stared at the others in the Kort. "What if he did bring food? He just wanted to spy on us, to plan this outrage. I claim justice!"

The assembled nobles stirred uneasily, ruffling their feathers and murmuring among themselves.

"Groh is right. This is Tok's vengeance against him for the matter of his father."

"It is a foul crime—Tok must be punished."

Then a deep voice spoke. "Wait, noble lords and ladies. I am no longer a ravenlord and have no right to vote in your final judgment. But I beg the Kort to hear me." It was Pruk.

"You may speak," said Lady Korak.

Pruk flew over to the Speaker's Branch. "There is still no evidence to prove Tok guilty," he pointed out. "We have only Grakk's word against Tok's."

Hope flamed in Tok's heart. "That's right!" he cried. "Let me go to the cache. I will bring back the frog—I will prove that I am innocent."

Grakk laughed. Puffing himself up, he stared at Tok. "Of course he will bring us back a frog—if he can catch one," he sneered. "It won't prove anything. Let *me* go, nobles of the Kort. I saw where he cached the body. I will bring it back for all to see."

Pruk shook his head. "No. There must be no doubt. Better that I go."

The Speaker turned and scanned the Kort. Many birds were bobbing their heads. "So be it," she said. "Pruk has nothing to gain or lose from this. Let the accused tell him the location of the cache. Pruk alone shall search it out."

Pruk glided down on silent wings and landed beside Tok. "Where did you hide the frog, Tok?" he asked. His voice was kind but very grave.

Tok swallowed hard. "At the edge of the South Woods in Lord and Lady Groh's territory. About fifty wingbeats from the near side of the pond. There's a half-dead spruce stub. I cached the frog there in a hole partway up, on the mossy side. There were dry leaves in the hole, and I put them on top of it."

With a few flaps of his great wings, Pruk took to the air and banked over the treetops in the direction of the South Woods. Tok stood frozen, following Pruk with his eyes until he vanished from sight. Pruk would find the frog, bring it back. He would be saved. But Grakk had dishonored him by his accusation. Turning to glare at him, he hissed, "You'll pay for this!"

Grakk drew himself up to his full height, and stared up into the Kort Tree, pretending to ignore him. But when Tarkah hopped closer to Tok, Grakk roused his feathers and moved toward her menacingly. "Keep away, Tarkah," he warned. "He's a murderer."

"So *you* say," snapped Tarkah.

"Quiet, all of you!" ordered the Speaker, and the ravenets fell silent.

Time passed. Tok closed his eyes, trying to think how many wingbeats it would be from the glade to the edge of the South Woods. What if Pruk couldn't find the cache? What would the nobles do then?

At last they heard the heavy swish of raven wings and Pruk circled over the glade. He flew directly to the Speaker's Branch and gently laid down what he had been carrying in his beak. It was the limp body of a dead nestling, still clad in its baby down.

High up in the Kort Tree, Lady Groh shrieked aloud.

"Lady Groh, my lord," said Pruk, bowing. "My deepest sympathy and sorrow." Then, gazing down at Tok, he went on, "I'm sorry, Tok, but this is what I found in the cache you described so exactly."

Now the accusing gazes of all were fixed on Tok. How could the dead nestling be there? he wondered dizzily. Had Pruk found the wrong cache? Then, seeing the gleam of triumph in Grakk's eyes, he suddenly understood. Grakk had done more than spy on him. Much more. *He* was the nest-breaker, and he had planned from the beginning to cast the blame on Tok. He must have replaced the frog with the dead nestling. He would have had time—he had been among the last to return to the roost that afternoon. Grakk was worse, far worse, than a bully and a braggart. He was a murderer!

At last Tok found his tongue. "What I hid was a frog! I would never harm a nestling. Grakk has done this, I swear it!"

"Of course Tok didn't do it!" Tarkah burst out. With an angry rustle of her feathers, she turned to the mob of ravenets. "Are we going to stand by and let these nobles condemn one of us?" she yelled.

Not one of the ravenets met her eyes. They shuffled their claws on the ground and muttered among themselves.

"Tok No-Name's not one of us!"

"He's an outcast, *unkora*. He might have done it. . . ."

"Grakk's a fine fellow. Why would he lie?"

"What a pack of cowards!" snapped Tarkah. "Lady Korak, I am Tarkah, Raak's daughter," she announced. "I will speak for Tok if no one else will. He is not guilty. He cannot be!"

The Speaker cut her off. "Silence! Ravenets have no

say in this Kort. Leave this to your betters!" Then, gazing down at Tok, she went on, "You have already admitted that the cache is yours. Don't think you can save yourself by accusing Grakk!"

Lord Groh dropped down beside her on the Speaker's Branch. "There has been enough talk!" he shouted. "In the name of my murdered nestlings I claim the justice of the Kort!"

At his words, each noble turned and plucked a twig from the Kort Tree.

"How finds the Kort?" demanded the Speaker. "Let the nobles cast their votes now. Those who find Tok guilty and *unkora* must drop their twigs."

Lord Groh's twig was the first to drop. Then another followed and another, twigs pattering down on the crusted snow in the deep shadows under the Kort Tree. When it was over, Tok saw that not a single raven still held a twig. His eyes searched out his mother, but she had turned away. Had she condemned him too?

An awful silence fell over the glade, and the ravenets drew back. Tok faced the Kort alone.

Chapter 6

Worst of all terrors under the sky is The Hunt.
                              —Dooms of the Kort

"Your sentence, nobles?" cried Lady Korak, turning to the Kort.

Pruk spoke up quickly. "You have found him guilty, lords and ladies. Why not let him be banished, never to return?"

Lord Groh hammered his beak on the branch. "No!" he thundered, glaring down at Tok. "The murderer must die. That is the only justice I will accept."

The nobles stirred on their perches, quorking among themselves.

"I demand The Hunt," shouted Lord Groh. "It is my right by *kora!*"

Heads nodded. Then from somewhere in the throng of nobles a voice croaked, "The Hunt!"

Slowly, others picked up the refrain.

"Hunt!"

"Hunt!"

"Hunt!"

"Tok!" screamed Tarkah.

"Get her out of here!" Grakk cried. He and his friends surrounded Tarkah. Buffeting her with their wings, they drove her from the glade. The rest of the ravenets scattered in panic.

"Hunt!"

"Hunt!"

The chant was deeper now, more ominous. The nobles were spreading their wings and clattering their beaks . . .

"Fly, Tok! Fly for your life!" Pruk's voice cut through Tok's fear, releasing him. He sprang into the air, wheeling away into the woods at the edge of the glade. It would be certain death to try for the open sky, he knew. They were too many. They would surround him, force him to the ground. Behind him he heard the deadly chorus, and the heavy swish of many raven wings.

He flew wildly, dodging tree trunks, tearing his feathers on the tips of branches. He could hear his pursuers crashing after him. Others, he knew, would be waiting in the air above the forest. He flew until he could fly no more, then plunged into the sheltering branches of a pine tree. Huddling in the darkest corner near the trunk, he tried to still the wild throbbing of his heart. Moments later, the hunters winged past him. Their voices faded into the distance, and Tok drew a shivery breath of relief. Then he heard them again. They were coming back!

"Lost him!" a harsh voice screamed in rage.

Tok trembled. It was Groh!

"Calm yourself, my lord!" said another voice, coldly. "He may have doubled back or hidden himself. Here is where we lost sight of him. Let's search more carefully."

They were all around him now. Someone rustled the branches of the pine tree, and Tok heard the scrape of claws. In panic, he bolted out the opposite side. Harsh voices yelled in triumph as the pursuers caught sight of him again. Once more the terrible chant began.

"Hunt! Hunt! Hunt!"

Other voices, many of them, echoed the deadly call from above the forest roof. Tok felt one of the pursuers slash at his tail feathers. No use to twist and turn now, no use to hide. They were right behind him.

Better to die under the open sky, thought Tok. He fled toward the light at the edge of the forest and burst out into a long narrow valley. Behind him, the hunters yelled in triumph; above, the sky was black with wings.

As he rose into the air, a raven dove at him, stabbing with his beak. Another followed, then another. There was no way to fight them, no way to escape. Tok used every trick he knew, but no matter how he turned and twisted in the air, they overwhelmed him. Under a storm of pecks and buffets he was beaten to the ground.

Pursuers and pursued crashed to earth in a tangle of wings. Flipped onto his back, Tok struck at his tormentors with beak and claws, but they pinioned him to the ground, a large raven standing on each wing. The rest gathered in a crowd around him. Tok stared from one pair of cold eyes to the next. Why were they waiting? Then Lord Groh stalked forward and planted one clawed foot on Tok's chest. Leaning forward, eyes blazing, he croaked, "Now, murderer of nestlings, you will feel my justice."

Bracing himself to die with *kora,* Tok thought of his father. Had death come to him like this too?

Groh leaned closer, and despite himself Tok cringed. Would Groh peck out his eyes while he was still alive?

"Stop!" commanded a harsh voice. With a swish of wings another raven landed beside them. To his astonishment, Tok found himself staring up at his mother. "Stop at once, all of you!" she repeated. Then, "Groh, I demand from you a life for a life."

Lord Groh drew himself up and roused his feathers. Gleaming hackles stood out stiffly all around his neck. "What does this squeamishness mean, Karah?" he barked. "Why should your murdering son go free?"

Lady Groh roused her own feathers and glared back at him. "Listen to me, Groh. Lord I made you *and can unmake you if I will.*" She paused to let her words sink in, then went on, "A life for a life, I say. You owe me blood-guilt. You killed my former lord, as all the world knows."

"He deserved to die. He was *unkora!*" snarled Groh.

"Even so," Lady Groh shot back. "The blood-guilt is mine to claim, and I claim it. Do you dare deny me?" Her eyes burned at him like flames.

Groh was the first to look away. Giving his feathers a peevish shake, he snapped his beak and stepped away from Tok. Then he took off with heavy wingbeats. The two ravens stepped off Tok's wings and he struggled to his feet.

"Thank you, Mother," he gasped.

Lady Groh cut him off. "I have already told you to leave this land. Now you must do it on pain of death. I have given you back your life, but you are still condemned by the Kort. If you are found here tomorrow, any raven will have the right to kill you. Do you understand?"

"Yes," said Tok. Then, as she turned away, "I didn't do it. Kill your nestlings."

Her cold eyes stared back at him. "I know," she said. "Murder is not in you. You are like your father in that." Then she spread her wings and flapped away over the forest.

By twos and threes the rest of the ravenhorde dispersed. At last only one bird was left. It was Pruk.

"That was well done of Karah," he said. "Without new evidence the sentence of the Kort must stand. A life for a life was the only way she could save you."

"I thought she hated me," confessed Tok, trembling. He could scarcely believe he was still alive.

Pruk shook his head. "I think not. But she chose Groh and out of *kora* she must stand by him. It will be long before he forgives her for this, though."

Shadows were creeping across the valley floor. In the west, Mount Storm still caught the last rays of the sun.

"Go now," Pruk went on. "It's a long journey to the edge of the Raven Mountains, and you must not be found here tomorrow."

Tok stretched his wings. They were sore from his struggles, and his battered body throbbed, but he could feel his strength returning. "Thank you, Lord Pruk," he said formally. "For standing up for me."

"I stood up for the truth. The lords and ladies are too busy with their territories to know much about you youngsters. But I keep my eyes open. I've seen this Grakk sneaking around and making trouble these past few days. His story stank like old carrion. He's the guilty one, I suspect. But there's no proof."

Tok clacked his beak angrily. "Someday I'll get even with him!" he hissed.

Pruk roused his feathers and settled them again. "No, Tok. Forget revenge. You must never come back. Now, wingspeed to you, son of Rokan, and wide skies for your dancing."

Tok froze. "My father's name," he gasped, staring at the older bird. "You gave me his name. You broke the law!"

Pruk blinked his whitelids. "Did I?" he asked. "I must be getting old and foolish! Anyway, the sky is open before you now. You can begin a new life in a new land, as you should have done long ago."

The two ravens spread their wings and beat up into the air. They circled once over the valley, gaining height, then Pruk banked away toward Black Ridge. "Farewell, Tok," he called down the wind.

Tok dipped a wing in salute, then flew west toward Mount Storm, following the dying light toward unknown lands.

Part 2

Kaa

Chapter 7

Now in the spring-stirring season
Roamed he the raven road, sky-skimming.
Westward flew he, wings unwearying
New lands knew he, and strange sights saw.
    —"Tok's Journey" from Sagas of the Tellers

Dawn found Tok beyond the Raven Mountains. He had flown all night across the lands he knew, dropping down to the forest twice to rest before winging onward. At first it had seemed that the mountains would go on forever, but by now they had dwindled into a range of low hills. Beyond them lay an open rolling country dotted with patches of woods. It looked very wrong to him. Where had all the trees gone?

He focused his eyes on another line of hills far to the west. Glimpsing two black shapes in the distant sky, he veered eagerly toward them. Local ravens could tell him much about this strange land below him. But when he got closer he could tell by their size and their slow wingbeats that they were only crows. Disappointed, he banked away. No self-respecting raven would ask a crow about anything!

Many thousand wingbeats on, a winding line of green caught his eye. It was a great river, thickly fringed with trees. He changed course and followed it a long way as it wound toward the south. At last he dropped down wearily among the huge poplars that lined its banks. Though it was still the Moon of Nestlings, it was already spring here. Heart-shaped leaves, newly opened, fluttered and danced around him in the breeze. Bright new grass pushed up at the feet of the trees, and clumps of wood violets and buttercups nodded in the dappled shade. Small birds dashed to and fro feeding their young, and the air rang with their singing. The cold and hunger of his homeland seemed no more than a bad dream here.

Dropping onto the grass, Tok walked down to the riverbank. The water ran clear over white sand, and he plunged his beak into it and drank thirstily. He could see hundreds of minnows darting to and fro, feeding. He waded in, striking here and there with his beak, but they escaped him easily. From a branch above, a kingfisher mocked him with its rattling cry, then dove straight into the water and emerged with a fish, as if to show him how things should be done.

In the grass and reeds farther along the bank Tok came upon a nest of water voles, and made a meal of the little squeakers. But even while he ate, a sound in the background troubled him. He flew up into a poplar and cocked his head, listening. It was a dull roar, followed by a whizzing sound, and it seemed to come from beyond the line of trees on the far shore. Curious, he soared across the river. From the air he could see a wide black path that followed that side of the river. As he watched, something that looked like a huge shiny beetle zoomed up the path. It approached with a roar and whizzed away into the distance. Tok had never seen anything like it.

But his sharp eyes had picked up something else. In the middle of the path lay an animal. Ever hungry, he angled down and landed nearby. The path felt hard and wrong under his claws, not like normal ground at all. But food was food. Hopping forward, he peered at the animal cautiously, then took a careful peck, jumping back in alarm at his own daring. But the animal, a very flat raccoon, certainly looked dead. Something seemed to have squashed it, and Tok had no trouble finding a way to get at the meat inside it. Stuffing himself, he wished he could cache some of it for later. But what was the use when he would soon be moving on?

So busy was he with his feasting that he didn't notice the roar of an another beetle-thing until it was nearly upon him. With a terrified quork he flapped heavily into the air just in time to escape being crushed by the round things it ran on. As he shot above it, he could see heads inside. Two-Legs! Tok fled back to the poplar trees. He'd seen Two-Legs in the mountains during the Moon of the Hunters when they came to shoot deer. This path and the beetle must be theirs. He shuddered.

Slowly his panic ebbed away. He was safe enough here on the far side of the river, he comforted himself. So he dozed for a while, then preened all his feathers one by one, getting rid of dust and oiling them. When he was satisfied, he spat out pellets that contained hair and bits of bone from his meals, shook his feathers into place and took to the air again. With strong sweeps of his wings he set out for the hills he had seen in the west.

The air had grown much warmer while he rested. Though the sun still shone, towering clouds were building up to the west. Flying closer, Tok could feel cooler air and sense the powerful updrafts at the heart of them. The air seemed to tingle inside his feathers, and for sheer joy he soared and tumbled above the plain, dancing his thanks to Skyah. The hills came closer and closer, and soon he could see the forests on their slopes. His heart beat faster, for it certainly looked like raven country. Tilting his wings against the gusty wind, he soared over range after range of hills, always on the lookout for shaggy black shapes in the sky. But there was none. At last he saw a towering white pine on the crest of a ridge and landed.

Still heavy with his huge meal, he felt no need to hunt. He settled himself comfortably near the trunk of the tree, rousing his feathers and settling them again. The forest seemed strangely still. No birds called, no insects buzzed, and he heard no rustle of animal feet. It was as if everything was waiting for something to happen. Uneasily, Tok began to quork and querk aloud, talking things over with himself. He went over everything that had happened—the Kort, the sentence, The Hunt. The more he brooded about it the angrier he got. Oh yes, he'd escaped with his life. But thanks to Grakk's lies his name was now *unkora,* just like his father's. The thought was like a thorn in his craw. No matter what Pruk said, he was going back there someday. He'd get even, he'd show them all . . .

But he couldn't go back now. So where should he go? He had thought he only had to leave the Raven Mountains to find other ravens. If only he had asked Tarkah and the other newcomers where they had come from last fall!

At last he fell asleep, only to awake much later when a flash of lightning lit up the inside of the pine tree. Thunder rumbled, and a sudden gust of wind shook the branches. Then came another dazzling flare. This time the thunderclap came right overhead, a ripping sound followed by a hollow boom. Wind lashed the tree, and Tok clung to his perch half-deafened. Then with a sizzling crash, lightning hit the pine, shearing off the top of it. In panic, Tok took off, but the falling treetop caught him. He crashed to the ground, wings pinned under a tangle of branches. Cold rain poured down, beating on his whitelids and soaking his feathers.

For a moment he lay there, stunned. Then he tried moving his wings. There was no pain, so they weren't broken, but the pile of branches held them firmly. He struggled to move first one wing, then the other. The branches seemed to yield a bit, but then the whole mass shifted down the slope, pinning him again. His muscles ached, but the fear of being trapped there, helpless, drove him to keep trying to free himself. One wing seemed less tightly held, but he still could not get it loose. At last he had to rest, and lay there, panting.

The sky had cleared, and a crescent moon was setting behind the treetops. Birds began to sing and the eastern sky brightened. Soon it would be full daylight, and what would become of him then? Tok thrashed his wings again, trying to escape from the twiggy trap that held him. Then he heard a low hiss and snapped his head around. Beyond the tangle of branches crouched a large tawny beast. Sleek and lithe, it was the deadliest thing he had ever seen. The black tip of its long tail twitched ever so slightly as its nostrils flared, sniffing his scent. Its eyes burned at Tok with a green flame. Then it drew back its lips in a snarl, showing long white fangs. Muscles rippled under its tawny fur—it was going to spring on him!

Tok scrabbled frantically against the branches with his feet and forced himself upward, twisting his left wing and yanking it hard. He felt it move a little, but then the beast was on him. He felt a searing pain as a fang sank into the muscles of his chest, and he screamed in rage and agony. He struck at the glaring green eyes with his beak, slashing the corner of one of them and drawing blood. With a snarl the beast drew back for a moment, shaking its head. Ignoring the pain in his chest, Tok thrashed desperately left and right. Then, suddenly, his left wing came free. With one more twist, he freed his other wing and fluttered over the mound of branches. The creature bounded after him.

Tok hurled himself into the air, but his damaged flight muscles could not power his right wing. He veered clumsily, flapping right over the beast. It leaped and its front paw grazed him at an angle, dashing him to the ground. Unable to take off again, he scurried into a thicket of briars. Folding his wings tightly, he squirmed deep among its spiny shoots, ignoring the pricking of its thorns through his feathers. Then he turned at bay, slashing at the beast's paw with his beak when it tried to claw him out.

With a snarl, it pulled its paw back. Then it got up and paced all around the thicket, looking for a way to get at him. It succeeded in getting one paw and its head through another gap in the brambles, but Tok struck at it, piercing its nose with his beak. The creature drew back with an angry hiss and sat licking its nose. Then it turned and padded away.

Tok wasn't fooled. The beast was only waiting for him to leave the thicket. He cocked his head, peering out through the brambles. After a moment he could see it standing just beyond the edge of the glade, almost invisible among the forest shadows. Trembling with fear and pain, he settled down to outwait it. At last it returned. It sniffed around the thicket and Tok quorked at the top of his voice, spreading his shoulders and raising his feather ears. At last, with a savage look at Tok over its shoulder, the beast trotted away in search of easier prey.

Chapter 8

First the Maker created ravens,
then crows from the scraps left over.
                                        —Raven myth

Tok watched it leave, focusing his eyes first near then far, to make sure it was really gone this time. Then he peered down at his chest feathers. They still oozed blood, and the muscles beneath throbbed where the beast's fang had pierced them. He eased himself out of the thicket and gave his wings an experimental flap, but pain stabbed through the right side of his body. He sensed that his right wing could not carry him, and that trying to fly now would only make things worse. Trembling, he looked around. He could not stay in the thicket—there was no food and the strange beast might return. But where could he go?

In the distance, he could hear the murmur of water, so he began to walk toward it. He moved warily from one sheltering bush to another, stopping often to look and listen. He had never had to walk such a long distance before, and it was slow work, for his claws kept catching in tufts of grass and tree roots.

The sound of the water grew louder and at last Tok reached a spring that splashed down the mountainside between banks overgrown by brambles and creepers. He waded straight into the water, its icy chill soothing the burning pain in his chest. Gulping great mouthfuls, he tilted his head back to let it trickle down his throat. When he had had enough he squatted down, dunking his breast feathers to try to wash the blood away.

Suddenly, out of nowhere, a loud voice demanded, "What are you doing?"

Tok quorked with alarm. Floundering out of the shallows, he backed up against a rock, ready to defend himself. But he could see no enemies on the banks of the stream. Then, looking up, he saw a sleek young crow perched on a branch. It was much smaller than he was, and still wore its brownish-black yearling feathers. From its voice he could tell it was a male.

Tok puffed himself up and glared at the crow. "What business is it of yours?"

"None," the crow admitted, with a flip of his tail. "I just wondered." When Tok said nothing, he went on, "I've never seen a crow as big as you."

A *crow!* Tok's temper flared. "I'm not a crow! I'm a raven."

The crow gave a mocking caw. "A raven?" he jeered. "Go on! Ravens are nothing but an old crow tale!" He peered more closely. "You *are* awfully big, though. And ugly too. You're sure you're a raven?"

Tok didn't bother to reply. Panting, he let his right wing droop.

The crow cocked his head. "You're hurt," he said, dropping from his perch to land beside Tok. He fixed his shiny brown eyes on the sticky feathers on Tok's chest. "How did that happen?"

"A beast nearly killed me," Tok muttered. "Tawny, with a long tail. Claws. Lots of teeth."

"*Caw-err!* A cougar!" The crow stared up at him, beak agape. "You fought off a cougar? That must be what I heard a while back—spitting and snarling and a lot of loud noise. I flew up here to have a look but didn't see anything."

"I hid in a thicket," said Tok. "The beast couldn't get at me so it left after a while. But it bit the muscles in my chest and I can't fly."

"*Tuk-tuk-tuk.*" The crow clucked in sympathy. "Bad. The ground's a bad place in the forest. Too many hungry things prowling around looking for a meal."

Tok nodded grimly. "I'll just have to stay close to the brambles until my wound heals."

"You're a tough one." The crow thought for a moment, then said, "Well, there's water here. Not much to eat, though. Snails, bugs, a few frogs. Maybe I could find you more food."

"You'd do that for me?" Tok was puzzled. Ravens sometimes helped other ravens, but never any of the lesser birds.

The crow spread his shoulders. "Why not? It's not every day I meet a real live raven. I can't wait to tell my family!"

"Is that one of them calling?" For a crow was cawing two sharp notes in the distance.

The crow listened for a moment, then called a two-note reply. "That's Kraa, my father," he replied. "He sounds angry, so Mother must be getting impatient. I'm supposed to be minding the nestlings. My name's Kaa. What's yours?"

Minding the nestlings? Tok had never heard of such a thing, and he stared at the young crow in astonishment. Then he replied, "I am Tok, son of Lord Rokan." For *kora* required him to give his lineage, even to a lowlife crow.

Kaa gave a cackle of laughter. "Son of a lord? My, how grand! We crows don't bother with all that title business."

Not bother with lineage? Crows really were *unkora*, thought Tok.

"I'd better see what my mother needs me to do," said Kaa. "But I'll be back. Meanwhile there's a big bramble thicket just beyond those rocks. You should be safe there."

Left alone, Tok cautiously made his way around the rocks and found the brambles Kaa had told him about. It was a good dense patch, and once inside he could easily drive off anything that tried to get at him. Weary and aching, he returned to the edge of the stream. Poking among the stones, he found a few snails. He cracked them in his beak and ate them, though he wasn't really hungry, then he bathed his wounded chest again. Satisfied that the bleeding had stopped, he clambered onto a low branch near the bramble patch and gloomily began to preen his feathers.

Not long afterward Kaa came winging back with a mouse in his beak. "Here you are," he said, landing beside Tok.

"You didn't have to . . ." Tok began, as he took the mouse. He hadn't expected to see the crow again—he seemed such a flighty fellow.

Kaa blinked his whitelids. "Of course I did," he said. "I said I'd help you, didn't I?"

Well! thought Tok, crunching the mouse, bones and all. Crows actually had some honor after all.

"Besides, it got me out of a bit of work," Kaa went on. "My mother has a nestful—five hungry mouths to feed. It keeps me and my sister on the hop, I can tell you."

"Your sister helps too?" Tok asked. "Don't you go away and find new territories?"

Kaa flipped his tail. "Some of us do. But a lot of us stay and share our parents' territories."

Tok thought of the way ravenets left their parents by autumn, never to return. That was the brave way, the noble way. He remembered his own yearning to leave and his shame when he could not because of his name. Yet Kaa had kept his promise about bringing food. Could there be more than one kind of *kora?* The thought made him uneasy.

He had gone on with his preening while Kaa talked away. Now to his astonishment, the young crow hopped up beside him on his perch and began to groom his head and neck feathers. Tok stiffened. A crow daring to preen *him?* But it felt wonderful, and little by little he relaxed. Half closing his eyes, he turned his head this way and that to let Kaa reach every feather. No one had ever preened him before. Maybe Kaa's chatter wasn't so bad after all.

Kaa wanted to know all about everything. Were there

really other ravens? Lots of them? And how did they and
crow folk get along? And how far away was this strange
land Tok had come from? And how did the cougar get
close enough to hurt him?

Tok tried to answer patiently. When Kaa had finished
preening him, he politely offered to return the favor,
though the thought of preening a crow seemed most
unkora.

Kaa eyed Tok's huge beak doubtfully and began to talk
even faster. "No, thanks, though it's *ka* of you to ask. But
you're awfully big, you know. Your beak looks pretty ferocious. What if it slipped? Around my eyes, I mean?
Besides, I'd really better be getting back. I wouldn't want
to be caught in the deep woods after dark."

"Why not?" wondered Tok, who spent all his nights in
the forest.

"Owls," whispered Kaa, glancing over his shoulder.
"Aren't you afraid of owls?"

"Not very."

"You mean they don't hunt you?"

Tok gave a deep quork of laughter. "If one did I'd make
nestling-pap out of him," he boasted. Well, if it were a very
small owl, he added to himself, for big owls did kill ravens
sometimes. But bragging helped keep his spirits up.

Kaa's eyes widened. "Just wait till I tell my sister. She
tries to stay awake all night because she's so afraid an owl
will get her."

"You'd better go quickly," said Tok, for the sun was low
behind the trees, and owls began to hunt at dusk.

"Will you still be here tomorrow?" asked Kaa.

"Where can I go with my wing like this?" grumbled Tok.

"See you then," said Kaa. With a worried glance over his shoulder, he sped away.

Chapter 9

No distance too far for a raven flying,
no distance too short for a raven walking.
—Raven proverb

Tok spent a miserable night. Despite his boasts to Kaa, the sounds of the forest suddenly seemed strange and frightening. Leaves rustled mysteriously, and the underbrush crackled as unseen creatures passed nearby.

The wound in his chest ached, and every time he tried to flex his right wing he felt a stab of pain. Unable to sleep, he brooded. What if the injury didn't heal properly? Would he ever fly again? Dance again? How would he survive? At last he fretted himself to sleep.

He woke to daylight outside the thicket. Mist was rising, and slanting rays of sun shone through it beneath the trees. Hopping to the edge of the brambles, he crouched there, watching and listening, but he could sense no danger. Crows called in the distance, and Tok thought of Kaa. His stomach felt very empty, and he could not help wondering if the young crow would bring him something to eat. Then he felt ashamed. A raven should not depend on a lowly crow. It was *unkora*.

He walked down to the stream. After drinking his fill, he foraged along the edge of it, turning over stones with his beak. In this way he caught some worms and beetles. They didn't satisfy him, so he was glad to see Kaa winging toward him with a garter snake twisting and writhing in his beak. The young crow dropped it in front of him.

Tok pinned it down with one foot to keep it from slithering away, bit it behind the head to kill it, then snipped off a hunk and bolted it down. "Want some?" he offered.

Kaa shook his head. "We ate in the Two-Legs' fields," he said. "The corn is beginning to sprout. Delicious."

Tok downed another chunk of snake. "You mean you raid the Two-Legs? Isn't that dangerous?"

"You sound like my mother. She'd prefer to live far away from them, but my father's territory is very rich—we have both the forest and the fields. There are lots of birds' eggs and other good things in the woods, but the fields have tender corn and fat grasshoppers. Yum," he added, clacking his beak at the memory.

"I told my family about you," he went on. "My father says I can visit you as long as I don't shirk helping with the nestlings." He sighed and gave his wings a flap. "I suppose I'd better get back, though I'd rather stay and hear more about ravens. I don't suppose you can fly yet," he added. "You could come back with me."

Tok flapped his wings but the pain made him blink. Yet he hated the thought of another endless night in the thicket. "I can't fly," he replied. "But if you scout the way for me, I can try to walk to your territory."

"Walk?" Kaa sounded doubtful. "It's not far as the crow flies, but it's different on the ground."

"I want to try."

"I'll have a look then," said Kaa, and he winged away downstream.

Soon he was back. "I followed the stream a long way," he reported. "There are no cougars or lynx or foxes moving around—they're the only ones likely to give you any trouble. And there are plenty of brambles along the stream for cover if you need it."

"Is there some place where we could meet later?" Tok asked.

Kaa thought for a moment. "A fallen log across the stream," he said. "It's quite far, though."

"I'll make it," vowed Tok, as Kaa flapped away.

Slowly, Tok worked his way downstream. The slope was rocky and his claws slipped and skidded, wrenching his body and making his wound ache fiercely. He soon became weary and bedraggled, but he marched on, all his senses alert for danger, stopping to rest and drink when he had to. He was terribly hungry, and thought longingly of his raccoon feast, the last time he had been full-fed.

It was not until late in the afternoon that he reached the fallen log. Kaa was waiting for him with a beak full of grasshoppers.

Not even a decent snack, thought Tok, though he munched them eagerly. Then he bathed and Kaa helped him preen his ragged feathers. They found a thicket that seemed safe enough, but Tok shivered at the thought of another night on the ground.

Kaa noticed his misery. "Don't worry. You'll be out of the woods tomorrow," he promised as he flew away.

The next day passed much the same way. By now Tok was so hungry that he could scarcely believe his luck when he spotted a rotten log lying some way from the stream. It had been ripped open and its surface was crawling with juicy white grubs. Saliva dripping from his beak, Tok hopped over and began to stuff himself. He had not swallowed more than a few beakfuls, though, before a black shape loomed up on the other side of the log.

The bear cub sniffed at him. Tok jumped back and hissed, beak agape, hoping to scare it off. But the cub lolloped over the log and batted him playfully with its paw. Tok flinched and backed away again, still hissing. The cub followed, batting him again and then again. Tok could sense that it meant no harm, but the blows made him hurt all over. If he didn't do something, he might have a wing broken. So he pecked the cub's paw hard. When it still came after him, he slashed its tender nose with his beak. The cub began to squall. Tok hopped toward the stream just as a mother bear lumbered out of the woods with another cub at her heels.

There were no thickets Tok could reach in time. He flapped his wings wildly and got into the air despite the pain, but his right wing buckled and he crashed to the ground in front of the bear. Rousing every feather, he stood at bay, beak agape, and screeched at the top of his voice.

The injured cub ran whimpering to its mother, and she stopped in the midst of her charge to sniff it over. After licking its hurt nose, she glowered at Tok, wicked red glints dancing in her little eyes.

Suddenly, a black shape zoomed close over the bear's head with a wild *"Cak-caw!"* That seemed to decide her. With a grunt she turned and hustled her cubs off into the forest.

Kaa fluttered down beside Tok. "I heard your cry, and knew something was up! Do you often take on bears like that?"

"Not if I don't have to," grumbled Tok. He shook his shoulders and let his feathers settle. "That fool of a cub tried to play me to death! And I've only myself to blame. That torn-open log meant 'bear' for sure, but I was just too hungry to be careful."

"Never mind," said Kaa. "We're nearly there."

Tok looked around. It was true. The slope was much less steep now, and the woods were thinning out.

And so he came at last to the country of the crows.

Chapter 10

When the owl flies, every crow is alone.

—Crow proverb

Kaa flew on ahead of Tok, cawing at the top of his voice. Within moments a large glossy crow flew back with him. Landing on a branch, it fixed its bright brown eyes on Tok.

"*Caaak?*" it asked, turning to Kaa, who was bouncing up and down on the branch beside it.

"*Caw-err,*" replied Kaa. "This is the raven I've been telling you about." Then to Tok, "This is Kraa, my father."

"*Cuk-ca!*" A smaller crow with brownish feathers like Kaa's winged up to join the others. Kaa turned and gave its feathers a quick stroke with his beak. "And this is Kiraa, my nosy sister."

Kaa's father was big for a crow, about two-thirds the size of a raven. He stared down at Tok suspiciously. "Who are you?" he demanded.

"I am Tok, son of Lord Rokan. I've come from the Raven Mountains to the east and north."

Kraa blinked his whitelids. "What are you doing in my territory?" he asked. "And why are you walking about on the ground like one of the Two-Legs' fowl?" He gave his own sleek wings a flip.

"Because I'm hurt," Tok shot back. "A tree I was roosting in was lightning-struck, and then a cougar got at me."

"And today he fought off a bear," Kaa added proudly. At this Kiraa gave a surprised caw and roused all her feathers.

"Your friend seems to have more adventures than are good for him," said Kraa dryly.

"He can stay with us, though, can't he?" begged Kaa.

Kraa didn't answer at once, and Tok grew impatient. No crow could tell *him* what to do! But until he could fly again he was going to need all the friends he could get, he reminded himself. So he shuffled his claws in the grass and tried to look humble.

"Well," Kraa said at last, "I suppose he can, since there's only one of him." Spreading his wings, he added, "Just one thing, Tok. Stay away from our nest. From what little I've heard, your kind are notorious robbers." He flapped away through the trees.

Tok grumbled under his breath. Of course ravens robbed other birds' nests. There was nothing *unkora* about that. Many birds did the same—especially crows. Who was Kraa to scold him about it?

Kaa fluttered down beside him. "Don't mind my father," he said. "He's always grouchy when he and mother have nestlings. Now come along. Kiraa and I will show you the best places to hunt mice."

○

With a mouse feast in his stomach, Tok began to feel more

cheerful. The land of the crows was rich and pleasant—an open pine wood on the edge of wide fields. There was a pond nearby, too, full of frogs and fish. He could live well here, he told himself—if only he could fly.

He knew he had to try in spite of the pain. The next day he waited until Kaa and Kiraa grew bored with watching him and flew off to find food for the nestlings. He couldn't stand the thought of the young crows seeing him flap clumsily about. Crows always made flying look like heavy work, and ravens scorned them for that. Now he was more stone-winged than any crow.

First he flapped up onto a stump. The pain bit deep into his chest, but it was duller now. He could bear it. Next he jumped off into the air, wings beating furiously, and made it onto a low-hanging branch. His chest muscles were burning now, but at least he was off the ground. Locking his toes around the branch, he spread his wings wide and flapped them until it hurt too much to go on. After resting for a while he did it again. And again.

That night he roosted off the ground for the first time since his injury. By the next day an itching deep in his chest told him that the damaged muscles were truly healing.

As his wing got stronger, Tok began to go about with Kaa and Kiraa. At first the other crows kept a safe distance away. But as the days passed the younger ones grew bolder. They would sidle up to him, cawing loud comments to each other about his size. Meanwhile, Kaa told and retold Tok's adventures, with more details each time.

"Some day I'll have adventures of my own to tell about," he would add wistfully.

Once Tok could reach the high branches, he had to get used to having Kaa and Kiraa cuddled up on either side of him, their shoulders pressed against his. Still, it *was* cozy deep among the branches at night with friends close beside you, he thought. Not like the lonely life he had led before.

As soon as he could fly longer distances, Tok joined the crows for morning raids on the fields, and found that Kaa was right—newly sprouted corn was delicious. One day, though, a Two-Legs came to the edge of the field in one of the beetle-things. For a moment it stood staring at the crows, then, reaching into the beetle, it pulled out something long and thin and shiny. Tok had seen Two-Legs shoot deer with such things. It was a firestick! He squawked in fear, and at the same moment a sentry crow cawed a warning. The whole flock took off into the woods just as the firestick went off with a bang. No crows fell. After watching the woods for a while, the Two-Legs got back in its beetle and went away.

This scare did not defeat the crows. The moment the Two-Legs was out of sight they flew right back, and they returned the next day and the next. But though they ate many corn sprouts many more survived, and soon the fields were full of lines of waving green corn plants.

"No more corn for now," Kaa told Tok, with a wink. "But lots more to come—just you wait!"

Even without corn there was plenty to eat. Life was soft and easy in this warm land, Tok told himself lazily. No need to fret about finding other ravens. There was plenty of time for that. He scarcely noticed as the Moon of New

Leaves slipped into the Moon of Flowers. Then, unbelievably soon, it was the time of long days, when the sun stood farthest north in the sky.

One warm night, Kaa did not appear at roosting time and Tok found himself pressed between Kiraa and another crow. Just before dawn, something awakened him. He took his head from beneath his wing and peered about in the warm darkness. There was a faint whir of wings, a moving shadow . . . then Kiraa vanished from the branch beside him with a shrill scream.

Owl! thought Tok, as other crows wakened around him with loud cries. For a few moments he clung to the branch, cold with fear. If only he hadn't bragged about not being afraid of owls! If he did nothing now he'd be *unkora*. So he dropped from his perch, trying to guess what direction the owl would take. Outside the roost, the night seemed strange and menacing, and the shapes of the trees loomed close, reaching for him. Was the owl close by, ready to strike? Then a shadow swooped ahead of him carrying something in its talons. Tok pursued it, dodging wildly among the trees, terrified that he might dash himself to pieces among their branches.

At last the owl landed in a tall elm. Putting its back against the trunk it perched with one feathered foot holding the limp body of Kiraa. Tok shuddered as he swept past it. It was a great horned owl, the enemy of every bird. He knew he couldn't harm it, but he might be able to make it drop its prey. He'd have to keep attacking, he told himself. If he gave it a chance, he would be seized like Kiraa.

Grey as a ghost, the owl stared at him out of blazing

yellow eyes and whispered, "Go. I am death, and this is mine."

"No!" yelled Tok. Swerving in midair, he struck at the owl with claws and beak. Hissing, it pecked at him, its head swiveling on its shoulders as it followed his attack. Tok struck again, and this time the owl lunged at him, trying to seize him in its talons. Kiraa's body slid from its grasp and dropped to the ground.

If only the others would come! From the roost tree, crow voices answered Tok's cries, but he heard no beating of friendly wings. They are too afraid of the owl and the dark, he thought desperately. He pecked at the owl again and again. Its beak gaped and the great talons reached for him, but each time they closed on nothing as he twisted and turned just out of reach. At last the owl took wing and swooped toward him. Tok dodged, and it glided silently away between the trees.

Kiraa still lay at the foot of the tree where she had fallen, and Tok feared that she was dead. But then she opened her eyes and stared up at him in terror.

"Tok! Oh, I thought you were *it*, come back to eat me." She shuddered.

"Are you hurt?" he asked.

Kiraa struggled to her feet. "Half-crushed," she wheezed. "I felt its talons close around me and then I just . . . went numb. I couldn't even struggle!"

Dawn was breaking when Tok and Kiraa returned to the roost. The crows were wailing and crying loudly now, but they fell silent when they saw Kiraa.

"I was in the claws of death," she told them. "But Tok

saved me. He attacked the owl and made it drop me. Then he chased it away!"

There was a great outburst of cawing.

"Chases owls? I never heard anything like it!"

"*Caw-err!* He must be crazy. Lucky for Kiraa!"

"Tok the owl-fighter! Tok Owl-bane!"

Kaa arrived just in time to hear the second telling of the adventure. Kiraa made it much longer this time and added many details.

When he had heard it all, Kaa puffed his feathers up. "Didn't I tell you he was brave?" he cawed, strutting along the branch. "He's *my* friend. *I* found him!"

"He's my hero," said Kiraa. "He saved my life." She sidled up to Tok and pressed herself against his shoulder.

Tok shuffled his feet on his perch. No one had ever called him a hero before. And he knew in his heart that he didn't deserve it. He hadn't really gone after the owl for Kiraa, only to save his own *kora*. And he hadn't chased it away, it had just decided to go. "Now it's daylight you should mob that owl and drive it far away," he told the crows gruffly. "If you don't it'll only come back again."

"Tok's right!" cried Kaa. "Let's go!" The crows were brave enough in daylight, and he had no trouble raising a search party to scour the mountainside. A chorus of caws from the woods soon announced the finding of the owl. Tok watched as crows flew in from all directions to scold and dive-bomb it.

Kaa soon came winging back to settle on the branch, every feather standing on end with excitement. "We found it all right!" he boasted. "We mobbed it until it moved on.

And Kraay's lot from across the river will drive it even farther. So you can sleep in peace tonight, Kiraa," he added. Leaning over, he gently preened his sister's head.

Kiraa roused her feathers and settled them again. "I'll never be afraid now Tok's here to look after me," she said, bowing toward Tok and blinking her whitelids at him. He looked away, embarrassed.

Chapter 11

What crows don't know isn't worth knowing.
                                    —Crow proverb

After that, the younger crows began to imitate Tok, swaggering about and cawing in deeper voices to sound more like ravens. Even Kaa's crusty father thanked Tok, and Kaa's mother begged him to keep an eye on her youngsters, who had long since left the nest.

As for Kiraa, she told him frankly that someday she was going to have him for her mate. "That way I'll always be safe," she announced, with a flip of her wings.

Tok found he did not mind all the attention. It was certainly better than being an outcast, he thought. Days passed now when he did not even think of trying to seek out other ravens. Maybe I'm turning into a crow, he told himself one day, then almost fell off his perch in shock.

His wound was healed now, except for a dull ache in his chest when he flew long distances. He began to practice his dancing, sometimes watched by the admiring Kaa and Kiraa.

"It's amazing what you can do—all that tumbling and

rolling in the air," Kaa said once. "But what's it *for?*"

Tok scratched the back of his head with one claw. "Why, it's for fun," he said. "And to thank the Maker."

"Oh," said Kaa.

But Tok felt he did not really understand.

Hot days stretched into the Moon of Ripeness. Now the corn stood tall and the grain was golden in the fields. Plump berries clustered on the bushes around the pond. Each night bigger and bigger flocks of crows flew in to roost from far away. The twilight was full of their hoarse voices as they chattered excitedly before settling in to sleep.

Tok began to grow restless. Something felt wrong, something was missing. The days were shorter now, and the nights more chill. He sensed the coming winter, and brooded, the old desire for vengeance against Grakk stirring in him. He knew it was no use to go back yet. The sentence of the Kort still stood. Somehow he had to find a deed to perform that would prove his *kora.*

Kaa noticed his gloom. "You're fretting about something, aren't you?" he asked one day as he watched Tok preening his feathers after a long flight.

"There's something I have to do," Tok admitted. "It's hard to explain. It's about *kora.*"

"You've never said why you left your homeland," hinted Kaa, his eyes bright with curiosity.

What harm could it do to tell him? thought Tok. So he told the young crow about his father and mother, and Lord Groh, and Grakk's treachery and the sentence of the Kort.

"*Caw-err!* What a story," said Kaa when he was done.

"So you can't go back, can you?"

"Not unless I can prove my *kora*," agreed Tok. "And I don't know how to do that. You see, it would take a very great deed to make the Kort change its sentence." He shook his feathers with a dry rattle. "A raven I knew said he thought such deeds exist only in tales. I'm afraid he is right."

Kaa pecked thoughtfully at the branch he sat on. "Life in the Raven Mountains seems hard. All that starving and dying." He shuddered, but then his eyes lit up. "You could go back and tell the Kort there are better, easier places to live," he said eagerly. "Tell them how much food there is in our hills, and offer to bring them here. Wouldn't you be a hero then?"

"No. For ravens will never leave the Raven Mountains," replied Tok. "It is our place forever, for Skyah sent us there. Only the young can leave."

Disappointed, Kaa hunkered down on the branch and was silent for a long moment, thinking. Then, *"Ca-caw!"* he cried. "Now I have it! Find those Grey Lords, the ones in that tale you told me. They helped the ravens long ago, didn't they? Maybe they could help again. Maybe then the Kort would forgive you."

Find the Grey Lords! Tok's feathers prickled with excitement. If he could truly find them, bring them back to the Raven Mountains, it would end all the starvation and suffering. It would be a matchless deed, the kind he had dreamed of doing! He would be praised and honored, an outcast no more. For a moment he could almost taste the glory of it, and his heart beat faster. Then it sank. "But there are no Grey Lords anymore," he said. "They're all dead, killed long ago by the Two-Legs. They live only in stories."

"Are you sure?" said Kaa. "What if they're not all dead? What if there still are Grey Lords somewhere?"

"But where? How would I find them?"

"Crows go everywhere, and they talk to each other. They would know if anyone does," replied Kaa. "Oh, not our lot around here. We're stay-at-homes. But now others are coming in from all directions on their way south. We could ask if anyone has seen or heard anything."

Tok was suddenly dizzy with questions. What if there *were* still Grey Lords? What if he could find them? What if he could persuade them to go with him to the Raven Mountains? Would the Kort give him back his *kora?*

That night he and Kaa hopped among the birds in the roost, asking questions. However, many of the newcomers had never seen a raven and were not eager to talk to one now they had the chance. They shifted nervously away from Tok, muttering amongst themselves. It wasn't until many nights later that they found a crow from the north. He was a shaggy old bird with white feathers in his wings, and didn't seem much afraid of anything.

"Grey Lords?" he shook his head. "Never heard of them. What are they?"

"I don't really know," confessed Tok. "Great birds, I think. Mighty hunters. They are grey and swift."

The crow peered at him closely in the twilight of the roost. "You're a raven, aren't you? I've seen your kind in the north woods. Big brawling fellows. But Grey Lords—I don't know anything about them. I do know a raven saying, though. Every crow in the north knows it." Spreading his wings he lifted up his head and croaked:

> "Ravens, dark dancers,
> Riding the north wind
> Sharp-eyed, with wing-dip
> Signal the Singers.
> Keen-nosed they follow,
> Partners in prey."

"Singers!" gasped Tok. "But the Grey Lords are singers—our stories say so. They work with the ravens to hunt prey. What are these Singers?"

The crow folded his wings. "I don't know. It's just something I heard. Maybe the saying doesn't mean anything. But it does talk about the north wind. If you want to find more ravens and maybe find out who the Singers are, you must go north."

The others settled down to roost, but Tok couldn't fall asleep. The words "Go north" echoed in his head, and his heart beat strong and fast. While other birds flew south he would go the other way, he told himself—north into the teeth of the oncoming winter. For he was sure now what he had to do. He had to search for the Singers.

Chapter 12

Caw! Caw! Caw!
Corn today and more tomorrow.
Crow delight is Two-Legs' sorrow.

—Crow feasting song

The corn was ripe in the fields now and early the next morning a huge flock of crows swooped down on it. Kaa showed Tok how to strip the green husks away from the ears of corn to feast on the milky-sweet kernels inside.

"I told you there would be lots more corn coming," he said, stuffing himself greedily.

Tok hung back at first, worried as always about the Two-Legs. And sure enough, not long after they arrived, a Two-Legs' beetle came jouncing up the dusty path by the field. At once the sentry crow cawed a warning, and the flock took off into the woods. Safe among the branches of a pine tree, Tok peered down at the Two-Legs. It got out of its beetle, but this time it did not carry the firestick. It walked into the field and examined the damaged rows of corn where the crows had been feeding, straightening bent and broken plants, and picking up spoiled ears that lay scattered on the ground. It turned and stared for a long moment at the woods, then, shaking its head, it turned and walked back to the beetle and went away. The sentry crow watched until the beetle disappeared, then cawed "All's well." Within moments the entire flock was back feasting again.

"You're going to leave soon, aren't you?" Kaa asked Tok between beakfuls.

"How did you know?"

"You've been practicing your flying more. And when you're not flying you sit around muttering to yourself. And now with all this about the Singers. Anyway, don't worry. I won't tell the others," Kaa went on. "Especially Kiraa."

"I'll miss you," said Tok. "All of you."

"You won't have to miss me," said Kaa, stripping more corn from a cob. "I'm coming with you."

"Coming with me!" spluttered Tok, choking on kernels. "But you can't!"

"Yes, I can," said Kaa confidently. "Why not? I'm grown up now and can do what I like. And what I like is to go with you. Anyway, I'm bored with all this. I want to have adventures. Like you."

"There's no corn where I'm going," Tok warned him. "To find the Singers I'll have to go north. Winter is coming, and life there will be hard. Very hard."

"*Caw-err!*" said Kaa. "I *know* that. But wherever we go there are bound to be crows, and what they eat I can eat. So don't bother trying to talk me out of it. I'm going with you, and that's that!"

Tok's heart sank. Kaa must not go! The journey would

be too hard and cold and dangerous for him. And besides, no crow could fly as far and fast as he could—he'd have to coddle Kaa every wingbeat of the way. He might never get far enough north to find the Singers.

Later, when they had finished feeding, Tok soared alone, brooding. It was no use trying to argue with Kaa—he was too stubborn. He would have to slip away in the dark and put many thousands of wingbeats between himself and the roost before morning. It seemed *unkora* to sneak away without telling Kaa and the others, but he had to do it, he told himself. There was no other way.

In his long flights over the countryside Tok had learned to watch the black paths of the Two-Legs for oncoming beetles. He had made many a fine meal from the animals they killed. Today there was nothing to eat, but he saw the red beetle of the Two-Legs who grew the corn scurrying down the path that led to the many-roosts. Tok had seen the strange shape of this place from the air, but fear of the Two-Legs had kept him well away from it. Kaa had been there often, though, and said that hordes of them lived together in the tall roosts he could see on the horizon.

Now Tok idly watched the red beetle move out of sight. He was just descending from his flight some time later when the beetle came scurrying back. He focused his eyes on it as it followed the path that ran past the cornfield. Then it turned onto a faint track that led into the woods, heading in the direction of the roost tree. Curious now, Tok kept the beetle in sight. At last it stopped at the end of the track, and the Two-Legs got out. Another of its kind was with it.

Swinging lower, Tok landed in the top of a tree right over the beetle. The Two-Legs pulled out two big lumpy things. Carrying them, they tramped away toward the roost tree. Tok shadowed them, flying from treetop to treetop, always keeping them in sight through the screen of branches below.

It was still early afternoon, and the roost was deserted. One of the Two-Legs took out a strange object and put it up to his eyes, carefully scanning the woods and the fields beyond. Tok made himself invisible, angling his shiny feathers to reflect the light so that he blended into the background of branches.

The Two-Legs made strange noises to each other. Tok watched as one of them began to climb the roost tree. When it got near the top it stopped and let down something long and thin like a vine. The other fastened one of the lumpy things to the vine and the Two-Legs in the tree hauled it up. It began taking small roundish things out of the lumpy thing and fastening them deep among the branches, moving down the tree little by little. When the big thing was flat and not lumpy, the Two-Legs dropped it, hauled up the other one and went to work again. When it got near the bottom of the tree, it jumped down, pulling some long thin threads with it. These the other Two-Legs attached to another object, which it fastened to the trunk of the tree. Then it bent over for a moment, twisting something on the front of it. After that, both Two-Legs walked back to the beetle and went away.

Tok flew at once to the roost tree and searched among the branches until he spied one of the roundish things.

Fearing the strangeness of it, he hung back, cocking his head to focus on it up close, first with one eye, then with the other. The thing was dull grey, the shape of a fat pine cone, and had grooves on it. Summoning his courage, he hopped closer and pecked at it. It felt hard as stone, but had a cold smell that was not stone. It didn't smell like food, either. Why had the Two-Legs fastened it to the branch? Tok had no idea, but his fear of them told him that they meant to harm the crows. He took to his wings and flapped off in search of Kaa's father.

He found Kraa back in the cornfield with the rest of the flock. When he told him what he had seen, the older bird cocked his head. "Put things in the roost tree, did they? I've never known them to do that."

"I think they mean us harm," said Tok.

Kraa shook his feathers "Who knows, with Two-Legs? Firesticks we know all about. But things in the roost tree? It's a mystery. Have the Two-Legs gone away?"

"Yes. But I think we should stay right away from the tree," Tok insisted.

"You do, do you?" snapped Kraa, touchy as ever. "Well, you can please yourself, of course. But this is a matter we crows will decide for ourselves. I'll tell as many as I can about this, and we'll soon see what to do." He flew off cawing the assembly call at the top of his voice. Other crows answered excitedly, and soon a large flock had gathered near the roost tree. First they all went to look at the objects hanging in the tree. Then they gathered again to caw it all over. More streams of crows began to flock in toward the roost, and they were warned away. Soon all the trees nearby were black with crows, and the air was filled with cawing and cackling.

Tok listened impatiently to the long discussion. Some said anything the Two-Legs did was dangerous, and the roost should be abandoned. Tok loudly croaked his agreement with this. But others said the Two-Legs were nowhere in sight and the strange objects couldn't possibly harm them. All they had to do was post lookouts to watch in case the Two-Legs tried to creep near with firesticks. This met with many caws of approval.

"Let's do that. And to be safe, we'll stay outside the roost until well after dark. If nothing happens, we'll know it's safe and that the raven is worrying for nothing," Kraa suggested. And the rest agreed.

The lookouts were posted. As darkness began to fall they called "All's well." The Two-Legs were nowhere in sight. Crows cawed back and forth nervously, impatient to settle down for the night. Parents scolded their youngsters, who were as big as they were now, but clumsy and in everyone's way.

Tok listened to the uproar. It's all so *crow*, he thought. But they had been good to him, he told himself. And later tonight he would be leaving them behind forever.

Time passed slowly. It was quite dark now, and the crows began to stir restlessly.

"Nothing's going to happen," one cawed. "The raven is wrong."

"Let's not be hasty, though," replied another. "We should wait a while longer."

And so they did. The moon rose, and by its light the

lookouts reported that there was still no sign of the Two-Legs. Now the crows began to fidget on their perches. A few flew boldly into the roost tree and settled down comfortably. Still the rest waited. Bats fluttered through the air, scooping up insects, and far away an owl hooted.

Kiraa shivered. "That's enough for me," she said loudly. "An owl could pick us off easily sitting out here. Even with you around," she added, with a glance at Tok. She flew toward the roost tree, and her father and mother and their youngsters followed. The other crows had decided too. The whole flock took to the air and landed in the roost tree to settle in for the rest of the night. Soon only Kaa was left sitting beside Tok.

"You were right to warn everyone, Tok," he said. "But nothing has happened. Whatever those things in the roost are they can't be dangerous or we'd know by now. And the Two-Legs are nowhere about to do mischief. Let's go to the roost."

Tok thought it over. Whatever the Two-Legs were up to didn't seem dangerous now. And if he stayed outside the roost Kaa would stay with him. He didn't want that. The two of them flapped across to the roost tree and settled in with the others.

It took the crows a long time to settle down to sleep. Slowly the caws and cackles died away, and at last there was silence. Tok allowed himself to doze lightly, but kept waking to watch the moon. When it stood high in the sky above the treetops, he knew it was time to go. He would need time to get well away before Kaa woke and found him gone.

They had come last into the roost and Tok had taken care to place himself near the end of a branch. All he had to do was ease along it until he could launch himself into the air. Quietly, he shuffled sideways. Kaa slept on, but Kiraa roused on the branch above. Tok froze, but after a moment, she sleepily tucked her head under her wing again. Reaching the end of the branch, he glided away from the tree. With a few powerful wingbeats, he swung up over the woods and circled once, feeling the starry sky imprint itself on his brain like a map. Then he wheeled and flew in the direction he knew was north.

Chapter 13

Heavy is the vengeance of the Two-Legs.

—Crow proverb

Tok had flown no more than a few hundred wingbeats when he heard a cry far behind him.

"*Ca-caw! Ca-caw!* Tok!"

It had to be Kaa. Tok hissed angrily, and increased his wingspeed, but the cry came again and again, though fainter. He slowed a bit, trying to decide what to do. If he just flew on he could easily outdistance the young crow. But would Kaa give up then, or would he wander on, trying to catch up, and get himself into trouble? At last, with a dip of one wing, Tok banked, wheeling back in the direction he had come from.

"Tok! Tok!" The cry was louder now, and soon he could make out a frantically flapping crow.

"You sneaked off!" panted Kaa as the two came together and circled. "You were going to leave me behind! No fair! It was *my* idea for you to find the Grey Lords. You know it was!"

Tok quorked with annoyance. "I told you—the journey

96

is too far, too hard for you."

"Crows aren't weaklings. I can do it!" Kaa insisted. "You don't have to wait for me if you don't want to. I'll follow as best I can."

But that was exactly what Tok didn't want. "Let's talk it over with your father, then," he said, veering south. "Maybe *he* can talk some sense into you!"

Kaa tagged after him, complaining all the way.

When they reached the roost, all was silent. Then, just as they circled in to land, a shattering blast tumbled them in midair and a burst of flame leaped toward the sky.

Struggling against the violent updraft, they banked away from the flames. "It's the Two-Legs!" shrieked Kaa. "They've killed them all!"

Below them, black bodies shot out of the burning tree, some of them on fire. Calling and crying, they blundered into nearby trees, seeking shelter. The roost tree was a torch of flame now, the resin in its needles making it burn with a crackling roar.

Kaa was flying in circles, screaming. Tok managed to get above him, forcing him down into a tree near the edge of the fields. "You can't do anything now," he shouted over the roar of the flames. "Many escaped—with luck your family will have too. We must wait until morning, then try to find them."

By dawn, the shattered roost tree had burned itself out. Only a thin column of smoke curled up from it into the clear sky. In the trees around the wrecked roost, the surviving crows moaned, parents looking for children and mates for mates. The ground below the roost was littered with hundreds of black bodies.

Tok and Kaa fluttered from tree to tree. "Has anyone seen Kraa?" begged Kaa. "Or my mother? Or Kiraa?" But no one had. At last, with all hope gone, they searched among the dead under the tree and found the scorched bodies of Kaa's family huddled together where they had fallen. Kaa hopped forlornly among them. He smoothed Kraa's feathers and stroked his mother's. Then he tried to raise Kiraa's head, but it fell back limply.

Tok felt sick with pity. "Come away," he said gruffly. "It's no use."

Now crows were flying in from many directions to join the survivors. Grieving and crying, they perched in the trees, weighing down the branches with their black bodies. For a long time the air was filled with wailing, and then with mournful caws the crows began to abandon the woods one by one.

"They'll all go," mumbled Kaa. "No one could live here—not now."

"We must go too," urged Tok, spreading his wings.

Kaa made no protest. Lifting himself into the air with a last sad cry, he followed Tok northward.

Tok knew he had to take Kaa along now. He couldn't leave him behind to grieve alone. So he took care not to fly too far that day. In the early afternoon they landed near a small lake surrounded by berry bushes.

"Eat," ordered Tok. "Or you won't be strong enough to fly."

Numbly, Kaa obeyed.

They roosted that night among the yellowing leaves of

an old poplar near the pond. Kaa kept waking up with loud cries, and pressing himself close against Tok. But Tok stayed awake for a long time, thinking about what lay ahead for them both. He imagined Kaa, heartsick and wing-weary, falling farther and farther behind. Kaa half-frozen, shivering and starving in falling snow. It would be better, far better, he told himself, if only Kaa would stay with other crows. They would surely find many along the way. Then he would be free to find the Singers.

But when Tok mentioned staying with other crows the next day, Kaa refused. "I go where you go," he said, gazing reproachfully at Tok. "You're my family now."

There was nothing else that Tok could say.

At first they journeyed many days over a countryside golden with autumn. There was food in plenty—berries, spilled grain in harvested fields, and mice and shrews in the meadows. Many flocks of birds were heading south, but they saw only a few crows now and then. Kaa flew to question them, but none knew anything about the Singers.

Little by little the nights grew colder, and the last leaves flew from the trees, driven by blustery winds. The moon rose full and stark white. The Moon of the Hunters, thought Tok, remembering the boom of firesticks among the Raven Mountains, and raven feasts on the carcasses of slaughtered deer.

○

After many more days the landscape began to change beneath their wings. There were more forests than open country now, and long narrow lakes set between low rolling hills. With the change, Kaa's spirits began to lift a little.

"Look—crows! Lots of them!" he cawed late one afternoon. And sure enough, a ragged flight of black shapes was flapping along below them. Kaa zoomed down to join them for a few moments. "There's a good roost not far away," he told Tok when he returned. "A big one." His voice trembled with excitement and he blinked his whitelids. "We can roost there, can't we? There are no Two-Legs anywhere near," he added. "I asked."

Tok had got used to roosting alone, and did not fancy the company of noisy strangers. But he could see how eager Kaa was to be with his own kind. Maybe, just maybe, he would decide to stay with them after all. "Let's go," he replied.

With a caw of delight, Kaa dived down toward the other crows, and they began to call back and forth. In the distance Tok could see dark ribbons of crows flying in from all directions. As newcomers he and Kaa were careful to land far from the roost, making their way slowly toward the central tree. The sky above was black with birds, circling and cawing against the sunset sky. Inside the roost there was a great hubbub as crows gossiped and complained while they settled in for the night. They nudged and jostled each other in the dim light, each trying to get the best place.

Tok and Kaa settled in too. But it wasn't long before Tok sensed that something was wrong. In the midst of the joyful racket of the newcomers, other crow voices sounded plaintive and shrill. Some birds perched trembling and silent on the branches. Their eyes were closed, but they were not sleeping, for their beaks opened and closed, panting.

"What's wrong with them?" he asked Kaa.

"Who knows? Different crows have different ways. Maybe these are local birds who don't like the rest of us taking over their roost. Is that right?" he asked the silent bird beside him. When it did not reply, Kaa turned away and fluffed his feathers. He gazed around eagerly, enjoying the noise and the crowding.

Tok was still uneasy. There was something wrong with some of these crows—he was sure of it. But what could it be?

When the crows had settled a bit, Kaa started asking questions of the other birds. Some were from far to the north, and were flying ahead of cold weather close behind them.

"I woke up yesterday with frost on my feathers," one complained. "I'm for warm sun and easy foraging in the south."

Then Kaa asked about ravens and the Singers. This time several birds nodded in the gathering dark. Yes, they said, they had heard of the Singers, though none had actually seen one.

"Oh, they live much further north," one replied. "Far beyond the Shining Lakes."

"How can I find them?" Tok broke in.

For a moment the speaker fell silent, frightened by Tok's deep voice. Then, "Raven, are you?" he asked, peering at Tok. "Why ask? Your kind know the Singers better than anyone. But finding the Singers is not so easy. I've heard they don't live in one place. They cover great distances, always on the move, always hunting."

Tok's heart beat faster. The Singers *did* exist. And they had to be the same as the Grey Lords—everyone said ravens knew them well. In his excitement he found it hard to sleep. When he did, he was awakened several times by a swishing sound followed by a thump. He could see nothing in the darkness, but he could hear rustles and whispers as crows shuffled on the branches and resettled themselves. What was happening?

At first light the crows began to caw and mutter among themselves. Some flew off at once, but many remained behind, making faint sounds and stumbling about among the branches. Outside, crows suddenly began to caw the alarm call.

Now Tok was sure that something was terribly wrong. "Let's go!" he urged Kaa.

But the young crow stayed stubbornly on his perch. "Why hurry?" he complained. "This is a good place. And good company. I want to stay a while."

It was what Tok had hoped for, yet now he was terribly afraid. "The alarm call—can't you hear it?" he demanded.

"Whatever it is, we're probably safer in here," said Kaa. "Don't you . . . " he began, turning to the bird perched right beside him. Then he uttered a terrified squawk. The other crow was clearly sick. It sat trembling on the branch, and its eyes had turned milky white. Then with a pitiful mewing sound it closed its eyes and dropped from its perch, plummeting like a stone to the ground.

Tok and Kaa burst from the branches of the roost and flapped away as fast as they could. Outside, all was confusion. There were more dead crows under the tree. Others, unable to see, were trying to fly but were crashing into tree branches. The luckier ones were cawing danger calls and fleeing.

"What was it?" gasped Kaa as they headed north.

"I don't know. A sickness. They looked as if they had gone blind," Tok replied. "The crows that had it must be the ones that live there. And the others . . ." He said no more, but thought of how the sick crows had pressed close against healthy ones in the roost. He shuddered as he flew.

Chapter 14

The greatest kora *of all is courage.*
—Wisdom of the Kort

After that Kaa never spoke of roosting with his own kind again. Day after day the two of them flew northward. The skies were empty now, for the great flocks had long since gone south. The land seemed to hold its breath and wait for winter. Then one morning they woke to find the ground dusted with snow, though it soon melted in the rays of the sun. More snow fell the next night, and in the morning there was a thick crust of ice on the edge of a nearby pond.

"Winter is coming," Tok told Kaa as they began their day's journey. "But it can't be far to the Shining Lakes. Once we get there, we'll stop to rest and forage before we try to cross."

"Rest? What's that?" muttered Kaa. "I didn't think ravens needed any."

Tok glanced at him sharply. He had not complained before on their journey and now he seemed to be having even more trouble than usual keeping up. Grudgingly, Tok slowed his wingspeed, though he longed to hurry ahead to the land of the Singers.

Wingbeats and more wingbeats across the leaden skies—to Tok the journey began to seem endless. Then one day the sky cleared and a chain of broad blue lakes appeared ahead of them. Tok gazed down eagerly. Somewhere beyond were other ravens and the Singers. In just a few days he might actually find them!

They fed near some woods at the frozen edge of a lake. Tok's head was so full of ravens and Singers that it was a while before he noticed that something was wrong. Kaa wasn't having much luck with his hunting, and more mice escaped him than he caught. Puzzled, Tok killed a few extra and left them nearby. Kaa pounced on them eagerly and killed them again, not seeming to notice that they were already dead.

That night he trembled on his perch, and Tok began to worry. Perhaps they had traveled too far, too fast after all. "We'll stay a while longer," he told Kaa. "There's no hurry now that we've reached the Lakes."

"Good idea," Kaa mumbled.

So they spent a lazy day, flying little and feeding until they could eat no more. Tok watched Kaa closely. Rested now, he seemed a bit more like his old self. But he still missed most of his prey, and Tok had to help out. And the young crow seemed ill at ease in the forest, blundering into branches he would once have dodged easily.

"What's wrong with you?" demanded Tok when they roosted for the night. His voice sounded sharper than he'd meant it to, so he added, "I mean, are you all right? Have we flown too far these last days?"

"I . . . I do feel tired," admitted Kaa. "It will be good to sleep." A tremor shook his wings.

At first light Tok turned eagerly to Kaa, hoping to find him better. Then he stared in horror. The young crow's eyes showed the first milky traces of the white blindness.

Kaa blinked miserably. "It's no use," he said, shivering. "I've been feeling strange for days. I tried to tell myself I was just tired. But Tok, I can hardly see you." After a moment he added, "You must go on now. You see how it is. I won't be able to come with you after all."

Tok gave a great cry of sorrow and rage. "Wrrrakkk! Go without you? Don't be foolish. We'll stay right here until you feel better. I'll look after you—you'll get better. Just wait and see."

"But what if . . . what if you get the sickness too?" quavered Kaa. "I got it from roosting with those sick crows. I must have. There was nothing wrong with me before."

"Then I must already have it too," Tok told him. "Or maybe ravens don't catch the sickness. Anyway, I'm going to look after you. Remember how you fed me when I was hurt? It's my turn now."

Kaa shuffled his feet on the branch. "But your journey . . . the Singers . . ." he protested.

"Never mind all that!" thundered Tok. Suddenly his own problems no longer mattered. Now there was only Kaa. He'd known all along how much the young crow loved him, yet all he'd wanted was to leave him behind and get on with his journey. Even after Kaa's family died he had grudged having to travel more slowly because of him. What kind of *kora* was that, to hope Kaa would just decide to stay with other crows along the way? Well, now he would guard Kaa and make him better somehow. Those other crows, the ones who had died, had probably been starving. That was why they didn't get better. It would be different for Kaa. He'd make it be different.

He guided Kaa down beside the lake, and brought food for him. Kaa ate little, but when the morning sun melted the skin of ice on the water he walked into it and drank great gulps, tilting his beak up to let the liquid trickle down his throat. "I'm thirsty," he muttered. "So thirsty."

Tok found him a safe perch nearby and he dozed most of the day, shivering in his sleep. By late afternoon, the milkiness on his eyes had thickened into staring white.

"I can't see at all, Tok," he said in a small voice.

"Never mind. Just do as I say," replied Tok. "There's a branch straight above you. Just a jump and two wingbeats. Do it!"

Kaa obeyed. Little by little Tok guided him to a perch a safe height above the ground.

"There," he said, when Kaa was settled. "That wasn't so hard, was it? You're going to be fine. I can find plenty of food for both of us. When you feel stronger we can fly farther south. Where it's warmer." He was talking faster and faster now, trying to convince himself as well as Kaa. "You'll get better. I know you will."

Kaa said nothing. Instead of pressing close against Tok as he had always done, he stepped a way along the branch, putting plenty of space between them. Just before they went to sleep, he said, "Thank you, Tok. I'd be so frightened to be like this alone." Then he put his head under his wing.

Somehow Tok managed to fall asleep, but when he awoke in the middle of the night and looked around, Kaa was no longer on the branch! "Kaa!" he shouted, diving for the ground. "Here I am, Kaa. Why didn't you call?"

There was no reply. Tok hopped about under the tree. Kaa could not have gone far, yet he did not seem to be anywhere near. So Tok flapped onto a bare branch, his eyes searching the moonlit glade for the tiniest movement. Nothing. He called Kaa's name and called again. No answer.

Slowly Tok realized the truth, and a terrible sadness welled up inside him. Kaa hadn't tumbled from his perch. He had gone on purpose, gliding to the ground on silent wings, hiding himself away where Tok could not find him. Now he was waiting for some kind of death to claim him. For a blind bird on the ground it would not be long in coming.

He's doing it for me! Tok thought in anguish. Because he doesn't want to stand in my way, keep me from my quest for the Singers. "Kaa, let me help you!" he pleaded. "I don't care about the Singers. Not anymore!" But there was no answer, and he knew now that there would not be one. And so he sat sorrowing alone. He had thought ravens were the brave ones, he told himself bitterly. But what were their quarrels and strutting compared to this?

Slowly the night wore away. Just before dawn Tok heard a sudden scuffle in the bushes, then a scream. Then silence. When the sun rose his eyes picked out a small drift of black feathers under a bush at the far edge of the glade. With a mournful cry he launched himself into the air and with heavy wingbeats set out across the Shining Lakes.

Part 3

The Country of the Two-Legs

Chapter 15

Skyah made one world for us all. The Two-Legs,
not content, have made themselves another.
—Truths of the Tellers

Below Tok, the water of the lake rolled dull silver under a sky thick with clouds. He flew fast, with powerful wing strokes. There was nobody to hold him back now, he told himself. He'd wanted his freedom, hadn't he? Well, now he had it. But he would have given it up gladly if Kaa could only be alive again.

He gazed ahead, yearning to catch sight of a forested shore. But the lake was too wide—it stretched ahead as far as he could see. At last, he saw a distant shoreline, but there was no forest. Instead he saw ranks of great tall objects, unnaturally straight. He knew them at once for the work of the Two-Legs, like the many-roosts in Kaa's country. But this place was much greater. It lined the northern edge of the lake as far as he could see. Some of the roosts were so tall that their tops were lost in the bellies of the low clouds that hung over them. Tok shuddered to think of how many Two-Legs might live there.

Trying to avoid the danger, he swerved west, hoping to find the end of the lake. But it seemed to stretch on forever. Then he tried flying east, but the result was the same. The distance was too great for even his strong wings, for there was no place to land and rest. Reluctantly, Tok turned north again. He'd have to fly straight into the roosts of the Two-Legs. Either that or give up his quest and return to the south shore. And that he would not do. Kaa had died because of his search for the Grey Lords. He had to go on to the end now.

The closer Tok got to the great roosts, the taller they loomed. Like a great row of jagged teeth they cut him off from the northern woods he was seeking. He could see now that the roosts were set into a web of the Two-Legs' hard black paths, the ones their beetles ran on. As far as he could see there was no ground at all—just the thick crust of the Two-Legs' unnatural makings covering the ground to the horizon.

Trembling, he plunged among the towering roosts that lined the shore of the lake. There were even taller ones behind them, and still more after that. He found himself flying along a canyon of not-stone, its walls set with a strange shiny substance that reflected confusing lights and shadows. A silvery flying thing roared high overhead, and Tok flinched as the sound echoed off the canyon walls around him. Another terror of the Two-Legs! Wild air currents buffeted him as they gusted between the giant roosts, and he struggled to control his wings. From the depths below him rose a dull roar pierced by strange honkings. The paths below were jammed solidly with beetles.

The canyon funneled him northward for thousands of wingbeats. At least it seemed to be taking him in the right direction, Tok thought dizzily, but would it never end? He glimpsed a few green open places, and yearned to land, but he did not dare to. On and on he flew, his senses numbed by the sheer *wrongness* of everything around him. Stone that was not-stone, wind that was not-wind, sky that was not-sky. Would he ever escape? Or would he struggle on until his wings failed and he smashed into one of the structures around him?

At last, when he had almost given up hope, the height of the roosts began to grow less, though the ground was still crusted over with them. Now he could see farther than he had been able to in the nightmare canyon. Clusters of big roosts still dotted the landscape among many smaller ones, but in the farthest distance he thought he could see a line of clean white. That meant snow—open country!

Then, straight ahead of him, he saw a giant path carved across the heart of the terrible many-roosts. Along the broad swathe of open ground marched a line of trees that were not-trees with long vinelike things stretched between them.

Just a little rest, Tok promised himself as he dropped down toward them. He was almost out of the many-roosts now. The worst was over. The closer he came, though, the more he sensed something wrong about the not-trees. There was a queer feeling to them—they seemed to give off an unseen vibration and a low hum. But Tok was too tired to care. He had to rest before he fell like a stone from the sky. He circled in, claws outstretched, and grasped a strange hard limb on one of the not-trees, locking his toes around it. His outstretched wing brushed against one of the vines. Then it was as though a million suns burst in his head. His body seemed to explode and he felt himself plummeting earthward. He never knew when he hit the ground.

○

Darkness. Burning pain. Tok opened his eyes, but saw only dim masses against a field of grey. He closed his whitelids. Every nerve in his body tingled, and his wing muscles trembled in spasms. He tried to flex his toes, but they wouldn't obey. They felt thick, heavy, and they hurt with a continuous, throbbing pain. His mind drifted toward nothingness again.

Then a voice, shrill and high, came from close by. So close that Tok's eyes shot open again. He blinked his whitelids several times, trying to clear his blurred vision.

A deeper voice spoke too, rumbling in Tok's ears. Two cloudy shapes loomed close, and Tok struggled to focus on them. When he did, his heart almost stopped with panic. He was lying in some kind of enclosure, and peering in at him through the sides of it stood a pair of Two-Legs!

Chapter 16

Enemies are always more surprising than friends.
—Raven proverb

Tok's beak gaped and he hissed in fear. Frantically he tried to get to his feet, to spread his wings ready to fight them off. But he could barely move his wings. And now that he could focus on his feet he saw that they were covered with some kind of thick white wrappings. The Two-Legs had bound them! And what had they done to his wings? he thought in terror. He could see no wrappings there, but they felt so weak that he knew the Two-Legs must have harmed him in some way.

The one with the squeaky voice put its face right up against the side of the enclosure, and Tok hissed again. The other Two-Legs rumbled something and Squeaky Voice stepped back. Then, to Tok's relief, they both turned and walked away. Whatever they wanted with him they weren't going to hurt him—yet.

After a few moments, Tok tried again to struggle to his feet. He managed to get one wing half open, and using this as a prop, he rolled over and got his feet under him. The wrappings on his feet bothered him, so he drew them under him and began to peck at the material. Little by little, with much tugging, he pulled the white strips off, snipping each one into bits with his beak. They wouldn't wrap him up in those again!

Standing on his feet made them hurt even more sharply. Peering down at them, he could see that they were coated with some kind of sticky substance. He tasted it and found it bitter, like pine resin. Maybe it was poison, he thought. Best to leave it alone.

There was water in a round thing in one corner of the enclosure, and Tok hop-dragged himself over to it. He drank deeply, washing away the bitter taste on his tongue. Then he tried again to spread his wings. There was just room in the enclosure, and this time he managed to do it, though like the rest of his body his wings kept trembling. Had the Two-Legs done that to him? Or . . .

He could remember landing on the tree-that-was-not-a-tree, but nothing after that. So perhaps it was the tree that had hurt him. But whatever had happened, the Two-Legs had him now. They probably had firesticks or worse things. He would have to stay alert. But he felt so hurt and so weary . . . his head drooped and he fell asleep where he crouched.

When he awoke, he found he could see better. The enclosure seemed to be inside a roost of the Two-Legs, but one whole side of the roost stood open and he could see outside. A shiny beetle of the Two-Legs stood close beside him. It did not move or make any noise, so he quickly lost interest in it. He could see from the angle of the shadows on the ground that the sun was low, so it was late in the day. He stretched his wings. The pain in his body was less now, though he still trembled all over. His feet hurt him, but tough and scaly as they were, Tok knew their hurt was not deep. They would heal fast.

He set about examining the enclosure. It was made of thin hard threads that Tok thought would be easy to break through. But when he champed them in his beak, he found he could not cut them. Frustrated, he shuffled around, testing and tapping. There seemed to be no way out. He heard a loud *thud*, and turned around quickly. Through the open side of the roost he could see an even bigger roost some distance away. The smaller Two-Legs was coming toward him from it, carrying something. Not a firestick.

Tok flattened himself against the side of the enclosure, as far away from the Two-Legs as he could get, and hissed a warning as it approached.

He hissed again as the Two-Legs fiddled with something at the far end of the enclosure. Then the whole end opened, and the Two-Legs removed the empty water-thing, replacing it with a fresh one and another object piled high with chunks of . . .

Meat! Tok salivated at the sight and smell of it. He had not eaten since he had hunted for Kaa, and despite his shivery weakness, his hunger was great.

The Two-Legs closed the end of the enclosure and stood looking down at him. Then it squeaked something that grated in Tok's ears. He roused his feathers, making himself as big as possible, hoping to scare it away, and shuffled his feet, refusing to go near the food with this strange creature staring at him. After a while it walked back to its roost and disappeared inside.

Tok hopped closer to the meat, then jumped back in alarm at its strangeness. But nothing happened. After another try he got close enough to sniff it. He yearned to bolt it down, but a Two-Legs had touched it, and they were tricky. Perhaps the meat was poisoned—ravenlore had taught him that was a favorite trick of theirs. But his body told him he needed food, needed it desperately. And these Two-Legs hadn't hurt him so far. Cautiously he pulped a piece of meat in his beak, testing its taste and smell. There seemed to be nothing wrong with it. He'd eat just one piece, he promised himself. But he was so hungry that in the end he ate two. Then he drank a lot of water and put his head under his wing.

ↄ

The small Two-Legs came back in the morning. Opening the enclosure, it took the meat out and added fresh water.

Tok watched longingly as the Two-Legs carried the meat away. It had tasted wonderful, and it had not made him sick. If only he had thought to cache some of it! But soon Squeaky Voice returned with a plate piled high with more food and placed it inside the enclosure. There was meat—a different kind—and a flat piece of something white, and a yellow lump of something else that smelled delicious.

The Two-Legs squeaked some more. Then it backed

away from his enclosure and stood waiting to see what he would do.

Tok hopped over to the dish of food. He was terribly hungry now. He would never get his strength back if he didn't eat. And though he still didn't trust the Two-Legs, last night's meat hadn't been tainted. So he fell upon the food, bolting down the meat first. Then he put one foot on the white substance and pulled off bits of it. Not much taste, but he finished it anyway. The wonderful-smelling lump was much better, like the best, richest fat from a carcass. And there were small crispy orange things too. Tok crunched one thoughtfully. It was very tasty, like nothing he had ever eaten before. Eagerly he ate the rest of them, saving only two, which he cached at the far end of the enclosure.

The small Two-Legs patted its front paws together and gave a little jump. Then it turned and ran back to its roost, making those annoying squeaking noises all the way.

His hunger satisfied at last, Tok dozed for a while. Then he preened himself feather by feather. He was beginning to feel much better, though his wings trembled and his feet still hurt him.

He shuffled up and down the enclosure, quorking and querking to himself as he thought things through. The Two-Legs—at least Squeaky Voice—weren't going to kill him after all. In fact, he'd just had the best meal of his entire life. That bore some thinking: ravenlore taught that the Two-Legs were the deadly enemies of all ravens. He'd seen their terrible firesticks with his own eyes. And look what they had done to Kaa's people! Yet these Two-Legs were actually feeding him. It was a mystery.

The sun rose and set two more times before Tok began to feel more like himself. Squeaky Voice brought him more delicious food twice each day, and no Two-Legs tried to harm him. But they had shut him up in this enclosure for some strange reason of their own. His heart rebelled at being not-free—he had to get away! He knew now that there was a way out, for he had watched Squeaky Voice open the end of the enclosure. He had to find out how it was done. First though, he ate the crispy orange things he had cached, closing his eyes as he savored the taste. Then he inspected the end of the enclosure. He tested every bit of it with his beak, and shoved against it with his shoulder, but it held fast. He just couldn't make out how it opened. Angrily he banged on the hard floor of the enclosure with his beak until the water-thing danced around, spilling a puddle.

Squeaky Voice brought him another wonderful meal later on. This time, Tok stationed himself near the end of the enclosure and focused his eyes on what the Two-Legs did to make it open. He could see now that there was some kind of fastener on the outside. Squeaky Voice slid a slender round piece of it back, and the end of the enclosure swung outward.

As soon as it had left him again, Tok sidled up and peered at the fastener, first with one eye, then with the other. There were two hollow things and a piece like a twig that slid through them. He worried at the slider with his beak, but it was made of the same hard substance as the rest of the enclosure, and was too slippery to grasp. He eyed it again—was there nothing he could get hold of? Then he saw a kind of tooth on the side of the slider. He pressed his beak against this and felt the slider move. He pushed again, and it moved some more. He could open it!

Turning back to the food, he gobbled it down, savoring every bite. There were more of the crispy orange things and he ate them lovingly. When would he have such delicious food again? Then he drank the water and hopped back to the fastener. He nudged the tooth with his beak until it would move no farther, then he pushed hard on the end of the enclosure. It swung open, and he was free!

Tok hopped to the ground, and spread his wings. A couple of flaps took him outside the roost, then he launched himself a little higher into the air and made a wobbly beeline for a tall evergreen nearby. But his wings felt strangely weak after even so short a flight, and this worried him. He wouldn't be able to cover much distance at a time until they strengthened. But he would have to try. The Two-Legs would soon discover he was gone, and might try to catch him again.

He took to the air, wheeling once over the Two-Legs' roost. He did not feel strong enough to try to gain much height, so he tree-hopped as best he could, always heading north toward the horizon of pure white snow he remembered. It took all his courage to keep going, for he was still in the terrible many-roosts of the Two-Legs. If anything, it was more frightening than in the daytime. For at dusk bright lights sprang on everywhere and the sky above him took on a strange pinkish glow. There were terrifying noises too, a ceaseless dull roar overlaid with the honking of the Two-Legs' beetles and an occasional wailing sound. Half-deafened, half-blinded, Tok struggled on until he could stand no more. At last he crept among the sheltering branches of a spruce tree and huddled there until dawn. Taking wing again, he circled and turned northward. Would it be another day of terror like yesterday? But no. Not too many wingbeats away, the many-roosts ended and the clean snowy fields began. With a croak of joy, Tok flung himself forward.

Chapter 17

Many strange things under Skyah.
—Truths of the Tellers

His heart lifting with every wingbeat, Tok flew toward a small patch of woods in the distance. Swooping among the trees, he found no evergreens to shelter him, but even the bare limb he perched on seemed welcoming. Peace flowed about him, and his panic began to subside. Feeling hungry again, he thought wistfully of the delicious piles of food the Two-Legs had brought him. Then he shuddered. Better to go hungry in the wild than be full-fed by *them!*

From his vantage point high in the tree, Tok scanned the surrounding countryside. It was mostly open fields covered deep in snow. To the south rose the jagged teeth of the great many-roosts. Hard paths led to it and he could see the beetles of the Two-Legs scurrying to and fro along them. He could hear other sounds now, over the distant roar from the place of the many-roosts. The creak of bare tree branches rubbing together, the whisper of the wind among the twigs. And a harsh cawing in the distance. Tok cocked his head, listening. Crows, he thought. But among their calls he could pick out other voices, deeper, hoarser. . . .

Ravens!

His weariness forgotten, Tok beat away northwest, closing in on the voices. He could see no mountains, no forests, nothing that looked like raven country. Smoke hung in the air ahead of him. It was rising from a stretch of low uneven hills, around which grew a fringe of stunted trees. The bristles over Tok's nostrils quivered as the wind brought the smell of burning and of . . . carrion? No, not exactly. Yet the hills stank of decay.

He swooped lower, then back-pedaled in the air. The hills were black with the shapes of hundreds of crows and ravens!

He dropped down next to a large party of ravens. The nearest one, a big bird with rough unpreened feathers, stared at him.

"You're new. Who are you?" it croaked.

"I am Tok, son of Lord Rokan," replied Tok.

The other raven clacked his beak. "Never mind the titles," he jeered. "There's no need. Plain Gork is good enough for me." He jabbed his beak into the ground and yanked out something juicy.

"No titles?" asked Tok.

"None." Gork eyed him curiously. "Tell me, why do ravens have titles where you come from?"

"Why, to honor lordship over a territory, the right to take a mate . . ."

"Bah," scoffed Gork. "It all comes down to food. Being a lord means you hold enough territory to feed yourself and a family. That's all. We don't need territories here."

"How do families get enough to eat, then?" Tok wondered.

Gork gave a harsh quork of laughter. Then, turning to the other ravens nearby, "Did you hear that, you grubbers? He wonders how we get enough to eat!"

There was a mocking chorus of querks and grunts.

"Can't you see for yourself?" Gork went on. "You're standing on mountains of food. We're all lords here!" He scrabbled something else out of the soil and swallowed it.

Tok peered at the uneven ground under his claws. It seemed to be a jumble of things piled together and mixed with soil. The crows and ravens were busy tearing open hummocks of green or white slippery material and strewing the contents about the hillside. There was a strong stench of well-rotted food.

"But what *is* all this?" he asked Gork.

The raven wiped his beak on his breast feathers, leaving a greasy smear. "It's from the many-roosts of the Two-Legs. They bring more here every day. Very kind of them, I say," he added with a hoarse chuckle. The other birds cackled and wheezed in agreement.

Another raven swaggered up, with a band of followers trailing behind it. Around its neck it wore a ring of some slippery-looking grey material. Noticing Tok's stare, the raven roused its feathers and stretched its neck, showing off its strange collar. "I see you admire my ruff. Handsome, isn't it?" he boasted. Then, when Tok didn't answer, he added sharply, "This is my badge of honor. I'm Porag, the lord of these hills."

Tok glanced at Gork. "I thought there were no lords here," he said.

Gork grunted. "There aren't. Pay no attention to Porag. He just got his head stuck in that thing one day and now he gives himself airs about it."

Porag drew himself up, erecting his feather ears. "That's enough from you, Gork," he hissed. "Teach him some manners, the rest of you!" At this the others rushed forward and attacked Gork, who defended himself fiercely with beak and claw. At last, though, the big raven was driven off, closely pursued by Porag's followers.

Porag stared coldly at Tok. "You see how it is. Show respect, and you're welcome. If not . . ." He took to the air and flapped off over the reeking hillside.

Left to himself, Tok found a slimy lump of meat and gobbled it down, then tried a piece of squashed fruit. You'd never have to worry about caching things for hard times here, he thought. He could scarcely grasp the idea of such plenty. In his home there had been starvation and death, but here there was food for all.

Suddenly a squabble broke out nearby. A young raven had unearthed a large tasty morsel and a couple of bigger birds were trying to steal it. From the ravenet's voice, Tok could tell she was a female.

"It's mine! I found it!" she croaked, clutching the morsel tightly in her claws. But the other two worked cleverly as a team, one yanking her tail feathers, and the other snatching the tidbit away when she turned to defend herself.

With two swishes of his wings, Tok landed among them.

"Drop that!" he cried. He gave the thief a buffet with

his wing, and it let go of the prize.

"Mind your own business," croaked the other raven, puffing out his feathers. "We're of Porag's crew, and we rule here."

"Oh, you do, do you?" roared Tok, giving him a buffet too. "Clear out, I tell you. Leave her alone!" Rousing his feathers and erecting his ears, he stalked toward them with half-spread wings. They gave ground before him, then with angry quorks they took to their wings and drifted off over the hills.

Meanwhile, the ravenet had hopped over to reclaim her find. She was a small bird with untidy feathers, but her amber eyes were clear and bright. "I suppose *you'll* try to snatch it now," she rasped, putting one clawed foot on it and staring defiantly at Tok.

Despite her rough looks, her boldness reminded him of Tarkah, and Tok's heart suddenly felt sore. "Keep it, it's all yours," he said. With a couple of wing-flaps he glided higher on the hillside.

After a moment the ravenet followed him. Spreading her wings, she made a little bow. "Sorry," she said. "I needn't have been so rude. Help yourself," she added, pushing toward him the lump of meat she had carried with her in her claws.

Tok snipped off a piece with his beak and tossed it down. It was rich and rank. Delicious.

"Are you a stranger?" asked the ravenet. Tok nodded, and she went on, "I thought so. You have a different look about you."

"Different?"

She cocked her head. "You look worn, as if you've traveled far. Not like this greasy lot who never go anywhere."

When Tok said nothing, she continued. "My name's Brekka." She sighed. "I shouldn't talk against the others. I never go anywhere either. I've lived here all my life."

"You mean you were hatched here? You didn't come from . . . from away?"

She nodded. "Almost all of us were hatched here."

Despite the rich food in his belly, Tok shivered. What a life. No fall flights, no adventures. No clean wind to ride, no wild forests to roost in. Nothing but stinking hills and stunted trees. He gazed at Brekka in pity. "My name is Tok," he said. "And you're right. I've traveled far. Part of the way with the help of those folk," he added, as a ragged flock of crows flew cawing overhead.

"You went with *crows?*" Brekka lifted her head and stared down her beak at him. "How *unkora!*"

Tok's temper flared. "*Unkora?*" he burst out. "How would you know what's *kora?* You live off the Two-Legs. What kind of ravens are you, anyway?"

"Better than you . . . you crow-lover!" Brekka taunted, angrily tearing off a chunk of her meat and bolting it down.

Tok opened his beak to yell at her, but closed it again. Hadn't he thought the same way himself? It had taken Kaa to teach him that a crow could be as noble as any raven.

"Tell me," he asked in a lower voice, "why do ravens quarrel over food here, when there's plenty for all?"

"The more you have the more you want," snapped Brekka. "And even if food is easy to find, it's easier still to steal it." She tossed her head. "Besides, it's exciting. Nothing else ever happens here—every day's the same. Except Porag's lot are getting bolder all the time now."

Tok raised his throat hackles and growled in disgust. Grakk would be right at home among that greasy-beaked, oily-feathered crew, he thought bitterly. Even if he didn't have to search for the Grey Lords, he would not stay here. Not for all the easy pickings in the world.

Brekka went on pecking listlessly at her chunk of meat.

"Have you ever heard of the Grey Lords?" he asked her.

"No," she replied. "We know nothing of the world outside."

"Have you no Tellers, then?" wondered Tok.

"Tellers? What are they?"

"Keepers of the raven way, tellers of tales and traditions."

Brekka uttered a harsh croak. "Traditions?" she scoffed. "We have no traditions!"

Tok gaped at her in amazement. "You mean you don't tell stories, don't sky dance . . . ?"

"I don't even know what those things mean."

"But you must have rules . . . a Kort!"

She shook her head. "Here it's every raven for itself." She thought for a moment. "Some say that we didn't always live here like this," she went on, "that we came from somewhere else. An older bird might know, but I don't know how you'll find one who does—you'll have to ask every raven on these hills. And there are hundreds."

Tok's heart sank. These were the only ravens he had found, and they knew even less than he did!

Chapter 18

Not seen, yet there. Not there, soon seen.
What is it?
Kora.

—Raven riddle

"But you must at least know Skyah!" said Tok.

"Skyah? Who's that?" Brekka demanded.

"Why... the Maker of All," faltered Tok. "I thought all ravens honored Skyah!"

"Why should we? Skyah hasn't done anything for us lately!" she jeered.

There was no use talking to her, thought Tok. No use at all. He spread his wings to glide away.

"Wait!" cried the ravenet. "I've just thought of something. I did know an old bird last year. I've scarcely thought of her since and she may not even be alive. But if she is, perhaps she could help you."

"But how would we find her?" Tok asked hopelessly, staring out over the reeking hills stretching away into the distance.

"Craal never cared much for these hills," replied

Brekka. "She used to stay right at the northern edge, near the biggest trees. She might still be there." She flapped away through the smoke that veiled the hillside, and Tok followed. After a few hundred wingbeats they landed on a dead tree on the edge of the hills.

"This is where Craal used to forage," said Brekka, peering down at the crowd of ravens on the near hillside. "I met her when I was only just fledged and on my own."

She turned her head from side to side, scanning the hordes of birds. "There—I think," she said at last. "Yes, that's Craal." She glided down and Tok followed.

At the very edge of the hills they found a dusty old raven scrabbling in the ground. Her feathers, dull and lifeless, were flecked with white, and her eyes were veiled with a bluish haze. She was terribly thin, and poked about with her beak as if she couldn't see very well.

A chill went through Tok when he saw her filmy eyes, and he hung back. "Is she . . . is she sick?" he asked, remembering the terrible white blindness.

"Not sick, just old," muttered Brekka. She hopped closer. "Craal? It's Brekka. Do you remember me?"

The old bird peered at her. "Young Brekka, is it? Of course I remember. I recognize your voice, though I can scarcely see you."

"You look thin, Craal," said Brekka. "You can't be getting enough to eat." She flew a little higher on the slope and poked about, returning in a few moments with a juicy mouthful. "Now, eat that," she ordered. "Then we want to talk with you."

Craal bent her head low as if she could barely see the

food in front of her. Then she bolted it down, glancing over her shoulder as if afraid that someone would snatch it from her. "Thank you, Brekka," she said when she had finished. "It's not often I dine as well as that, even here on the Hills of Plenty."

"Is that what you call this place?" Tok broke in.

Alarmed by the loudness of his voice, Craal backed away.

"Wait, Craal," said Brekka. "It's all right. This is Tok. He's with me."

Craal lifted her head. "I've no cause to love young males," she explained. "They've given me many a drubbing for the sake of a mouthful of food. Imagine—a bird of my age knocked about by youngsters. There's no *kora* anymore, no *kora* at all," she added bitterly.

"I'm . . . I'm sorry, Craal," said Brekka. "I wish I'd known you were in need. You were so good to me when I was new fledged."

Craal drew herself up proudly. "Don't blame yourself for my need, young one," she said. "Independence is the raven way, the way of *kora*. Mates care for mates and the rest fly free. When you're old and going blind, as I am, it's time to die. But somehow I seem to go on living."

"Still, I wish I'd known. I was just too busy stuffing myself to think. I feel *unkora*." Brekka's wings drooped, and she drew her whitelids over her eyes.

"Brekka thinks you may be able to help me, Craal," Tok said into the awkward silence.

"If I can, I will," replied Craal, fixing her eyes on him.

"I'm looking for a raven old enough to remember tales

131

about the Grey Lords, the Singers," Tok told her. "Brekka says ravens haven't always lived here but came from a different place. Can you remember anything about that?"

Craal turned and gazed out over the hills, as if her dim eyes could see beyond to a different world. "Oh, yes!" she sighed. "I remember . . ."

"The Grey Lords?" Tok cut in eagerly.

"No, not them. I was too young, fresh out of the shell and only just fledged when we began our great journey. But my mother knew the Grey Lords. She told me that they and ravens once hunted freely together. But that's all over now. We ravens left before it was too late. Came here to the Hills of Plenty. But the Grey Lords were too proud to leave their old home in the Lost Hills, my mother said. And so they stayed. The Two-Legs must have killed them all by now."

Just like in the Raven Mountains, Tok thought, with a pang of disappointment. Was it the same everywhere, then? Were there truly no more Grey Lords? But the northern crow he and Kaa had talked to knew of the Singers! "You left your old home because of the Two-Legs?" he asked Craal.

"Who else?" Craal ruffled her dusty feathers. "The Lost Hills, where we dwelt, were encircled by the lands of the Two-Legs. Every year they cut down more trees, killed more wild folk. Living became hard, very hard. So we ravens sent out scouts to find a new safe place to live and they found . . . this," she said, with a jerk of her beak. "The Hills of Plenty, they called it. They should have called it The Hills of Shame. It's true that we're safe here, and well fed. But we've become *unkora*."

"How can you say that, Craal, and to a stranger, too!" protested Brekka.

"I didn't mean to criticize *you*, Brekka." Craal drooped her wings. "Not every one of us is *unkora*. But most ravens here don't even remember that there is such a thing."

She's right, thought Tok, remembering Porag and his gang, bullying and grabbing.

"Do you know the way to the Lost Hills, Craal?" he asked after a moment. For what else could he do but go on, though his hope of finding the Grey Lords had all but ebbed away.

"They must lie northwest of here," she told him. "For we came southeast aslant the rising sun on our great journey. How many days flight I cannot tell you, for I was very young then, and our group traveled slowly for many days to get here. But if you keep the morning sun at your back, and check the star-that-is-north by night, you'll find the Lost Hills, I know." Then she added wistfully, "And if I were any younger I'd go with you, Two-Legs or no Two-Legs. For anything is better than living as we ravens do here."

Tok thanked her. He and Brekka set about foraging and soon provided Craal with another good meal. Then they ate heartily themselves.

Snow began to drift down, veiling the ugliness around them. Tok turned to Brekka. The ragged little ravenet peered up at him through the falling flakes.

"Come with me to the Lost Hills," he said. "You don't belong here."

"But I do," she said harshly. "I'm no hero. I live very well here, and have no taste for hardship. Craal is right—we're all *unkora*."

"But—"

"Besides, there's Craal. I won't leave her now that I know her need. I'll look after her to the end, whenever that may be."

"You're not *unkora*," he told her.

She bowed her head.

"But some day you must leave this place," he went on. "You *must*, Brekka. Follow the rising sun and you'll come at last to the Raven Mountains, where I was hatched. It's a long journey, and there are many hardships there. But the life is *kora*."

"What about you?" she asked. "If you find your Grey Lords?"

"I'll lead them home," he said.

"And if you don't find them?"

Tok did not answer. Spreading his wings, he shook off a cloud of snow crystals and took to the air. He called a last greeting to the small black figure on the hillside, and beat away against the rising wind.

Chapter 19

I am the black heart of the white winter.
—Raven proverb

Tok flew into the teeth of the gale with heavy swishes of his wings. It was snowing hard now, and the Hills of Plenty soon vanished behind a curtain of swirling white. The light was fading and he could feel the temperature of the air dropping. But the cold didn't bother him. After rest and a few good meals he felt better than he had since he had crossed the Shining Lake.

The flying snow blotted out the great many-roosts of the Two-Legs and muffled their distant noise. The countryside felt cleansed of their presence, returned to itself. Tok's spirits rose and he did a barrel roll. A cross-draft caught him and tossed him upward, but he mastered it easily. He had left the Two-Legs behind, at least for now, he told himself. Somewhere ahead lay the Lost Hills. Grey Lords had lived there in the time of Craal's mother. There might be some left. There had to be!

When darkness began to fall, Tok roosted in a grove of evergreens. The good eating on the Hills of Plenty meant that he didn't have to forage now. So he tucked his head under his wing and rode out the last of the storm among the branches, rousing now and then to listen to the wind in sleepy comfort. Morning dawned clear and bright, with a sky of delicate blue and not a cloud in sight. The countryside lay under a mantle of snow, and it was sharp cold. Tok's head feathers were rimed with frost from his breath.

He dropped down out of the tree into the snow and began to give himself a bath, rolling and sliding in the powdery whiteness until every single feather was coated. A red squirrel, out exploring after the storm, stopped to watch in astonishment. Catching sight of it, Tok rolled and slid closer, pretending to be absorbed in his play. When he was between the squirrel and the nearest tree, he pounced on it. After a struggle, he managed to kill it with a blow of his beak. He ate it daintily, beginning at the mouth, gradually turning it inside out until only a neat bundle of hide lay on the trampled snow. Then he flapped up to a branch to preen himself, removing even the slightest taint of the Hills of Plenty.

When he was satisfied he mounted into the clear air, working his wings hard to set the blood circulating again. When he got high enough, he began to dance. His wings carved great swoops of sorrow for Kaa, then he rolled and tumbled his terror in the many-roosts of the Two-Legs, and the shame of the ravens on the Hills of Plenty. The best of his soaring flight he offered to Skyah. Heart-hungry, he wished for other ravens to dance with him, for his lonely journey had taught him that the skydance wasn't just one raven, no matter how nimble its wings. It was ravens together, honoring the Maker of the beautiful world.

At last, with the blood pulsing warmly through his veins, he put the sun at his back and set out for the Lost Hills. All that day he flew, roosting again at night. Before he slept he checked the star-that-is-north, as Craal had told him, and the next day he adjusted his course.

Below him the land was still gently rolling, dotted here and there with roosts of the Two-Legs. There were patches of trees, so Tok could find shelter and forage. But the Moon of Snows had come and gone. Now it was the Moon of Deep Cold, the season of long nights and bitter storms. Some days Tok felt he got no closer to the endless, level horizon that receded before him. Could Craal have been wrong about the Lost Hills? But then one clear, sparkling day he glimpsed a fine blue line ahead of him, like a distant bank of clouds. For long moments Tok did not understand what he was looking at. Then he did. Not clouds, but hills—at last!

Though he had already flown far that day, his wings shed their weariness like water. The air seemed to lift under him, pushing him forward. As he flew, the sky became overcast and the wind rose. By the time he reached the hills, it was beginning to snow again, and daylight was fading. It was too late to search now, he told himself. He would have to find somewhere to roost, if he could, for he could see through the drifting snow that what Craal had told him was true—all the nearer hills were shorn of their trees. In their place bushes and young trees had sprung up on the slopes, but there was not much shelter.

Tok lifted himself over one ridge and then another,

gliding on the wind currents that whined around the summits. He peered through the driving snow, hoping against hope to see the ghostly shape of a Grey Lord riding the wind, to hear its wonderful singing. But he saw nothing, and the only song was the voice of the gale.

At last he glimpsed a wooded slope and took shelter among the trees. Even if there were Grey Lords they wouldn't be hunting in weather like this, he reminded himself. But all the same he fell asleep listening for them.

By morning the Lost Hills were drifted deep in fresh snow. Tok took to the air early, circling high above the ridges, watching and waiting. His heart leaped when he saw a huge bird circling high above him, but it was only an eagle on the lookout for prey. He wished now that he had asked Craal if she knew what the Grey Lords looked like. But he was sure that they must be birds like him, only greater. What else could be both a swift hunter and a singer too?

Tok quartered the Lost Hills, searching from north to south and back again from west to east. The hills were not as large as he had thought at first, and were hemmed in on all sides by land crusted with roosts of the Two-Legs. Only the steepest slopes had kept all their trees. Soon, perhaps, even those would be gone. Besides the eagle, Tok saw only a pair of hawks soaring. Discouraged, he drifted down into the treetops. Perhaps Craal was right after all, and the Grey Lords were long dead. Had his journey been for nothing?

Very hungry now, he flew deep into the valleys among the hills, hoping to spy something to eat. He passed over a narrow glade among thick conifers. Then, glimpsing something, he backpedaled in the air. A deer carcass lay in full view, only lightly dusted with fresh snow. Entrails spilled enticingly from its opened belly and Tok's mouth watered. Had other predators already fed and left?

Then he saw that there was something else in the glade, a white creature crouching almost invisible against the snow. So the deer *had* been found. But the beast did not seem to be feeding. It was tethered in some way. A wide circle of tracks showed how it had gone this way and that, trying to get free. Bright splotches of blood flecked the snow. When Tok flew closer, he could see that the creature's right front paw was held fast in something. He dropped down on a tree branch above it.

It stared up at him with fierce golden eyes. "Well," it said coldly. "A croaker. You must be, you're too big for a crow. It's long since my kind have seen one of you traitors." It grinned mirthlessly, showing shining white fangs in its tapered muzzle.

Tok cocked his head, focusing on it close up. The creature had pointed ears. Its shaggy coat of cream-white fur thickened into a ruff below them, then into a dense mane over its shoulders. Its brushy tail lay half-hidden in the trampled snow. The only animal Tok had seen that was anything like it was a fox. But this was no fox. It was something bigger and much more powerful.

"If you've come to peck out my eyes you're too early," the not-fox went on. "I'm not dead—yet."

"You're caught in that thing, aren't you?" Tok asked it.

"I'm not lying here for the fun of it!" The voice of the

not-fox was sharp with pain. It struggled up on three legs and tried to pull its foot free of the trap, but blood oozed from its damaged paw, and it fell back on the snow panting. "The Two-Legs will be back to check its trap any time now," it gasped. "It will shoot me." The not-fox ground its teeth. "Maybe I deserve it. I should have known there would be a trap. But I could see and smell nothing. And I was so hungry, and the deer was tempting . . ."

"Isn't there a way to open the trap?" Tok asked, remembering the enclosure the Two-Legs had kept him in.

"There must be—for the Two-Legs," the creature replied. "But I've trampled on it, chewed it . . . Nothing seems to work."

"If I come down and have a look will you let me alone?" asked Tok.

The not-fox lifted its head and for a moment hope kindled in its eyes. "My people say croakers are clever," it said. "But what could you possibly do?" It whined, and lay its head on its paws.

Tok dropped down onto the bloodied snow. From close up he could see that two jaws of the trap held the creature's paw fast. He pecked at them. They were made of the same hard bright substance as the enclosure the Two-Legs had kept him in. So there was no way to break them. He walked all around, studying the trap, while the not-fox followed every movement with burning eyes. Tok tried to stay as far away from it as he could. After all, the creature hadn't exactly promised not to harm him. And even in its fear and pain it looked fierce.

He could see that loops of the same hard substance fastened the trap to a post driven deep into the ground. Mounds of churned-up snow lay all around where the not-fox had struggled with the trap. It must have been carefully buried, and the creature had stepped right into its open jaws. There *must* be some way to open the jaws again. He thought of how the fastener had slid back to open the door of the enclosure—one position, open, another position closed. But he could see no sliding pieces here.

Then he noticed something. It was an ear-shaped piece that stuck out at the edge of the trap below where the jaws met. He tried to move it sideways with his beak as he had done the fastener on his enclosure door. But it wouldn't slide. The piece was a different shape, too. Not round, but flat. Tok pecked the top of it, and a tremor went through the jaws of the trap.

The creature whimpered. It had gotten to its feet again, and was watching him closely, ears pricked straight up.

"I think I can see how it works," Tok told it. "But I don't know if I'm strong enough to shift it."

"Try," said the not-fox, its brushy tail moving ever so slightly.

"You must pull back when I hit it," warned Tok. "No matter how much it hurts." Drawing his head back he struck the flat piece with his heavy beak. The jaws creaked open a tiny bit, and the not-fox pulled its foot back hard. But the jaws snapped together again, and the creature sank down with a moan of pain.

"It's no good," it said, its golden eyes dimming with despair. "It's all over with me."

"Don't give up!" urged Tok. "You're only caught by

your toes now." The creature struggled up again and braced itself on its haunches. Rearing his head back, Tok struck a savage blow at the trap. The shock half-stunned him, and he felt a sliver shear off the side of his beak. But the cruel jaws opened just a little. The not-fox yanked its paw free and took a limping step backward as the jaws snapped shut again.

Suddenly a rough voice bellowed at them across the glade.

A Two-Legs! Tok flapped his wings, trying to gain height, but there was an enormous roar, and something hot blasted by him, knocking him out of the air. Firestick! he thought numbly, as he hit the snow. Then the jaws of the not-fox closed around him.

Part 4

The Lanna

Chapter 20

Truth often comes disguised.
　　　　　　　—Wisdom of the Tellers

Tok braced himself for crushing pain, but the not-fox held him gently between its teeth. It plunged into the undergrowth, dodging this way and that as it ran. Another blast from the firestick struck a branch above them, showering them with snow and bits of wood. The creature bounded up a steep slope, its breath panting hot around Tok as it climbed. The firestick exploded again, but it was distant now, its boom a hollow echo among the hills. At last the not-fox took shelter in a copse of stunted pines near the crest of a ridge. It dropped Tok on the snow-drifted bed of dry needles under the trees.

"Pah!" it said, taking a great bite of snow and chewing it. "Can't say I care for the taste of you."

Tok shook his ruffled feathers and settled them again. "Lucky for me. When your jaws closed around me I thought I'd breathed my last."

The not-fox threw itself down and began to lick its injured paw.

"I suppose I should thank you," Tok said. He noticed it didn't bother to thank him for setting it free. He fluttered up onto a low-hanging branch, and set about preening his rumpled feathers. But his eyes never left the strange creature on the ground. He could see now that its coat was not pure white, but was flecked with shades of golden brown. Its yellow eyes were slanted, its narrow face framed by its ruff. "What are you?" he demanded at last. "I've never seen anything like you before."

The creature cocked its head and gazed up at him. "You haven't seen much, then," it taunted. "I'm a wolf."

It turned back to its damaged paw now, whining a bit at the pain of its injury. Peering down, Tok could see that one of the toes on its right forefoot was nearly severed, and hung by not more than a shred of flesh. As he watched, the wolf lowered its head and bit the toe free with its sharp front teeth. Then it got to its feet, blood oozing from the stump. "At least the other bones aren't broken," it said, taking a few limping steps.

"Why limp now?" Tok asked. "You could run fast enough when you had to!"

"Easy for you to say, croaker," the wolf shot back. It limped to the edge of the copse and put its muzzle into the wind. "More snow coming, and soon," it added. Then it stepped out onto the hillside. Peering after it, Tok could see a single set of tracks leading down from the ridge, as if the wolf had crossed that way from the next valley. Without another word, it set off up the trail.

"Wait!" croaked Tok. With a couple of wing-flaps he caught up to the wolf, landing a respectful distance away in the snow. Whatever kind of truce they had established at the trap seemed to be over now.

"Well?" The yellow eyes were impatient.

"I'm searching for..." How to describe the Grey Lords? Tok asked himself. He knew so little about them. "...For huge grey birds, great singers, swift hunters. They're said to live in these hills. My people call them the Grey Lords."

The wolf shook its ears. "I know of nothing like that," it said. "Eagles are big and they hunt, yes. But not even a croaker would call their screeching *song*."

A cold wind gusted over the ridge, blowing a flurry of snowflakes into their faces, and the wolf moved off again.

Tok made a quick decision. "I'm coming with you," he said, flapping after it as it limped over the crest of the ridge and down the other side.

The wolf did not bother to turn its head. "At your peril. My kind have no love for croakers," it replied.

"Why?" asked Tok, trying to slow his wings to keep pace with the wolf. But a gust of wind sheared across him, and battling it he shot right over the wolf's ears and plummeted into a deep snowbank below the ridge.

The wolf stopped and ran out its tongue, laughing. "Tell me," it asked, "do all croakers fly as badly as you do?"

Ignoring the insult, Tok struggled out of the snow. "Why don't wolves like ravens?" he demanded, shaking his wings. "And you called me a traitor back there at the trap."

"It's an old story. Not one to be told on the top of a ridge in a blizzard," replied the wolf. "Well, come along if you must. But for the love of the Lanna, stop flapping about my ears!"

"I can't help it. The wind's too strong."

"Well, ride on my back if you must!"

With a flip of his wings, Tok landed on the wolf's back. Digging his claws into the mane on its shoulders, he held on for dear life, crouching down to make himself as small as possible against the wind.

"Umph," grunted the wolf. "You weigh enough. There might have been some good eating on you after all."

Tok uttered a mocking quork. "What do you call yourself?" he asked as they moved off through the thickening snow.

"Selaks."

"Are you a he or a she?"

"She. You talk a lot, don't you?" As if to discourage further questions, the wolf sprang forward down the ridge, Tok clinging desperately to her fur as her powerful shoulders worked beneath him.

"Doesn't your foot hurt you now?" he said into her ear.

"Of course it does," she said between her teeth. "I run through that."

And so they descended the ridge, black on white through the falling snow.

At last they reached the floor of the valley. Selaks began to cross it in great bounds, following a broader track drifted over with snow. Unable to stand the jostling any longer, Tok took to the air again. The wind was calmer here than on the ridge and he flew easily ahead, following the line of the trail until it met another. Then he landed and waited for the wolf.

"Which way?" he asked, as she loped up.

Selaks lowered her nose to the spot where the two paths met. Looking more closely, Tok could see a yellowish stain beneath the fresh snow. "The *skiffet* says they went this way. And not long ago," she said. Squatting, she over-marked the spot, then moved forward on the right-hand path.

It led them higher again, over a low pass between two hills, and down through thick woods on the other side. It was snowing hard now, the trail ahead vanishing before their eyes. Selaks stopped and pricked her ears forward, listening.

Then, lifting her muzzle, she began to sing.

The song began on a mid-note, then abruptly rose pure and high, hanging suspended until it trailed away, descending. The very sound of it roused every feather on Tok's body.

"*Ar-ooooooo!*" sang Selaks. Then she paused, listening intently.

Tok's ears were sharp, but he could hear no answer.

"*Ar-oooooo! Ar-oooooo!*" she called again.

Another pause, and then from far ahead of them, very faintly, came an answering song.

"*Ar-ooooooo-ahhhh!*" Another voice joined in, then another, the three songs pitched not together, but in harmony, creating a complex chord.

Selaks's tail waved to and fro. "Malik and the others," she said. "May their hunting have gone better than mine!"

She plunged confidently ahead now, breasting the

snow on the path. Unable to keep his balance in the whirl of air currents at the bottom of the pass, Tok landed on her shoulders and dug his claws into her fur again.

Down they went into the next valley, the woods looming dark around them through the storm. Near the bottom of the pass Tok saw a sudden movement ahead. Then out of the trees the figure of another wolf appeared. Huge and grey, it bounded toward them, vanishing and reappearing among the shifting veils of snow. Two other lean grey forms ran in single file close behind it.

"Malik!" cried Selaks, throwing herself on the lead wolf, giving it a shoulder bunt and biting at its muzzle. In response, it reared on its hind legs and wrapped its forelegs about her, play-wrestling her to the ground.

Caught by surprise, Tok lost his hold on her mane and spun off into the snow. One of the other wolves sprang upon him, pinning him by one wing and glaring down at him.

"What strange delicacy is this you've brought us, Selaks?" it demanded, curling its lip back to show its fangs.

Torn between fear and wonder, Tok stared up into its blazing amber eyes. *Grey singers, swift and fierce* . . . They must be—had to be—the Grey Lords. He had found them at last!

Chapter 21

Numon is always unexpected.

—Lore of the Lanna

Selaks got up, shaking snow off her thick coat. "It's a croaker, Rakal. Go ahead and eat it if you're hungry enough. It's nothing to me."

The wolf called Rakal bent closer, close enough for Tok to see every gleaming tooth in its head and feel its hot breath.

"What honor have wolves, then?" he cried. "I saved you from a trap, Selaks!"

"And I saved you from the firestick of the Two-Legs," retorted Selaks. "I owe you nothing!"

"Who dares question the honor of wolves?" growled the leader, swinging his rough head toward Tok. "And what's this about a trap, Selaks? Have you been stealing from the Two-Legs again?"

"To my cost," she admitted, holding up her injured paw.

Malik sniffed at it, then licked the wound. "Poor little sister," he muttered, giving her neck a nuzzle.

"Oh, it's nothing," she replied. "The toe was nearly severed, so I bit it off."

Malik play-bowed before her, stretching out his forelegs and raising his rump. "Hail, Selaks Three-toes!" he joked, grinning. "But what about the croaker?"

"Oh, let it go," she said, carelessly. "It doesn't taste good anyway."

Rakal stepped back, freeing Tok's wing. But it licked its chops wistfully. "Are you sure, little sister?" it asked.

"Quite sure, sister. Though I've known *you* to eat almost anything."

Indignant, Tok roused his feathers and put up his ears. "I've come a long way to talk to you," he told the wolves. "Are any of you ready to listen?"

Malik gave a short bark of laughter. "Listen to a croaker? We've better things to do!"

But Selaks stared down at Tok, her forehead furrowed. "What nonsense is this? Back on the ridge you said you were looking for big grey birds!"

"Birds?" asked the fourth wolf, which was a bit smaller than the rest. "This croaker thinks we're *birds?*" It began to prance about on its hind legs, pretending to fly; then it rolled over in the snow, snorting with mirth.

Rakal turned on it. "Be quiet, Timmax!" she snapped. "When you're senior enough to speak on the hunt we'll be sure to tell you!"

The wolf called Timmax put both paws over its muzzle, gazing up at the others with merry brown eyes.

"Oh, let him alone, Rakal," said Selaks. "The more attention you pay him the sillier he gets. Timmax is as

151

foolish as a milk pup."

Malik took a step closer to Tok and peered at him. "What's a croaker doing in our hills anyway? We were well rid of your kind long ago. What do you want of us now?" he growled.

"Selaks said your kind don't like ravens," replied Tok. "But she didn't say why. And I did tell her I was looking for birds. That was a mistake. I thought the Grey Lords I'm searching for had to be birds because they sang. But now I've heard *you* singing . . ."

"I know nothing of Grey Lords. We are the Lanna." Malik poked Tok with the tip of his nose, forcing him to hop backward. Then he nudged him again, and once more Tok gave ground.

"Do that again and my beak will teach your nose a lesson in manners," warned Tok, spreading his wings wide and puffing up his throat hackles.

"Oh, ho!" Malik's lips pulled back from his teeth in a ferocious grin. "Bold words. But what could you have to say that wolves would want to hear?"

"You're starving in these hills, aren't you?" demanded Tok. "You're hemmed in on all sides by the Two-Legs, scarcely able to feed yourselves. It's a wonder you've survived this long!"

Malik's eyes flashed. "Who told you these things?"

"Another raven far away, near a great many-roosts of the Two-Legs. Her ancestors came from here long ago. They knew your people and their troubles."

"So you *are* one of those traitors! Just as I thought!" Selaks cut in.

"The ones who left these hills? No, not one of them," said Tok. "I come from a land farther away, much farther. From a place where your kind don't exist anymore. Where no one even remembers you, except as an old tale."

Rakal shivered, the wind ruffling her coat. "The croaker's words sound like bad *numon*," she whined. "Besides, the storm worsens and it's getting dark. Why stand here arguing with him?"

"You're right," said Malik. "We're wasting our time." He turned and loped back along the trail, Rakal and Timmax falling into line behind him. Last of all went Selaks. One by one the Grey Lords disappeared into the snowy dusk.

Tok tried flapping after them, but the gale buffeted him and he could make no headway. He had come so far, and against all odds he had found the Grey Lords. Now he had lost them! "Why won't you listen?" he cried into the wind. "My people need you and you need them!"

Selaks reappeared in front of him so suddenly that he almost blundered into her. "Come on, then, if it's so important," she said impatiently. "Tell your story to our *vór* and *vóra*. They will decide."

Tok flew up onto her shoulders. "I thought Malik was your leader," he said, digging his claws into her fur.

"Malik?" Selaks gave a short bark of amusement. "Malik is my brother and I love him dearly. But he isn't *vór*, and isn't likely to be. Adanax and Bervenna are our *vór* and *vóra*."

Tok felt her muscles bunch beneath him, then she sprang away after the others.

153

The wolves ran in silence. Tok noticed that each stepped exactly into the tracks of the one before it, so that only a single line of paw prints marked their passage along the narrow trail. They flowed down it like moving shadows. It was impossible to see anything through the storm, but the movement of the air currents told Tok that they were emerging into another valley. On and on they ran, tireless, ignoring the gusting wind and driving snow. When would they get where they were going? he wondered. Any sensible raven would have sought shelter by now!

At last Malik stopped and howled, lifting his muzzle into the wind. They all stood silently waiting. At last through the bluster of the wind came a faint response.

"They're at east *skiffet*," muttered Selaks as the wolves began to run again. "Because of the storm. There's a bit more shelter there."

"You don't roost in the same place each night?" asked Tok, leaning close to her ear.

"Sleep, you mean?" Selaks shook her head. "Not in winter." Then, "No more questions. I need my breath for running."

Some time later, Tok began to feel air currents moving at an angle against the wind. They must be bouncing off something big, he thought. Another line of hills. In a few moments, the dark shapes of trees appeared around them through the snow. Malik howled again, still running, and this time the answer came at once, from very close.

A dark figure suddenly loomed ahead of them through the storm. It was another wolf, bigger than any of the others. It had a brindled coat of black and grey. Malik leaped to greet it first, crouching low before it, then pressing himself close against its shaggy flank. Then the others crowded around. Ears back, tails wagging, they touched noses with the big wolf, licking its face and nipping playfully at its muzzle.

"Greetings, my *vór*," cried Selaks, pressing herself against its other side.

"Malik, Selaks!" it said in a deep warm voice. Then, "What's that? Why, it's a raven!"

"And what in the name of the Lanna is it doing on your back, Selaks?" a chilly voice cut in. A silver-white wolf only a little smaller than the *vór* had appeared out of the snow.

"The croaker helped me out of a trap," explained Selaks, glancing from one to the other, ears lowered, tail pressed close against her side. "It says it has been looking for us, to tell us something important. So I brought it to you, *vór* and *vóra*. It had to ride—the gale was too strong for it to keep up with us."

"We have nothing to say to croakers," the big white wolf replied. "You should know that."

"I told her that, *vóra!*" Rakal put in eagerly. "So did Malik. But she wouldn't listen."

In a flash, Selaks whirled and nipped her on the rump.

Rakal raised her hackles and showed her fangs. "Remember your place, sister," she growled. "Or I'll teach it to you."

"Go ahead! You just try it!" challenged Selaks, raising her own hackles.

"That's enough, daughters," warned the *vór*, his voice a low rumble. At once they put down their hackles and pressed against him, nosing him under the chin. Then both sidled up to the white wolf and greeted her, too, with nuzzlings and lickings.

Tok still clung uneasily to his place on Selaks's back.

The brindled leader eyed him suspiciously. "Whatever you have to say, raven, this isn't the time for it," he warned. "Tomorrow will be soon enough."

"Never is too soon to listen to traitors," said the white wolf disdainfully. The two big wolves turned and trotted away among the trees. Malik and the others trailed after them, Selaks lagging behind the rest. Tok could feel her limping. So despite her boast her wound still bothered her, he thought.

When they reached the cover of the woods, he could make out the dim shapes of other wolves lying here and there in the snow. With a sigh, Selaks cast herself on the ground. Taking the hint, Tok flew up onto a branch over her head.

"Those were your leaders?" he asked.

"Our *vór*, Adanax, and our *vóra*, Bervenna." Selaks put her head down on her paws.

"They're your father and mother? And Rakal's and Malik's too? You're all one family?"

"Yes. Not that that makes the *vór* and *vóra* any easier on us!" With a huff of frosty breath, Selaks curled up and put her tail over her nose.

But Tok was still too excited to settle down. "Selaks? What's *numon?*" he demanded.

Her ears twitched. "Be quiet, croaker," came a muffled growl. "Haven't you caused me trouble enough for one day?"

So Tok was left alone with his thoughts.

Chapter 22

No more than one, yet always more. What am I?
A vór.

—Wolf riddle

Tok rode out the storm among the branches. Below him, snow drifted over the sleeping Grey Lords, turning them into mounds of white. Alone among the branches, he longed to be among his own kind again, as the wolves were.

He thought of Tarkah. Perhaps she would have chosen a mate by now. He shook his feathers with a dry rattle. What use was it to think of her? He was *unkora* in his own land, and would be forever, unless the wolves listened to him. But would they?

The blizzard blew itself out by dawn. With the first pale light, the wolves began to stir. Selaks got up, shaking snow from her fur, and a smaller tawny wolf jumped up to greet her, play-biting and nuzzling. Ignoring its attentions, Selaks bounded over to Malik and the two of them fought a mock battle over a stick, their hot breath steaming in the icy air. Timmax galloped over to join them and his older brother and sister grabbed him by the scruff of his neck and rolled him in the snow. Then the *vór* and *vóra* appeared and the pack gathered around them, tails wagging in greeting.

"Where's Rakal?" demanded Bervenna.

"Still asleep," said Timmax. He darted over to a snowy mound nearby and pounced on it, barking, "Up, lazybones!"

The mound exploded into the angry shape of his elder sister. Ears laid back, fangs bared, she chased him in and out among the trees till he surrendered.

Rolling over on his back, he waved all four paws in the air. "Don't blame me," he told her. "Our *vóra* was asking for you."

Rakal growled and snapped at him. But she hurried over to pay her greeting to the leaders.

"Always the last and the slowest," complained Bervenna, as Rakal nuzzled her.

Rakal's brushy tail drooped. "But I'm tired," she whined. "We had to run so far trying to find Selaks. And on empty stomachs, too!"

"Always thinking of your stomach, sister," teased Selaks, swaggering over to her. "Yet you're the fattest of us all!"

Rakal bared her teeth but said nothing.

"Speaking of Selaks . . ." the *vór* began. At once Selaks lowered her ears and sidled over to him.

"Rakal is right in one way," Adanax went on. "Roam if you must, but not so far alone. And in the future don't expect your brothers and sister to come looking for you."

Selaks hung her head. "I won't, my *vór*," she promised. "But the Two-Legs often hunt in winter in that valley, and I thought . . ."

"You didn't think nearly enough," Bervenna cut in. "Or you wouldn't have been foolish enough to get caught in a trap."

"It was well hidden," Selaks defended herself. "I could see no marks in the snow. And there was no smell of the Two-Legs."

"You've heard your *vór*," returned Bervenna. "A wolf who doesn't obey is a danger to its pack."

"I hear, my *vór*, my *vóra*." Selaks humbled herself, crouching low, ears back and tail curled between her legs.

"Enough, Bervenna," said Adanax. "Selaks has been punished, after all. Malik tells me the trap cost her a toe."

"Selaks Three-toes, Selaks Three-toes!" yipped Timmax, capering around his sister.

"Down, child," ordered a grizzled grey wolf, giving him a cuff with its paw as he passed. "Or you'll drive us all mad."

"Well said, Alkara," Adanax said, grinning. "Never has there been such a mischievous youngster."

The old wolf laughed up at him. "No? I seem to recall that when *you* were young . . ." it began.

Adanax pricked up his ears and raised his tail high. "What's this, Mother?" he grumbled. "Disrespect to your *vór?*"

She bunted his muzzle with her nose. "Disrespect? Oh, never, my *vór*. My oh-so-lordly son."

Bervenna tossed her head impatiently. "Enough nonsense," she said. "Adanax, what about the croaker?"

"Ah. I had forgotten." Adanax raised his yellow eyes and stared up at Tok, who was very glad to be out of reach at that moment.

"You have come among us uninvited, saying you have something to tell us," the *vór* continued. "Well, out with it."

The rest of the wolves moved in closer and there was no welcome in their eyes, either.

Tok wished that he had thought more about what to say, prepared a fine speech that might convince them. But it was too late for that now. "I come from the Raven Mountains far to the east of here, beyond the country of the Two-Legs," he began. "There are no wolves there, only old half-forgotten tales about creatures called the Grey Lords who used to hunt with ravenkind."

The wolves began to mutter among themselves.

"How could there be no wolves?"

"What happened to them?"

"Why would wolves bother to hunt with croakers anyway?"

"Quiet!" ordered Adanax. "Go on, raven."

"No one in my land ever knew what these Grey Lords were," Tok told them. "Just that they were grey and swift. And great singers."

Timmax had been bouncing up and down. Now he burst out, "Birds! They thought we were birds!"

Adanax turned and stared at the young wolf until he cowered in submission. Then he turned back to Tok. "Why don't your people hunt for themselves?" he asked.

"They can. They do," replied Tok. "But in winter, with most small game in their burrows, or sleeping under the ice, there are only deer. And those we can't hunt, can't kill. Even a dead deer we can't open—beak and claw aren't strong enough."

"What a puny folk!" sneered Bervenna.

"So you need wolves to hunt for you," Adanax said. "Why should we?"

"You need new lands, new hunting grounds. I know you do—I can see the shorn hillsides, and the Two-Legs are all around you. Our lands are empty—there would be plenty for all."

The old grey wolf lifted up her head. "May I speak, *vór?*" she asked.

Bervenna's eyes narrowed. "Why? This is for the *vór* and *vóra* to decide. What has this to do with you, Alkara?"

"Maybe nothing, maybe much," replied Alkara.

"Let her speak," said Adanax. "Perhaps in the end all of us must have our say about this."

Bervenna fell silent.

"As we all know, ravens once lived in these very hills," began Alkara.

An angry murmur ran around the circle of wolves.

"Yes, yes, I know," she said. "They left us when the Two-Legs came against us. It was long before my time, and I'm the oldest among you. But perhaps what we need to ask ourselves is this: Why do we call the ravens traitors? *Why did their going matter to us so much?*"

The wolves stared at each other, puzzled.

"You know the answer, I suppose," said Bervenna. "But

162

why does it matter now?"

"I don't know anything for sure, *vóra*," Alkara replied. "I can only guess."

"Guess what, then?" snapped Bervenna.

"How far can *you* see, my *vór?*" asked Alkara, turning to her son.

"See?" rumbled Adanax. "Why, in that direction . . . " He turned and stared out across the valley. "To that grove of evergreens. The rest is a blur."

"And you, my *vóra?*" asked Alkara.

"The same," replied Bervenna, with a toss of her head.

"And the two of you are the keenest-eyed among us," said Alkara. "Now you, raven," she went on, fixing her eyes on Tok. "How far can you see?"

Tok gazed out across the valley where the snow sparkled in the morning sun. "Past the grove, across the plain, to the hills beyond." He looked farther. "And with my long sight, to the pass and the range of hills beyond that."

"I thought so!" exclaimed Alkara. For the first time Tok saw a friendly light in wolf eyes. "You can see things afar that we cannot. Enemies . . . and prey." She turned to the other wolves. "That is the answer, I think. Once upon a time, the ravens were our far-seeing eyes. They helped us in the hunt sometimes, and perhaps even warned us of danger coming. That is why we hated them when they left us to face the Two-Legs alone!"

The wolves began to mutter among themselves again.

"She says we needed the croakers!"

"Nonsense!"

"But why else would we call them traitors?"

Tok gazed down at Alkara in wonder. "I only know that in my land wolves and ravens once hunted together. Until the Two-Legs killed all the wolves."

Malik spoke into the long silence that followed. "Croakers always manage to survive, it seems," he said. "No matter what happens to others."

Tok gave a quork of annoyance. "Not true! Many of us were killed too. The rest only lived because they could fly to the furthest mountains where the Two-Legs seldom go."

"Very well," barked Adanax. "You've told us your tale. And Alkara has explained why it might be true. But Bervenna is right. What does any of it matter now? What's done is done."

"But it doesn't have to be!" urged Tok, leaning low on his branch. "Come back with me to my land. It lies empty and waiting now. The deer are many; the hunting will be good. Whether you need ravens or not, we will still gain from your coming."

"By stealing our leftovers, you mean!" accused Selaks, and the pack yelped with laughter.

Tok roused his feathers. "Why not?" he retorted. "It is the way of ravenkind."

Adanax's forehead was furrowed. "You ask us to leave our own lands? To take a chance on a dangerous journey to a place we know nothing about?" He stared hard at Tok. "You ask much, raven."

"Too much!" Bervenna cut in. "And my *vór*, how could we trust him? His kind have betrayed us before."

The wolves growled their agreement.

"And yet," mused Alkara, "perhaps both wolves and ravens were better off before. When they worked together."

Adanax gazed around the circle of puzzled faces. Then, "We won't decide this now," he told the wolves. "Think, all of you, about what the raven has said. You know that we face great danger here. The Two-Legs are all around us. Every day they claim more of our sacred hills. They cut down the forests and their makings are thick on the ground. They show us no mercy, killing us on sight and hunting down the game we depend on. And they bait cruel traps to catch us. As Selaks learned to her cost," he added.

Selaks rubbed her shaggy head against him.

"In time, I fear, they will pick us off one by one," Adanax went on. "Now the raven offers us a way out. So think well on it. Before we decide, each of you will have a turn to speak. Meanwhile, we must eat," he added, staring up at Tok. "And you, raven, must prove yourself. You will find prey for us, as Alkara says you can. If you don't . . ." Leaving his words unfinished, he stalked off, and the others fell in behind him.

Chapter 23

Hunter and hunted recognize each other.
The rest is numon.

—Wolf proverb

With eager wingbeats, Tok climbed above the treetops. It was good to feel the wind under him again. He angled toward the hills, where he could feel a slight thermal form-ing as the slopes warmed in the morning sun. He rode it upward, turning his head anxiously this way and that. He had to find prey for the wolves, or they would never agree to follow him. But the fresh snow had covered all tracks, all signs of life.

Abandoning the thermal, he shot down over a ridge into the next valley. He flew low among the treetops, but saw nothing more than a squirrel ducking out of sight behind a tree trunk. It reminded him of how hungry he was. But it was hardly prey for a pack of hungry wolves, he told himself, swooping away.

The third valley over yielded nothing either at first. Had the Two-Legs left nothing alive in these hills? He thought of the juicy deer beside the trap where he had found Selaks, and his mouth watered. But no. The wolves feared the trap now and would never go near it. He had to lead them to fresh game.

As he wheeled low over a shorn hillside, a sudden movement caught his eye. Something was stirring in the underbrush that had sprung up where the trees had been cut down. Deer! Tok turned in the air and swept back for a closer look. There were three of them—two larger and one smaller. With a harsh croak, he banked away and climbed high over the hillside. As he glided down into the next valley, he saw a line of tiny figures moving far below. The wolves had already taken to the trail.

"Well, raven?" asked Adanax, stopping short as Tok landed ahead of them.

"Deer," replied Tok. "Three of them on the far slope of those hills. No sign of any Two-Legs."

Bervenna's pale eyes kindled. "Near west *skiffet*, then," she said to Adanax.

A tremor of excitement ran down the line of wolves and their easy trot stretched into a ground-eating lope. With Adanax breaking trail through the fresh snow, they left the main track and curved away northward, heading toward a pass between the hills. Tails high, eyes straight ahead, they followed their *vór* in single file.

Winging down the line, Tok found Selaks running behind Malik and dropped onto her back.

"Oof!" she complained. "Tired already, croaker?"

"Don't be so ungrateful. I've found you three fat deer!"

"You'd better be right, croaker," she grunted. "It's a long run to west *skiffet* and we haven't killed for days now."

"What is this *skiffet* you keep talking about?" asked Tok.

"Places we mark—where we meet or rest," she replied. "We have many in these hills."

When they came out of the pass into the third valley, Adanax stopped and raised his head. Nostrils flaring, he tested the wind. "The wind is toward us, raven, but I can't smell them. Are they still there?" he asked.

Tok launched himself into the air and flew toward the hillside. In a moment he saw that the deer had shifted higher up the slope, kicking snow off plant shoots and dead grass as they browsed. Swooping low, Tok dipped one wing and did a half-roll. Would the wolves see his signal?

Either they did or they suddenly caught the scent of the deer. As Tok watched, the pack gathered around Adanax, tails wagging. A moment later it split into two groups. Adanax, Selaks and Malik vanished into the woods at the bottom of the slope. The rest, with Bervenna and a tall grey wolf in the lead, flattened themselves against the snow and began to stalk the deer from down-wind. Moments passed as the wolves worked their way closer and closer.

Tok felt a sudden crosswind buffet his wings. At the same moment the deer lifted their heads and sniffed the air suspiciously. Then they bounded away across the slope. Abandoning their stalk, the wolves dashed after them up the slope. It was hard going, for the morning sun had made the snow sticky. Two of the deer vanished over a ridge, but one stumbled and lagged behind. Running flat out now, Bervenna moved after it like a silver streak over the snow, with the tall grey wolf on her heels and the rest of the pack trailing far behind. The distance between her and the deer narrowed every moment. Closer and closer she came, forcing the deer to turn toward the woods.

Suddenly Adanax and the others burst from the cover of the trees. Panicked, the deer hesitated for a moment before plunging uphill again. With a bound, Adanax fastened his fangs on its nose and the two of them crashed to the ground. The deer shook him loose and regained its feet. But the *vór* sprang at its throat, nimbly avoiding its slashing hooves. Meanwhile Selaks and Malik hurled themselves at its shoulders, trying to pull it down. Selaks was shaken off, but Malik sank his fangs into the deer's front leg and held on. It struck him with its other front hoof and somehow staggered onward.

Then Bervenna and the grey wolf sprang on it. They fastened their teeth in the deer's rump, while the others caught up and attacked its flanks. In a flurry of wolves, the deer went down, and this time it did not rise again. Blood stained the snow.

Caught up in the frenzy, Tok wheeled and spun in the air above them, his heart pounding at the sheer glory of their chase, their kill.

The wolves began to feed now, tearing great chunks of meat from the carcass of the deer. Tok landed in the snow beside them, snatching scraps of meat that were flung aside. He found himself not far away from Bervenna.

"Well run, *vóra*," he said.

She glanced at him, her silver face masked with blood from the kill. "It seems your kind have their uses after all, croaker," she growled, returning to her meal.

Soon much of the deer had been eaten. Stuffed with meat, the wolves withdrew to the edge of the woods. Some fell asleep, while others chewed bones and kept their eyes on the carcass. Malik was licking a wound where the deer's hoof had slashed him. Timmax was the only one with enough energy to lope over and try to drive Tok off when he settled in to feed.

Tok fluttered up onto the carcass and roused his feathers, spreading his wings. "Mind your manners," he hissed, clacking his beak angrily and striking at the young wolf when he got too close.

Startled, Timmax sat down hard in the snow. "Meat thief," he growled. But he ventured no closer.

"My meat. I found the deer," Tok reminded him.

"Our hills. Our deer. And *we* killed it," Timmax insisted.

Selaks heaved herself to her feet and ambled over, her stomach bulging with meat. "Timmax is right," she told Tok. "You're the outlander here." She made a halfhearted snap at him, but Tok easily avoided her fangs. Fluttering over her head, he landed behind her and pulled her tail. When Timmax sprang at him, he flapped off to a safe distance, snatching a shred of meat as he went.

"Oh, let him alone, Timmax," yawned Selaks, turning back toward the shelter of the trees. "I suppose we'll never miss the amount he eats."

We'll see about that, thought Tok. He flew back to the carcass and gorged himself on the rich meat until he couldn't stuff down another mouthful. Then he flew up to a tree branch, where he karked and quorked to himself as he preened his feathers.

Below him, Selaks opened a sleepy eye. "Must you make so much noise?" she complained. "No wonder we call you croakers!"

Tok coughed up a pellet and bounced it off her head. With a grunt, she closed her eyes again. He gazed down at the sleeping Grey Lords. Their dappled fur made them almost invisible in the shadows under the trees. Well, he had proved himself to them, hadn't he? Done what Adanax had asked him to do? So now they'd come with him, wouldn't they?

The sun had shifted far to the west before the wolves began to stir. They nuzzled and shouldered each other, licking the dried blood from each other's coats. Timmax play-wrestled with two smaller wolves who looked much like him. From their size, Tok guessed that these were last spring's pups, the youngest members of the pack. Rakal, still gnawing a bone, warned the three of them off with a growl when they tried to tweak it away from her.

One by one the wolves drifted back to the carcass. Adanax and Bervenna fed as they pleased, but the others approached cautiously now, ears and tails down, awaiting permission from their leaders before they ate again. Even the tall, gaunt wolf who had led the chase with Bervenna stopped a respectful distance away until Adanax growled, "Eat, Mantor." Only Malik trotted up boldly and began to tear meat off the bones. The *vór* and *vóra* turned on him angrily, fangs bared. Suddenly Adanax and Mantor leaped snarling on Malik and threw him to the ground. At once he rolled over on his back in submission. With low growls, they let him up.

"Why can't I eat? Was I not brave in the chase?" demanded Malik. "I held on as long as you did, Adanax. And have a wound to prove it!"

"You forget yourself, Malik," warned Adanax, staring him down. "*Karlán* is *karlán*. You may eat now—but only because *I* say so."

Malik dropped his eyes. "Yes, my *vór*," he muttered. Sweeping his tail low around his flank, he crept to a place at the carcass with the others. But it seemed to Tok that he cast sullen glances at the *vór* while he fed again.

Slowly the simmering excitement of the fight died down. The wolves fed peacefully, with only a little scuffling and snatching of favorite bits. When he had satisfied his hunger, Adanax took a hunk of meat and cached it some distance away under the snow. "To honor the Lanna, the ancestors," he explained when he saw Tok watching him. "So they will send us another kill as good as this."

The *vór* didn't notice when the ever-hungry Rakal sneaked over, dug up the cache, and gulped it down.

After the second feeding nothing remained of the deer but chewed bones and a few scraps of hide. With Adanax leading them, the pack set off downhill. Tok tree-hopped after them.

At the bottom, Adanax stalked over to a large rock half buried in snow and sniffed it. "No one has passed this way since we did days ago," he said. "Or, no one who wants us to know about it." Lifting his leg, Adanax over-marked the spot, then scratched vigorously with all four feet. His wolves gathered around him now, licking his muzzle and play-biting him.

"Time to move on," he told them.

Once more the wolves fell into line, and the pack moved off in the gathering dusk. Tok, uneasy traveling in the dim light, sought out Selaks and plopped down on her back. That night, the pack moved fast and far.

The next day they rested before hunting again. This time even Tok's sharp eyes found them no prey. But on the third day he spotted a few deer who had stamped out a feeding ground in the snow among a grove of evergreens. Again the wolves killed and feasted.

While the wolves rested, Tok took to the air to stretch his wings. Lazily he sifted the wind through the tips of his flight feathers, feeling the blood rush warm through his body. Then he began to dance, tumbling his joy at having found the Grey Lords, swooping a plea to Skyah that they would go with him.

"What were you doing?" demanded Selaks when he landed beside her. "At first I thought you were going to crash!"

"I was skydancing," retorted Tok.

"It looked like play—once I realized you were doing it on purpose."

"It *is* play. But it's more. It's being one with the world. With other ravens. With Skyah."

"Skyah?"

"The Maker. The Thought Behind the World," he explained.

"So croakers revere something the way we do our

Lanna," she said, her yellow eyes thoughtful. "Your danc-ing seems like our singing—it can mean many things. I like this about you, Skydancer." She put her head on her paws and closed her eyes again.

Skydancer. Pleased, Tok quorked the name to himself. He liked it—it felt *kora*.

More days passed, and on some they had good hunting. And then one evening Tok and the wolves were back near west *skiffet*.

"We have fed well these last days, my wolves," Adanax told them. "The raven has kept his word. Now is the time for council."

Obediently, they gathered around him.

"You all heard what the raven said about the new hunt-ing grounds," the *vór* went on. "He says he can lead us there, and that the Two-Legs won't bother us. Perhaps he speaks the truth." He glanced up at Tok, perched on a branch overhead.

"But the journey to the new land would be long and dangerous, and some of us might not live to see the end of it. For we would have to pass through the lands where many Two-Legs live."

The wolves whined and glanced at each other.

"But that isn't the worst," the *vór* went on. "To seek these new lands we would have to leave our home, these hills where wolves have lived since the First *Vór* and First *Vóra* came hunting down the Wolf Trail. These hills where the bones of our Lanna rest."

Bervenna lifted her proud head. "What life in a new land could replace the sacred hills of our Lanna?"

"Indeed," growled the wolf called Mantor, and Bervenna shot him a grateful glance.

The rest murmured their agreement.

"My *vóra*," said Alkara. "It grows harder and harder to feed as well as we have done these last days. You know it does. As our *vór* has already said, the Two-Legs leave us no forest, and soon there will be no deer. What then? Should we think of the future, not the past?"

"Can we trust the croaker?" demanded Malik, with a sharp glance at Tok. "He may be lying about this new land."

"We must choose," said Alkara. "To take a chance and go, or take a chance and stay. Which risk is the greater?"

"I . . ." Timmax began.

Bervenna rounded on him. "*You* have no say. You'll do as you're told," she snapped.

The rest of the wolves laughed, running out their tongues. Timmax's tail drooped and he sidled behind Selaks.

The sky had clouded over and snow began to drift down on a light wind. It powdered the wolves' fur white and eddied among the trees. Alkara lifted her head. "Snow," she said in a dreamy voice. Slowly she moved off alone down the valley, the wolves stepping back respectfully as she passed.

Adanax stared after her as she vanished into the whirling snow. Then he looked up at Tok. "We'll talk more after the Seeing," he said.

"What seeing, *vór?*"

"Among the family of wolves, the Lanna," Adanax

replied, "a rare few have the gift of Snow-Seeing—glimpsing visions in the falling snow. Alkara is such a one." He paused, then added with a sigh, "May she See something that helps us decide. Then we will continue the council. *Among ourselves*. Do you understand me?"

"I won't spy on you," Tok promised, as the *vór* and his pack vanished among the shadows.

Chapter 24

To the Lanna we sing
We wolves sing
We wolves rejoicing sing.

—from Songs of the Lanna

Alone, Tok waited as the snow sifted and swirled through the trees. The cold was bitter, and he shivered, fluffing out his belly feathers around his feet. Somewhere out there in the forest, the wolves were deciding. Would it be for him or against him? Burning with curiosity, he longed to slip silently through the trees to listen to their council. But he had promised the *vór*.

At last he saw a shadowy figure trotting toward him through the snow. It was Selaks.

"The *vór* sends for you, Skydancer," she said, looking up at him.

"What was the Seeing? What have you decided?"

Selaks shook her ears. "You'll hear. Come along." She headed back the way she had come.

The wolves were gathered in a glade deep among the trees. Adanax sat on one side of the group, Bervenna on the other. The clouds were parting, and the Moon of Deep

Cold rode high above the forest. Though it was waning now, it still cast a light almost as bright as day.

Tok fluttered down and landed in the snow before Adanax. The great wolf stared at him for a moment, his eyes like pools of shadow. "You are *numon*, raven," he said. "You come upon us uninvited and unavoidable."

Then the *vór* stood up and spoke in a loud voice. "The raven has reminded us of our past, and offered us a way forward for the future. Alkara has Seen a new land and wolves claiming it. She believes the journey will succeed. Even so we have argued about what to do. Many bitter words have been spoken this night, words best kept within the sacred circle. But now all of us have had our say. It is time to decide, but in this choice I will not rule you. Each of you is free to go or not to go."

Mantor spoke first. "I came to these hills as an outlander," the tall wolf said, glancing around the circle. "It is terrible to travel through the lands of the Two-Legs. I want no more such journeys. I will stay here."

Bervenna nodded. "I agree with Mantor," she said. "I, too, came from another place. Although that was years ago, I will travel no more."

"The journey will be long and hard," said Rakal, with a shiver. She glanced at her mother. "Our *vóra* is right. I will not go."

"And what about you, my *vór?*" challenged Bervenna.

There was a moment of silence, then Adanax raised his head. "It is in my heart to go," he admitted, "even though it means leaving our beloved hills. For I dread our future here. But if you, my *vóra*, and others too, choose to stay here, I will not leave you."

Bervenna gave a low growl of triumph.

Tok's hope ebbed away. He had seen how the wolves depended on their *vór*. If Adanax would not leave, how could any of the rest?

"I will go." Alkara's words rang out in the frosty air. "I have already told you my Seeing. The raven speaks the truth. We can make the journey."

"Alkara—" began Adanax.

"No, my *vór*," Alkara said gently. "You said each of us is free to choose. And I have chosen."

The *vór* gave her a long look, but he said no more.

"I will come with you, Alkara," said Selaks.

It seemed to Tok that Rakal's eyes flashed with satisfaction at her sister's words.

"Me too!" yelped Timmax.

"No!" protested Bervenna, leaping to her feet. "I forbid it. You're too young to choose for yourself!"

Timmax turned to Adanax. "You promised that each of us could decide, my *vór*," he said. "Don't I share the trail and the hunt with the rest of you? I'm old enough to choose. It is my right!"

Adanax glanced from Timmax to the *vóra*. "What Timmax says is true," he said at last. "He's no milk pup. He does his share in the hunt. How can I deny him?"

Timmax gave a yelp of delight and bounded over to stand by Selaks and Alkara.

"Don't worry, my *vóra*," said Selaks, as Bervenna sank back on her haunches, defeated. "I'll look after him."

"We both will."

To Tok's amazement, Malik now stepped forward. From the beginning Selaks's brother had distrusted him. Why would he choose to follow now?

"Alkara has Seen that the croaker speaks the truth about the new lands," Malik went on. "I'll go with him."

Then a small tawny wolf crept forward, glancing both ways as if expecting someone to bite it. Tok recognized it at once. Last and lowliest of the pack, it fawned on the others and hung back timidly after each kill until all the rest had eaten. "I'll go where Malik goes," it said in a low voice, glancing shyly at him.

He grinned and gave a wag of his tail. "Well done, Sirva," he said, and the little wolf quivered with delight.

"You're quite welcome to Sirva. *She's* no loss to us," sneered Bervenna, with a stare that made Sirva cringe.

Adanax gazed around the circle, but no one else spoke.

"It is decided, then." The *vór*'s voice was heavy with sadness. "Alkara, Selaks, Malik, Timmax and Sirva will go with the raven to the new lands. The rest of us will stay."

Tok's heart was beating wildly. They were going to come! Not all of them, but enough. He roused his feathers and spread his wings, bowing before Adanax. "Thank you, *vór*," he said.

Adanax didn't answer. Instead, he lifted his muzzle and began to sing. Bervenna chimed in, then the others, one by one. Their voices wove a web of shifting sound, and the wild music made Tok's feathers prickle. What singers they were! On and on the wolves howled until at last Adanax lowered his head and the song died away voice by voice.

"The council is ended," said the *vór*.

Alkara went over and rubbed her muzzle against his. "It's for the best, my *vór*," she said. "Fewer mouths to feed."

"But the pack is broken," he mourned. He turned and moved away among the trees, and Bervenna bounded after him.

One by one the other wolves drifted away to sleep, leaving Tok alone with Alkara.

"So, raven," she said. "Are you satisfied?"

"Your Seeing convinced them," said Tok. "Thank you."

She shook her ears impatiently. "Do you think I choose what to See? The Seeing *is*, raven. It's not my doing."

"This new land," said Tok. "Tell me, what did you See?"

"I Saw white peaks, and beyond them a land of high ridges and deep valleys, all black with forest. And a strange tall hill with a three-pointed rocky crest—much taller than any of our hills . . ."

"Mount Storm!" exclaimed Tok. "You Saw truly, Alkara."

"I Saw a raven tumbling in the sky and wolves going down into the valleys," she murmured, as if she hadn't heard him. "And I Saw . . . but that's for me alone to know," she finished.

"We'll leave for the Raven Mountains tomorrow," Tok said eagerly. "If the others agree, I mean. I promise you I'll find the safest and shortest way to lead you. You'll see your new home in the real world, Alkara."

"This I know," she replied serenely.

As Alkara turned away, Tok called after her, "The *vór* said I was *numon*. What did he mean?"

181

Moonlight glinted in the old wolf's eyes as she gazed back at him. *"Numon is fate, luck, but more than either of those things. It is a way of being that you cannot escape, a path that there is no turning aside from. Until tomorrow, raven."*

Tok watched her disappear among the shadows. Then he flew up into the branches of an evergreen on the edge of the glade. He ruffled his feathers, then settled them, and put his head under his wing. But he was too excited to sleep. His mind whirled with a thousand thoughts and questions. By what route should he lead the wolves? Not the way he had come—the land was full of Two-Legs. He'd have to find a way more to the north, then turn east.

He raised his head. The moon was sinking behind the treetops. Tok blinked. Something was moving against the snow, something almost as white . . .

Bervenna!

Tok half-spread his wings. "Are you looking for me, *vóra?*" he croaked.

"Yes," she replied. "I've come to plead with you, raven."

"With me, *vóra?* But why? You're staying, and the *vór* won't leave you."

"But he is terribly hurt by the breaking of his pack. I cannot bear to see him suffer. You are taking our children, raven. Please do not take our children!"

She stared up at him, silvered by moonlight, and Tok thought he had never seen another creature as beautiful.

"Malik, Selaks," she went on. "They're the future of the pack. And Timmax . . ." Her voice broke. "He's so young and foolish. How can he survive without us?"

"But Alkara Saw the wolves coming safe to the new land—"

"Saw?" she snapped. "I don't believe in the crazy visions of an old she-wolf. I want my children here. I want them safe."

"Safe, surrounded by the Two-Legs?" Tok reminded her. "Will they be safe when there are no more deer? When the Two-Legs cut down the last trees and drive you out?"

"Come down, raven," she said suddenly, stamping her front paws in the snow. "I tire of gazing up at you."

Tok stared at her. Could he trust her? She was fierce, utterly ruthless.

"Come down," she repeated. "I promise I will not harm you."

Yet if she killed him it would solve all her problems neatly, thought Tok. After a moment he launched himself from the branch and floated down to the ground in front of her.

Bervenna grinned, showing her fangs. "Good," she said. "If you had refused to trust my word I would have found a way to kill you, I swear it." Her eyes narrowed. "Why are you doing this, raven? Why?" she demanded. "You say it's for the good of your people. I don't believe that. There's something you want to gain. There must be. I understand these things!"

"You're right, *vóra*," Tok replied. "I want to gain honor among my own kind. For bringing back the Grey Lords. But it's still true that my kind need you. And your kind need us."

She stamped her forefeet again, in frustration.

"You yourself can solve your problem," Tok reminded her. "Change your mind. Come with us. The *vór* wishes it, and the others would follow him."

"But *I* do not wish it," she replied proudly.

"Then . . ." Tok raised his shoulders and half-spread his wings. "Then you must live with your choice."

Bervenna's eyes flashed, and her teeth ground together. Tok saw her muscles bunch under her fur, but he stood his ground. With a shudder she controlled her desire to spring on him.

"Ah, croaker," she said at last. "You have the mastery of me." She turned and walked away across the snow.

Not true, thought Tok. It wasn't he who had defeated her. It was her own iron will.

Chapter 25

Long journey, short farewell.

—Wolf proverb

The next morning, Tok found the wolves gathered at west *skiffet*.

"We go east," Tok told Adanax. "But we must keep well north of the many-roosts of the Two-Legs. They're as thick on the ground there as maggots in a six-day carcass."

"How many days' running?" asked the *vór*.

"I don't know," admitted Tok. "I was flying, remember. And I went far to the south and then came north again after I left the Raven Mountains. We'll have to travel more directly now—I'll try to find the shortest way," he added.

"Do you hear that?" Bervenna exclaimed, turning to her children. "The croaker doesn't even know the way! Malik? Selaks? Won't you change your minds and stay with us?"

"The raven is keen-eyed. He'll find the safest way for us," replied Alkara.

Bervenna gave her an icy stare.

The others in the little group said nothing. They gathered around the *vór* and *vóra*, rubbing against them and licking their muzzles. Selaks leaned her head against Adanax's broad back, squeezing her eyes tight shut. Alkara nuzzled him and pressed close against his other side. The rest of the pack, even Bervenna, surrounded them, whining and touching noses with the departing ones.

At last the *vór* broke away. "Enough," he ordered. "Go now."

For the last time, Alkara and the others obeyed him. With many backward glances, they set out on the trail that led east along the floor of the valley.

Tok lingered for a moment, gazing up into the sorrowful eyes of Adanax. "Forgive me, *vór*, for breaking your pack," he said. "But I'll lead your children to a place where they can live without fear. Trust me."

"Trust *you*? Never!" snapped Bervenna, glaring at him. "I curse the day you came among us, croaker."

"But *I* trust you, raven," said Adanax. "For Alkara's Seeing agrees with what you have said. Go safely."

"Somehow I'll send word to you," promised Tok. "Someday."

Adanax nodded. Then he lifted his head and howled. One by one the others joined in, but the chorus was thinner now. Then back from the trail came the missing voices, and for a few moments the song was whole again before the singers parted forever.

Tok launched himself into the air and flew after Malik and the others. They ran as they often did, in single file. First went Alkara, with Selaks close behind. Timmax and Sirva followed, with Malik bringing up the rear.

His Grey Lords, thought Tok. Really his now. He must not fail them.

The valley ran east among the Lost Hills, and clearly the wolves knew every step of the trail. They paused now and then to sniff *skiffet*, marking and over-marking it. After gorging themselves the day before, they should have no need to hunt, thought Tok. But he remembered only too well his own hungry journey across the lands of the Two-Legs. Now the land lay even deeper in the grip of the frost. Food would be harder to find than ever, and he had five more hungry mouths to feed. To make things worse, the wolves could not cover distance as fast as he could.

Hoping for advice, he dropped down onto Alkara's back. "I'm worried about food on the journey," he told her.

The old wolf grunted at his unaccustomed weight. "I, too," she said. "We should hunt again before we leave the hills. Then we can go without food for days if we must."

Like ravens, thought Tok.

"Last *skiffet* marks the boundary of the *vór's* territory," Alkara went on. "It lies beyond this valley where the hills come to an end. There are still some woods there. Perhaps we will find game."

Tok lifted off her back. Seeing the wolves bounding along so eagerly lifted his heart. He did a barrel roll in the air before thumping down on Selaks.

"Must we carry you all the way, raven?" she growled.

"Why not, Selaks?" teased Tok. "When my eyes aren't needed my wings might as well rest."

She snorted, then, "Do your kind have names, raven?" she asked.

"Of course. Mine is Tok," he replied, pleased she had bothered to ask.

"Tok." She rolled the word on her tongue as if tasting it. "It suits you," she said at last. "Tok Skydancer."

The sun was high now, sparkling off the snow, and the sky was pale blue above the white shoulders of the hills. The shorn forests were less ugly now, with the slopes deeply mantled in snow. It was a beautiful land, Tok realized, with a sudden pang. Even with all its dangers, the wolves must hate leaving it.

"Why did you decide to come?" he asked Selaks.

She gave a huff, her hot breath sending a plume of steam into the air. "You ask hard questions, Skydancer," she replied after a moment. "Something inside me, something I don't understand myself. Once I heard about your new lands I couldn't stop thinking about them. About being able to run free, with no Two-Legs crowding in on us. Even so, I nearly didn't come in the end. It was terribly hard to leave the *vór*."

"And Malik?"

"Even harder to say. I don't understand him at all. For he distrusts you."

"I know," said Tok. "Yet he came. What about the others?"

"Alkara? Who can tell? She's a deep one, and her Seeing gives her strange knowledge. But as she said to the *vór*, without her, there'll be one less mouth to feed. An ex-*vóra* cares about things like that."

"Ex-*vóra*?"

"Yes. Alkara was pack *vóra* before her mate was killed

188

by the Two-Legs. When Adanax became *vór* she gave up her place to Bervenna."

"What about Sirva and Timmax, then?"

"Oh, Sirva. That's easy—she wants Malik to choose her for his mate," said Selaks with a contemptuous sniff. "As if he'd choose that low-*karlán* creature!"

"*Karlán?*" Tok recalled the unfamiliar word. Adanax had used it after he punished Malik.

Selaks thought for a moment, twitching her ears. "*Karlán* is who matters most in the pack. It's strength and courage, but also honor. Of course the *vór* has the most *karlán* of any of us, male and female. Everyone respects him and obeys him. The *vóra* is the she-wolf with the most *karlán*. She is usually the *vór*'s mate, and they rule the pack together."

Tok thought it over. It was something like the raven lords and ladies. "What about the rest of you, though?" he asked.

"Well, Mantor is next in *karlán* to Adanax. If anything happened to Adanax, he would be *vór*. Then come Malik and Timmax. We she-wolves have our own ranking. Alkara comes after Bervenna—Rakal and I and Sirva must all give way to her. Rakal thinks she's next because she's a year older than I am. But she's lazy and one of these days she's going to get a big surprise," she added, tossing her head.

She ran a little farther, then said, "Oh, but she doesn't have to worry about me anymore, does she?"

And she knows it! thought Tok, remembering the flash of triumph in Rakal's eyes when Selaks said she would go to the new land.

"Anyway," Selaks went on, "Sirva has the lowest *karlán* of any of us, male or female. Except for the two youngest pups, of course. Malik would never chose *her* as his mate."

"And Timmax? He wants to come because you and Malik are?" guessed Tok.

Selaks ran out her tongue, laughing. "That's so. And he probably thinks the whole thing is going to be *fun!*"

"He's going to be awfully disappointed," said Tok, taking to the air again.

As Alkara had said, the hills were drawing back from the valley, and from the air he could now see snowy fields stretching beyond a narrow fringe of dark woods. He felt a twinge of doubt. How under Skyah would he get a pack of wolves across open ground with little cover? If the Two-Legs sighted them they'd surely try to kill them.

Soon Malik led the pack into the shadows of the forest. He went directly to a huge tree that stood near the foot of the last hill. Tails wagging, the others gathered around, sniffing the base of the tree. Then Malik stalked forward and marked it.

"Last *skiffet*," he said, staring back at the rest with blazing eyes. "Now *I* am *vór!*"

Part 5

The
Crossing

Chapter 26

It takes more than cunning to make a vór.

—Wolf proverb

"No! I forbid it." Alkara's voice was icy.

"You dare to deny me what is mine by right?" snarled Malik, glaring at her.

"What right? You have not proved you are fit to be *vór*." Alkara walked over and stood face to face with him, lips curled back, fangs bared.

"Who has a better claim?"

"No one has a claim for now. It's too soon. Our hearts are still with Adanax. You can't replace him."

"And how do you expect to get to the new lands without a *vór*?" sneered Malik.

"Do *you* know the way?" Alkara shot back. "Of course you don't. The raven must lead us. And I will be *vóra*, as I was before," she added. "I gave up my rank in Adanax's territory, but I am taking it back now. Do any of you dispute my claim?" she added, staring fiercely into the surprised faces of the others.

No one answered.

Tok's mind was whirling. Now he understood why Malik had agreed to come. In the Lost Hills he had less *karlán* than Adanax and Mantor. He might never become *vór*. But in the new lands who else could be?

"Who stands with me?" demanded Malik, swinging his shaggy head toward the others.

"I do!" Sirva stepped forward eagerly.

"Good," said Malik. "Selaks?"

There was a long pause. Then his sister said, "No, Malik. Not now, not yet. Alkara's right. Adanax is still my *vór*. When we reach the new lands—"

"Timmax?" Malik asked.

The young wolf cast a worried glance at Alkara and his sister. "I . . . I . . . I . . ."

"Out with it!"

Timmax gulped and sidled over to Alkara. "I agree with Selaks," he said. "It's too soon."

"So, three against two," Alkara said softly. "You are *not vór*.

The big wolf ground his teeth.

Selaks went over and nuzzled him. "Don't be angry," she pleaded. "No one doubts you will be *vór* someday. It's just that it's too soon."

He turned his head away. "Let it be, Selaks," he said. "The decision is made—for now." Then he walked away into the woods. After a moment, Sirva followed him.

Alkara sighed. "He won't let go of this. There'll be trouble."

"Why should he let it go?" demanded Selaks. "Who else can become *vór* when we're ready to choose one—

Timmax?" she added mockingly.

At once Alkara sprang at her and gave her a shoulder slam that sent her staggering. Then the new *vóra* stood over her, ears pricked, tail raised high. "Don't use that tone with me, Selaks," she growled. "*Karlán* is *karlán*. And I'm prepared to teach you a lesson if you forget it!"

Selaks opened her mouth to reply, but the *vóra* clamped her muzzle between her jaws and pressed until Selaks whined in protest. A moment passed, then Alkara released her, but the old wolf's eyes were cold. "I'm *vóra* now, as I was before. You'd better remember it!"

Selaks flattened her ears. "Yes, my *vóra*," she said, as Alkara walked away stiff-legged.

"She's *vóra* all right!" muttered Timmax. "It's as plain as *skiffet*."

"Of course she is," snapped Selaks. Then she gave him a nip on the rump. "Just so *you* don't get any big ideas," she said over her shoulder, as she bounded after Alkara.

"Now, why did I deserve that?" complained Timmax, as he followed the others.

Tok tree-hopped after the wolves. How would he be able to lead these unruly creatures anywhere? he wondered. They were barely out of the Lost Hills and already they were at each other's throats.

The wolves were casting about in the woods now, trying to find something to eat. Suddenly they were in high spirits, as if their quarreling had cleared the air somehow. Even Malik seemed to have recovered his temper.

Timmax was pouncing with his forefeet on a mouse tunnel in the snow. As Tok watched, he tossed a panicked

194

mouse into the air before bolting it down.

Tok's mouth watered. "If I find more tunnels for you, will you share?" he asked the young wolf.

Timmax nodded, grinning, so Tok fluttered about until he located tiny tracks in the snow that led to two more tunnels. When Timmax pounced on one of them, Tok headed off the terrified squeaker that shot out of the snow, and crunched it. The two of them kept it up until both were satisfied.

Meanwhile, Selaks and Sirva had cornered a large snowshoe hare, driving it back and forth as it zigzagged between the two of them. At last it froze in its tracks, bewildered. Then Selaks sprang on it and snapped its neck. Casually she gulped down most of it. Then she swaggered away, leaving only scraps of fur and a few entrails in the snow for Sirva.

"Mice. Rabbits. Is this the best food you can find for your pack, *vóra?*" Malik taunted Alkara.

"I've eaten worse. I suppose you've found a whole herd of deer?" she shot back.

"No, but my nose tells me there's plenty of warm meat not too far away," said Malik, licking his chops.

The wind had shifted. The other wolves froze, lifting their noses and sniffing. Tok flapped up into the treetops. Beyond the edge of the woods was an open field that contained two of the strange roosts of the Two-Legs. Malik's nose, keener than his, must have picked up the scent of them. "Two-Legs," he called down to the wolves. "That's what Malik has smelled. But it would be asking for trouble to go anywhere near them."

Malik ran out his tongue and grinned. "It's not Two-Legs I smell. It's something else. Big meat. Why should we journey on empty bellies if we don't have to? I'm going after it." He set out toward the edge of the trees at a jaunty trot.

The others whined and stared longingly after him. Then they glanced back at the *vóra*.

"Come back, Malik!" ordered Alkara. But Malik kept going.

"The Two-Legs have firesticks," Selaks called after him.

"Poor little Three-toes. Stay behind if you're afraid!" laughed Malik.

At once she loped after him.

"Selaks!" yelped Alkara. But the white wolf kept on running. Alkara sighed and turned back to the others. "Very well, let them try if they want to take the risk. But you, Sirva and Timmax, will stay here with me," she added, glancing sternly from one to another. "We can't put the whole pack at risk for the sake of a meal."

They cowered. "Yes, *vóra*," they chorused.

"I'll go after them," said Tok. Taking wing, he soon caught up with the two young wolves. The light was fading, and their coats blended into the shadows as they moved toward the roosts of the Two-Legs. "It's too risky. Go back!" he told them as they stopped to sniff the air again.

"Oh, be quiet!" said Selaks. She and Malik were staring at the roosts ahead of them, one bigger and one smaller.

"The smaller one smells strongly of Two-Legs," said Malik, swinging his head from side to side. "The meat smell is from the big one. Make yourself useful, croaker, and see if any Two-Legs are outside."

Quorking angrily under his breath, Tok flew ahead of them and landed on the smaller roost. Peering down he could see a hole right through the side of it, where light poured out onto the ground. He fluttered down to a narrow ledge below the hole and peered inside. Then he jumped back, beak agape, and almost fell off his perch. There were four Two-Legs right in front of him! But the hole seemed to be covered by some substance like ice, and they didn't notice him.

Taking off silently, he flew over and landed beside the bigger structure. Its walls were solid and there was no light showing. Right beside it was a small wooden roost. Tok cocked his head, listening. A sleepy clucking told him there were fowl inside. He turned back to the big roost. There was a crack in the front of it just big enough for him to poke his beak through. Prying the opening wider, he pushed his whole head in. Now the warm musty smell of animals was very strong. In the dim light he glimpsed the big shapes of them. Their jaws were working as they champed at something.

Tok pulled his head out and made off on silent wings. The wolves had crept up near the roosts by now. "The Two-Legs are all in the small roost. There are big animals in the other one. And fowl outside," he reported.

Their eyes kindled. "Fowl," muttered Selaks, licking her chops.

With Tok flutter-hopping after them, they flattened themselves and moved silently forward over the ground toward the big structure. When they got there, Selaks slid off toward the wooden roost, while Malik put his nose through the space where Tok had peered in. He wiggled his muzzle this way and that until, with a slight creak, it opened wider and he slipped inside.

Meanwhile, Selaks was breathing in the smell of the fowl, saliva drooling from her jaws. She pushed eagerly against the door of the roost, but it wouldn't open.

Suddenly there was a loud *slam* from the small structure, and Tok and Selaks both froze.

"Hurry up!" urged Tok. "The Two-Legs may be coming outside!"

"I can almost taste those fowl!" muttered Selaks.

"Skyah give me patience," groaned Tok. But he hopped up on her back and peered at the door of the roost. It had a fastener like the one he had opened before. He fluttered down and slid it aside. Selaks clawed the door open and sprang inside.

At once a great screaming and cackling arose from the fowl. At the same moment the animals inside the big roost began to bawl and stamp. Panicked by the sudden noise, Tok bounced into the air and saw a large dog rushing down on him, baying at the top of its voice.

"Dog!" he yelled, as Selaks dashed out of the roost with two fowl struggling in her jaws. Tok flew straight at the dog, striking at its head. It skidded to a stop and snapped at him.

Then a Two-Legs ran out of the small roost just as

Malik tore out through the door of the big one. There was a terrific *bang*, and snow flew up at Malik's heels.

"Firestick!" screamed Tok. "Run for your lives!"

Selaks vanished around the corner of the big roost with Malik right behind her. The Two-Legs ran after them, and the firestick exploded again. Selaks stumbled, but in an instant she was back on her feet and running. With Tok wheeling overhead, the two wolves darted across the field and plunged into the woods.

Chapter 27

Hard as ice if you fight it. Soft as snow if you yield.
What is it?
Karlán.

—Wolf riddle

"Close!" panted Malik, as the two wolves threw themselves down onto the ground. Then he noticed the fowl in Selaks's mouth and snatched one for himself. In two snaps of his great jaws there was nothing left but feathers. Selaks finished the other one just as quickly.

"I hope you're both satisfied," complained Tok. "The Two-Legs certainly know we're here now. And your tracks will lead them straight to us."

Selaks gave him a half-guilty glance, but Malik ran out his tongue, laughing. "What's life without a bit of excitement?" he said. "They didn't catch us, did they? By the time they get here we'll be long gone!"

"Leaving more tracks behind you," snapped Tok. "And don't forget we're going to be crossing open country from now on."

Alkara appeared out of the shadows with the other

wolves behind her. She stood over Malik and Selaks, staring down at them with cold eyes. "We heard firesticks go off," she said. "So the Two-Legs must have seen you. They'll be on the lookout for us now."

Sirva sidled over and nuzzled Malik, who paid no attention to her.

Selaks casually began licking her hind leg. "My fur's creased. The firestick must have just missed me," she announced.

"It serves you right," said Alkara. "What did you two gain by your recklessness?"

"A couple of fowl," boasted Malik. "Much tastier than mice or rabbits. And I had a bite out of something delicious in the barn. Wish I could have stayed to finish it!"

"You'll do no more raiding," ordered Alkara. "Understood?"

Malik's hackles rose and he got to his feet. "Don't give *me* orders," he warned.

Without a word, Alkara sprang at him. Using her full body weight, she knocked him down. He jumped up and snapped at her, but she ducked and his teeth buried themselves harmlessly in her mane. With a fluid movement, she seized his throat in her jaws, then turning her shoulder under his, she threw him to the ground and held him there.

"Bones!" muttered Timmax. "She's pinned him like a pup!"

A moment passed, then Malik laid his ears back and whined to be let up. Alkara let go of his throat and stepped away.

"I said, no more raids," she repeated. "Agreed?"

"Agreed," growled Malik, getting up and shaking himself.

"Agreed," echoed Selaks, with a sideways glance at him.

Ears back, bodies low to the ground, the two wolves humbled themselves before the *vóra*.

Alkara looked up at Tok. "I think we'd better get away from here. What do you say, raven?"

"You're right," replied Tok. "If the Two-Legs don't come after us this very night, they will in the morning. But I don't know the way. Let me fly ahead and try to see something by moonlight. Wait for me at the north edge of the trees."

He launched himself into the air. It was a strange feeling to fly at night, but the moon reflected off the snow, giving enough light for him to see a good distance. Below him the roosts of the Two-Legs were brightly lit up, and he could see figures outside. The fool of a dog was still barking. Malik and Selaks had stirred up serious trouble, he told himself. Alkara was right—they had to get away while they still could.

He could see the straight line of one of the Two-Legs' hard paths. It would be easy running for the wolves, but it was too risky, he thought. Even though it was dark, he could see a few of the Two-Legs' beetles rushing along it, each lighting its way with strange round shining eyes on the front of it. Beyond the woods lay open country, but not far away the land became more rolling. At the base of a line of low hills, Tok could see a band of darkness.

Swooping lower, he could make out a shallow ravine thickly overgrown with bushes. He followed it for a while. The ravine ran roughly northeast, toward a glow of light at the horizon. That would be more roosts of the Two-Legs, thought Tok. Any route that brought the wolves closer to them was dangerous. But what choice did he have? There was no other cover in sight.

He wheeled back toward the woods. The wolves were waiting at the northern edge.

"You'll have to risk crossing open country," he told Alkara. "But beyond there's a ravine you can follow. That should be safer."

The wolves left the cover of the trees. Alkara took the lead again, with the others strung out behind her. The *vóra* set a fast pace, and the wolves moved out across the snowy fields like a ribbon of shadow.

Tok kept to the air for a while, alert for trouble. But when no danger threatened, he flew down and landed on Alkara's back.

"Will Malik obey you now, *vóra?*" he asked.

"For the moment," she replied. "But he'll keep testing me."

"Will he be *vór* in the new lands?"

She didn't answer him directly. "He has boldness, strength, cleverness," she mused, half to herself. "Every quality a *vór* needs. Except one."

"What's that?" asked Tok.

"Heart. The ability to put the pack first."

She's right, Tok realized, thinking of Adanax. The *vór* ruled his wolves sternly. Yet he had broken his own pack, freeing some of them to seek a better life. And he had denied himself the same chance, staying behind with those too stubborn or too timid to leave.

On they raced under the moon, distance melting away under the flying paws of the pack. They skirted far to the north of the lighted roosts where the dog still barked, then bore east across the rolling lands. At last Tok's eyes picked out the faint line of the ravine.

"Over there," he told Alkara. "Right below that near hill. The ravine begins at the base of it."

"I thank the Lanna for your sharp eyes, raven," said the *vóra*. "I can see nothing."

Once they reached the shelter of the ravine, their pace slowed, but they kept on moving. Alkara was trying to put as much distance as she could between them and the Two-Legs, thought Tok. Bush-hopping above them, he marveled at the wolves' endurance. They had run all day through the Lost Hills, and now how much farther?

At last Alkara stopped, and the wolves flung themselves down, falling asleep as they hit the ground. Tok eyed the sinking moon. It must be nearly dawn now. With open lands all around them they must sleep through the day and be ready to run again at dusk. It would give him time to scout the lands ahead. Realizing how tired he was himself, he put his head under his wing.

He roused at first light. Wearily, he forced his eyes open and looked around. The wolves still lay where they had thrown themselves down. Tok checked the sleeping figures one by one. A wolf was missing.

Malik.

Should he take wing and try to discover where Malik had gone? Just as he was about to lift himself from his perch, the big grey wolf came trotting back along the ravine.

Tok hunched his shoulders, trying to look as though he was still asleep, but his eyes missed nothing.

With a quick glance at the sleeping pack, Malik curled up where he had lain before. He put his head down on his paws and licked his muzzle.

His jaws were stained with blood.

Chapter 28

In every pack a rebel heart.
—Lore of the Lanna

Tok didn't even try to sleep again. Where had Malik gone? And what had he killed—some wild creature, or an animal that belonged to the Two-Legs? Below him the wolves slumbered on. Should he warn Alkara? But he was sure of nothing, really. Malik had promised not to do any more raiding. If he chose to do a little hunting on his own, what harm was there in that?

It was more important to find a route for the wolves to follow, he told himself. So he took to the air and flew farther along the ravine. To the north one of the hard paths ran into a many-roosts of the Two-Legs, though it was not nearly as large as the great one by the Shining Lake. Tok shuddered. At least they wouldn't have to face *that*—it lay well to the south. This place was dangerous too, but if the ravine ran far enough, the wolves would be able to skirt it unseen.

But after many thousand wingbeats Tok saw that the ravine came to a sudden end. The widest hard path he had ever seen cut straight across the countryside from north to south, and it was jammed with the beetles of the Two-Legs. Even from high in the air he could hear their restless roar. It would be sure death to try to cross it by daylight. Even at night it might be deadly.

Worried, he turned and flew northward. The path passed right through the many-roosts and disappeared into the distance as far as even his sharp eyes could see. He turned southward until he saw the terrible shapes of the great many-roosts in the distance. There was no way around the path. They would have to cross it.

Beyond the path was open country again. But in the distance he could see a loop of shining water thickly fringed with woods. A river. If they could only cross the path, he could lead the wolves to shelter there.

On his way back, Tok swooped low over the ravine, looking for tracks that would tell him where Malik had gone. The snow was unmarked, and Tok's heart lifted. Perhaps Selaks's brother had kept his hunting to the ravine after all. Then, only a little way from where he had left the wolves sleeping, he saw a line of paw prints that left the ravine and curved up over the hilltop. Tok glided uphill following them. As he shot over the crest of the hill, he saw more open land and another roost of the Two-Legs beyond it. And there in the field right below him, the half-eaten body of a strange woolly animal lay on the blood-spattered snow. More of the creatures stood huddled in the far corner of the field making frightened baahing noises.

Tok swooped down and landed beside the carcass. The killer had surely been a wolf—paw prints led right to it, and the carcass showed the marks of fangs. The rich smell of the meat made him dizzy, and saliva dripped from his beak. But he held himself back. Alkara had forbidden raiding. To eat the Two-Legs' beast would be *unkora*. He scanned the snow. There were no signs that the Two-Legs had discovered the dead animal yet. But when they did . . .

On heavy wings he flapped over the hilltop and glided down among the wolves in the ravine below. They were stirring now, chewing balls of snow from between their toes and greeting each other with sniffs and nuzzlings. Selaks slunk behind a bush and ambushed Malik, beginning their morning romp. Tok watched the wolves, troubled. If he left them to hunt freely they'd surely pick up the scent of the kill. Even the *vóra* might not be able to control them if they discovered fresh meat so close by. And then the Two-Legs would find them and kill them.

He fluttered over to Alkara. "We must go at once," he told her.

The *vóra*'s eyes narrowed. "Right now? Without hunting?"

Tok nodded. "Something has happened. We'll soon be in danger here."

She stared at him for a moment. "Malik?" she asked.

"I think so, but I can't prove it," replied Tok.

She got to her feet, and at once the others gathered around her. "We run, my wolves," she told them.

There was a chorus of yelps and whines from the pack.

"Now? We've hardly rested!"

"What about time for hunting?"

"I'm hungry!"

Tok noticed that Malik was the only one who made no protest. Instead, he watched the others with a gleam of amusement in his yellow eyes. "Are you wolves or just whiners?" he jeered. "The *vóra* has said we must run. So we run!" He trotted to his place in line and stood waiting.

"Malik's right," said Selaks. "If Alkara says we go, then we go."

Shamed, Timmax and Sirva slunk into line.

Tok watched them with pity. Hungry and footsore, they had another long run ahead of them. And then the terrible path to cross.

Alkara started off and Tok flew up the line to talk to her. "We'll follow the ravine as far as we can," he told her, dropping down on her back. "But then we come to a great danger." He did his best to explain to her about the hard path and the hordes of giant beetles that whizzed up and down it. "There's no hope by daylight," he finished. "There are too many beetles now, and the countryside is open, with no place to hide. We'll have to try to cross the path in the dark."

The *vóra* sighed. "We have seen these things the Two-Legs ride in," she said. "They use them to take away the trees they cut down in our hills. We call them *grawls* because of the sounds they make. They're huge and noisy, and they stink in our noses like a sickness."

Tok felt a shudder ripple down her back.

Grawls, thought Tok. A good word for the awful things. Better than beetles. Beetles are harmless.

By afternoon they were nearing the end of the ravine. Alkara allowed the pack to stop and hunt, for they had a better chance of finding food there than in the open fields beyond the path.

Tok and Timmax went back to their mouse catching. Tok scanned the snow for telltale tracks, while Timmax, head cocked, listened for the squeaking of the mice in their tunnels under the snow. Both did well, and after a while they began to keep score. Tok was in the lead when he noticed Sirva hovering timidly nearby.

"Selaks caught herself a rabbit," she said. "But mine got away. And I can't seem to manage the mouse catching." She shivered hungrily as Timmax sent another mouse flying into the air and crunched it.

"Stop stuffing yourself, Timmax, and give Sirva a lesson," said Tok.

Timmax trotted over, tail wagging. "It's easy! The tracks tell you where the ends of the tunnel are," he explained. "The squeaks tell you exactly where the mouse is. Then you do *this*," he added, pouncing with his front feet. A hapless mouse popped out of the snow, and Timmax picked it up delicately in his front teeth and presented it to Sirva. She swallowed it in one gulp.

"Let me try," she said, licking her chops.

After a bit of practice, she was doing much better. Ears pricked and eyes bright, she even *looked* better, thought Tok. At least she was getting a decent meal for once.

As soon as she had satisfied her own hunger, Sirva carried a mouse over to Malik, who was dozing under a bush. "You keep it," he told her, opening a lazy eye. "I don't need a snack."

"But you haven't hunted . . ." began Sirva. Then, baffled, she bolted the mouse down herself.

Well after dark, Tok led the wolves to a tumble of boulders that marked the end of the ravine. Their eyes widened as they gazed out at the hard path and the strange things that rolled along it. The bright lights on the front of the *grawls* made them even more fearsome than they were by day.

"They are like the *grawls* the Two-Legs use in our hills," Alkara reminded them. "Only they're smaller and much faster. And so, more dangerous."

"These . . . *grawls* run in two directions," Tok put in. "Two lines go north on the far side, and two more lines go south on this side. So look both ways before you try to run across."

"We'll go in turn," added Alkara. "Once across, wait for the rest to follow. The raven says there's a river not too far away, and we'll make for that."

The land near the path was rolling, and it was hard to see far in either direction. "You watch to the north and I'll watch to the south," Tok said to the *vóra*. "We can tell each runner when to go."

"Good," she said.

The wolves slipped down the hillside and flattened themselves at the bottom of a ditch beside the path. A *grawl* rushed toward them from the south, its lights half blinding them. They cowered as it tore past in a blast of wind, leaving a choking stench in the air behind it. Before they had time to recover, another zoomed by from the north.

If the wolves didn't cross soon, thought Tok, they

might lose their nerve. But who would be bold enough to try first?

Malik stood up and shook himself. "No use skulking here," he said. "We must cross. I'll go first."

However rash he might be, the big wolf was brave enough, thought Tok.

"Wait for our signal," Alkara reminded him. "And once you start, don't stop for anything until you're across."

Malik sprang up onto the side of the path. Selaks whined and gazed anxiously after him.

"Clear to the north," said Alkara.

"Clear to the south. No, one is coming, but it's still far away," said Tok, calculating the distance as best he could.

"Go!" growled Alkara.

Malik dashed across the path. The lights of the approaching *grawl* outlined him for a moment before he plunged into the ditch on the far side.

"He did it!" yelped Selaks, leaping onto the side of the path. "I'm next!"

"Clear!"

"Clear!"

"Go!"

Selaks bounded safely across.

They had to wait for some time after that, as a rush of *grawls* roared past in both directions.

Then, "Timmax!" said Alkara, and the youngest wolf sprang forward. At her command, he disappeared after his older brother and sister.

"Your turn, Sirva," said Alkara. "The others have done it. You can, too."

Trembling, the little wolf jumped up onto the edge of the path.

"Clear!" said Alkara, gazing northward, and Sirva leaped forward.

"No, wait! One's coming from the south—very fast!" cried Tok.

But it was too late. Sirva had bolted ahead in panic. She was already partway across, and the *grawl* was bearing down on her.

"Run!" barked Alkara.

Half-blinded by the lights of the approaching monster, deafened by its roar, Sirva cowered in the middle of the path. Then she tried to run back to them, but now two more *grawls* were thundering down on her from the north.

It was useless to shout to her now. She couldn't hear them. Tok and the *vóra* watched helplessly while she darted back toward the far side where the *grawl* hurtled down on her.

"I've got to help her!" Tok cried above its roar. Hurling himself into the air, he flapped after Sirva, but another *grawl* rushed right under him, and the whirlwind of its passing sent him spinning. He got control of his wings just in time to see Sirva plunge into the oncoming lights. There was a screeching sound, and the *grawl* veered on the path. Then it straightened its course and sped on.

Tok flapped across the path and landed by the crumpled form that lay on the far edge. A moment later, Alkara arrived panting beside him. She sniffed at Sirva's ruffled fur, licked her . . .

"She's dead," mourned the *vóra*. "My fault. I knew she

was the weakest, the most timid. I should have tried to find another way across for her."

Tok tried to comfort her. "There *is* no other way, *vóra*," he said. "She had to take her chance. There was nothing you could do."

Chapter 29

Suspicion chokes like a bone in the throat.
—Lore of the Lanna.

The other wolves crept out of the ditch. Cowering in the midst of the roar and glare of the terrible *grawls*, they gathered around Sirva, heads low, ears laid back.

"I was hateful to her," Selaks muttered. "What harm did the poor thing ever do to me?"

At that moment, Tok saw a faint twitch in Sirva's left hind paw. "She's not dead!" he shouted over the roar of the *grawls*. "Get her off the path."

Alkara's eyes widened. Sinking her teeth into the thick fur at the back of Sirva's neck, she dragged her down into the ditch.

"She can't be alive!" gasped Selaks. "I saw that awful thing run right over her."

But moments later, Sirva opened her eyes. When she saw the *vóra* staring down at her, she tried to get up, but fell back with a moan of pain. "I'm . . . I'm sorry, my *vóra*," she faltered. "I failed you."

"Rest a while," said Alkara. "But how can you be alive?

Didn't that *grawl* run over you?"

Sirva shuddered. "It swerved, then some part of it knocked me flying, and everything went black."

Alkara shook her head in amazement. "Praise the Lanna!" she murmured.

Timmax grinned down at Sirva. "You are one lucky wolf!" he told her, and she moved her tail feebly.

Tok glanced anxiously up at the road above them. They had to get away. "Can you walk, Sirva?" he asked.

"Lean on me," offered Selaks.

The little wolf struggled up, but when she tried to put weight on her left hind foot she cried out with pain. "I can't walk on it," she whimpered, leaning against Selaks.

"Then you must go on three legs," said Alkara. "We can't stay here." Then she looked around. "Where's Malik?" she demanded.

They stared into the darkness, and barked his name. But the big grey wolf was gone.

"But he was here!" cried Selaks. "We were in the ditch, watching Timmax cross."

"I didn't see him when I landed in the ditch," said Timmax. "And then I turned back to watch for Sirva."

Tok and Alkara exchanged glances. The *vóra's* eyes were cold and steady.

"Perhaps Malik has gone to scout ahead for us," she said smoothly. "I said we'd be heading toward a river. He may have gone to look for the shortest way."

Tok noticed that she didn't mention he had disobeyed her order to stay and wait for them.

"Yes! That must be it," said Selaks, with a wag of her tail.

"It would be just like my brother to do something like that."

Timmax looked puzzled, but said nothing.

"We must go northeast now," Tok told the wolves, "and try to reach the river by morning. There's no other place we can take shelter." And we're going to need it if Malik kills again, he said to himself.

They moved out across the fields, Sirva hobbling on three legs and leaning on Selaks. The little wolf struggled forward and made no complaint, but she moved slowly, and as time passed, Tok grew more and more worried. What if daylight caught them before they reached the river? He kept flying ahead to check the distance, and in his impatience it almost seemed as if the wolves were standing still.

The sky began to grow pale in the east. Sirva glanced at the horizon, then she stopped. "I'm too slow," she said. "I'm a danger to you. Go on to the river. I'll follow your tracks and catch up when I can."

"No," said the *vóra*.

"Keep walking!" ordered Selaks. "Timmax, help on her other side."

And so it was broad daylight when they saw the trees along the river ahead of them. Something buzzed high overhead. Focusing his eyes on it, Tok could see a winged object. Not a bird, for its wings didn't move. It was like the strange thing he'd seen flying over the great many-roosts by the lake, but smaller. He told the *vóra* what he saw, for it was beyond the reach of her eyes.

"It must belong to the Two-Legs. Some kind of air-

grawl, I suppose," she muttered, as it buzzed away over the river. "What next?"

They moved through the trees and found the river. It was broad and looked deep, and it was not frozen over. Plunging their muzzles into it, they drank deeply.

"*Here* you are!" said a cheery voice from behind them.

It was Malik. He trotted forward, ears pricked, tail high and waving. "What took you so long? The trail I broke for you was clear enough."

"Trail? We found no trail," said the *vóra* coldly. "Sirva is injured. It took us all night to get here. Where have you been?"

The grey wolf wrinkled up his forehead, puzzled. "Why, here, of course. Waiting for you. I thought it was best to go ahead of you and break the trail. That's one thing the croaker can't do for you," he added, with a sideways glance at Tok. "You mean you didn't find it? But I left *skiffet!*"

"We . . . we must have missed the track in the dark," said Selaks, glancing at Alkara.

"Yes," the *vóra* said after a long moment. "That's what must have happened."

"But what's wrong with poor little Sirva?" asked Malik, turning to sniff her.

"A *grawl* got me," she said wearily.

"Well, rest then," he told her. "And eat. I've done some hunting while I waited. I find I'm getting used to mice and rabbits after all." Darting behind a nearby bush, he dragged out a dead rabbit and dropped it before her.

Sirva sank down on the snow and stared at it, overcome. "Thank you," she whispered.

Selaks bounded over and licked his muzzle. "That's kind of you, Malik. Have you any more leftovers?"

"Too lazy to do your own hunting?" he teased. They play-wrestled for a few moments, then Malik threw himself down near Sirva and put his head on his paws. Selaks trotted off alone among the trees.

Tok caught himself a few mice, but he was too worried to be very hungry. Had he been wrong about Malik? Maybe he really had accepted Alkara's authority. But he had disobeyed her all the same.

When he had eaten enough, he perched on a branch and put his head under his wing. But roosting by day felt wrong to him, and he couldn't sleep. After a while he lifted into the air and flew back over the open lands, following the track the wolves had made. He found the place where they had crossed the great path, but there was no sign of a trail other than theirs heading toward the river. Unless Malik had not gone to the river by the shortest way, as he had said. And if he hadn't, why hadn't he?

Tok wheeled farther away from the road. In the distance he could see the structures of another Two-Legs roost. Had Malik scented something there and gone after it? Tok flew low overhead, but could see nothing wrong. All was quiet, and fowl pecked peacefully by one of the roosts.

It wasn't until he flew farther, beyond the roosts, that he found trouble. Some of the Two-Legs' *grawls* were pulled over at the side of a path. In a nearby field, he could see a group of Two-Legs standing around the carcass of an animal. Beyond it lay two others. He flew lower for a closer look. The animal on the bloody snow was partly eaten. The throats of the ones beyond had been slashed, but they had not been otherwise touched.

One of the Two-Legs screamed something at Tok and lifted a firestick. It went off, but Tok banked away safely over the fields. He did not want to return to the river with their eyes on him, so he floated down into a small copse of evergreens some distance away. As he watched, the Two-Legs fastened the carcasses one by one to a *grawl* and towed them to the path. With much heaving they loaded them onto the back of another *grawl*, then they went away.

At once Tok flew back over the blood-spattered snow. The Two-Legs had trampled the ground so much that he could see no tracks at all. He veered toward the river. If Malik had done the killing, he would have had to go this way to reach it. Then, in the next field over, he saw a single line of tracks circling back toward the river. He swooped low over the snow. Wolf tracks.

Had the Two-Legs seen them? he fretted, as he flew on. They hadn't tried to follow them. Perhaps the wolves would be safe for a while longer. He hoped so, for Sirva could go no farther that day.

Tok's wings felt leaden. He almost wished he had not found the killings. Because the killer had to be Malik. Didn't it?

In the woods beside the river, most of the wolves were asleep now. Selaks was nowhere to be found, but Alkara was lying on a hillock near the riverbank, watchful and silent. Tok could see her nostrils twitch as she sifted the scents that flowed to her through the air.

"Have you gone where I think you've gone?" she asked, as he fluttered down beside her.

"I flew back to the great path."

"And?"

"I found no trail from the great path to here except our own," Tok told her.

"I thought as much."

"There's worse news. Some animals belonging to the Two-Legs have been killed. Three of them, one partly eaten. Wolf tracks leading away toward the river. The Two-Legs haven't tried to follow them yet, but they may have seen them all the same."

Alkara stared at him for a long moment. "Was that what was wrong yesterday too? When you told me we had to go on without stopping to hunt?"

"There were tracks from the ravine to the Two-Legs' field. A half-eaten animal. But no proof that it was Malik."

The *vóra* sighed. "He's not hunting as he should be. I've been watching him. He's getting food some other way." She got to her feet. "I'll have to find Malik, try to talk him out of this," she said.

"Out of what, my *vóra?*" They turned to find Malik standing behind them. How much had he overhead? Tok wondered.

"Out of killing the Two-Legs' animals," said Alkara.

The grey wolf ran out his tongue. "Have you become tender-hearted, *vóra?*" he teased. "Fond of eating only mice, perhaps?"

She stiffened at his tone and took a menacing step

toward him. "Killing the Two-Legs' animals is dangerous to all of us," she said coldly. "Don't forget, we're in strange country with no hills to hide in. The Two-Legs could wipe us out. Easily. Is that what you want?" She stared at him until he dropped his gaze.

"Of course not. Anyway, I never said I killed any of their stupid animals, did I?"

"No," she echoed mockingly. "You never said. And you promised to do no more raiding, remember?"

Then Selaks ambled out of the woods. "What's the matter?" she asked, glancing from one to another.

"The *vóra* accuses me of breaking my word," said Malik.

"I accuse no one—yet," replied the *vóra*, as Selaks's eyes flashed angrily.

"Good," Malik shot back. "Because I've done nothing these last days except run loyally behind you and hunt rabbits. And break a trail to try to make things easier for you all. If killings were done, it wasn't by me."

Killings, thought Tok. He said *killings*. If he's not guilty, how does he know there were more than one?

A breeze sprang up, rattling a few last dry leaves that clung to the boughs above them. As the wind shifted, the wolves suddenly went on the alert. Hackles rising on their backs, they swung around and stared down at a grove of trees at the river's edge.

Out of the depths of it stepped a shadow-black wolf. It was huge—bigger than Malik, bigger even than Adanax.

"There!" said Malik, a note of triumph in his voice. "There's your killer, Alkara!"

Chapter 30

Numon often comes as a stranger.

—Wolf proverb

The *vóra* stood her ground, ears pricked, hackles raised. "Who are you?" she demanded.

"I might ask the same question," the newcomer replied coolly. "This can't be your territory—you mark no *skiffet.*"

"Nor you, that I've discovered."

"Why did you sneak up on us?" Malik broke in. He stalked stiff-legged toward the stranger, lip curled back, fangs bared.

"I don't sneak," the dark wolf replied. "I was watching to see what you would do."

"I call that sneaking," snarled Malik. He stopped a short distance away from the stranger and glared at him.

"Leave this to me, Malik!" snapped the *vóra.* Then, "So this isn't your territory?" she asked.

"No."

"Nor ours. So I see no need to fight about it."

"Agreed."

The two of them approached and exchanged sniffs head-to-head and head-to-tail. The stranger put his hackles down, and the *vóra* lowered hers.

"You lead this pack?" he asked.

"I am the *vóra*," she replied. "My name is Alkara."

"My respects, *vóra*. My name is Durnál." The strange wolf's eyes shifted to Tok. "Well! A raven. I haven't seen your kind for a long time."

Tok stared back at him. The stranger's eyes were as green as pond water, and as deep. Tok thought that a great sadness lurked in the depths of them.

"You've seen ravens?" he asked after a moment.

"Far to the north of here. On the borders of the barren lands."

No matter how far he traveled his own kind always seemed to be far away, thought Tok. Except for the miserable birds on the Hills of Plenty. Would he never find another ravenland?

"The raven's name is Tok. Skydancer, we call him. He leads us," Alkara said. "We seek a new home in the mountains to the east."

The stranger's eyes showed a spark of interest. "There are mountains to the east, then? Forests?"

"Tall mountains," Tok told him. "Thick woods where the Two-Legs come only seldom to hunt. Many deer."

"Will you join us?" offered Alkara. "Our pack is small, and the raven tells us the journey ahead is still long and hard."

"Thank you," the other replied. "But I'm not good company, and would rather keep to myself."

"Just as well," said Malik. "The *vóra* is too generous. We don't need killers among us."

The wolf called Durnál stared back at him. "Killers?" he said, puzzled. "Don't all wolves kill to live?"

"Killers of the Two-Legs' animals, he means." Alkara's tone was even, but Tok could see that she was watching the stranger closely. It seemed to him that the strange wolf flinched when the Two-Legs were mentioned.

"That's a dangerous game," Durnál replied. "Such animals are stupid and easy to hunt. But killing them brings down the wrath of the Two-Legs on the killer and all his kind."

"You seem to know a lot about it," said Malik.

Selaks stared suspiciously at the strange wolf. "He certainly does," she agreed.

The stranger gave her a long look. "It's a lesson every wolf must learn sooner or later," he said. "The lucky ones learn it before it's too late." He turned back to Alkara. "Good hunting, *vóra*, and a safe journey," he added.

"Wait! Listen!" she replied. She had turned to face the west, and stood with her ears pricked forward.

Durnál's head swiveled in the same direction. "I hear it," he said, after a moment.

Though Tok's ears were less keen, he could hear the barking of dogs in the distance, punctuated by the explosions of firesticks.

"It sounds like a hunt, *vóra*," said Durnál.

"Because of your killings," accused Malik.

"Not so," he replied. "I haven't hunted these last two days."

"Liar!" yelped Selaks, bounding over to stand beside Malik. "If it isn't you, who else could it be?"

Durnál gazed at her calmly. "One of you, perhaps?"

Selaks bared her teeth at him.

"We're wasting time," snapped Alkara. "We must run while we can."

"But what about Sirva?" demanded Selaks. "She can't run fast enough!"

As she spoke, Sirva hobbled forward. Though she limped badly, she was able to put four paws on the ground. "I'm ready to try, my *vóra*," she told Alkara, her eyes bright and steady.

"Good," said the *vóra*, with an approving glance.

There was a shattering roar overhead, and all of them cowered.

"The air-*grawl*," muttered Alkara. "Much lower this time. But at least it can't harm us."

"But it can!" Durnál shuddered. "There will be Two-Legs aboard it with firesticks. They'll shoot you down as you run. Whatever you do, don't try to cross open ground!"

Alkara stared at him for a moment. "Thank you for the warning," she said. "I've never been hunted that way."

She turned and bounded off with the rest of the pack behind her. The lone wolf watched them go.

Tok flew up into a treetop. To the west he could see movement at the edge of the woods that lined the river. Groups of Two-Legs with firesticks and dogs. As he watched, the dogs were set free. They bounded baying under the trees. The Two-Legs followed slowly, shooting off their firesticks now and then.

He karked and quorked to himself. What were the

Two-Legs up to? They must have seen the tracks after all, so they knew that at least one wolf was in the woods. But they weren't trying hard to catch up to it, they were just making a lot of noise. Were they trying to frighten their quarry into the open?

There was a roar as the air-*grawl* flew low overhead. The wind of its passing lashed the evergreen Tok sat in, and he clung to his branch for dear life. Staring up, he glimpsed the pale faces of Two-Legs looking down, and the glint of their weapons.

It must be as the strange wolf had said, Tok decided. If the wolves left the shelter of the trees, they would be shot down. He peered toward the east, trying to catch a glimpse of the running wolves. Could Sirva keep up the pace long enough to escape? Where were the dogs now? Turning to the west, he caught sight of the dark coat of the lone wolf through a break in the trees. He was running back toward the oncoming dogs!

What under Skyah was he doing? Tok wondered. Taking wing he followed, and dropped down through the trees just in time to see wolf and dogs meet. The stranger was actually going to try to fight them!

Durnál had chosen a clearing for the battle. The pack of dogs ran baying into it, then skidded to a halt as they saw the huge black wolf waiting for them.

"Come on, brothers," he taunted them, lolling his tongue and laughing. "It's many against one. I'm ready if you are!"

The pack whined uncertainly. Then the lead dog rushed snarling at the wolf and the rest followed. Durnál neatly sidestepped the leader's rush and whirled, slashing the dog's flank open with his fangs. The leader crumpled bleeding to the snow. Then Durnál turned on the others, teeth bared. The pack fell upon him, and before Tok's astonished eyes he disappeared under a wave of dogs.

Caught up in the frenzy, Tok swooped low over the struggling forms, striking where he could with beak and claw. Durnál reappeared a moment later, shaking off dogs. Some fell in limp heaps on the snow, others dragged themselves painfully away. The rest fled yelping back the way they had come.

Chapter 31

What goes on two legs and kills with three?
Two-Legs with a firestick.

—Wolf riddle

Croaking with excitement, Tok harried the stragglers out of sight. Then, the blood racing in his veins, he did a victory roll in the air. "Well fought! Well fought!" he rasped, landing in the snow beside the big wolf. Now that he was close enough, he could see that the stranger was bleeding from many small wounds.

"Fools!" snarled Durnál, the light of battle fading from his eyes. "What did they think they were dealing with? A raccoon?" He gave himself a shake, then, "Thanks for the help, raven," he added gruffly.

With a roar, the air-*grawl* appeared overhead, and a shot rang out. Raven and wolf dived for the shelter of the trees.

"I hope the *vóra* remembers what I told her," Durnál growled, "and doesn't leave the woods."

"It's the injured one I'm worried about," said Tok. "She won't be able to run far."

Without another word the wolf bounded off eastward.

Tok took to the air and flew ahead of him over the tree-tops. As long as the woods lasted, the wolves were safe for now, he thought. He circled higher, trying to gain a better view. Below him, the river wound its way through the countryside in a series of broad loops. Around the nearest curve, a steep rocky bluff rose on the south shore. There the woods ended—only a few trees clung to the base of the bluff. The wolves would have to leave the shelter of the woods.

And right at the base of the bluff waited a large party of Two-Legs.

They had no dogs, but Tok could see their firesticks gleaming in the pale winter sun. Overhead the air-*grawl* was flying in lazy circles, ready to pick off any wolf that broke cover. The wolves must either run out into the ambush or turn back to face the hunters and dogs behind them. It was a trap!

He had to warn Alkara. Tok dived down among the treetops, and dodged frantically among the branches. Where were the wolves now? At last he found them a short distance away from the bluff. Sirva crouched panting on the ground, while Alkara paced to and fro.

"Leave me," the little wolf was pleading. "I can't run anymore."

"No!" exclaimed the *vóra*. The others exchanged glances and licked their lips nervously.

"No use to run anyway," Tok said, dropping down onto the *vóra*'s shoulders. And he told her of the battle in the woods and the ambush ahead.

"Durnál bought you some time with the dogs," he finished. "But sooner or later the Two-Legs from the west will arrive and you'll be caught between two sets of firesticks."

The others whined and exchanged glances.

"Praise the Lanna for what Durnál did," said the *vóra*. "There has to be a way for us to escape. There has to be!"

At that moment, Durnál loped out of the underbrush. He stopped short at the sight of the others. "I'd hoped you'd got away," he said, disappointed.

"The raven has told us how you fought the dogs," said the *vóra*. "Thank you. But now the Two-Legs have us pinned between two sets of hunters." And she told him about the ambush. "We could try to hide until dark," she said, "and then chance the fields. The Two-Legs in the air-*grawl* wouldn't be able to see us then."

The wolves' heads turned sharply as the wind brought them the sound of distant baying.

"But what about the dogs?" asked Selaks. "They're still after us."

Durnál flashed her a quick glance. "You're right. The dogs will scent us wherever we try to hide. And there's more. When the hunters from the west catch up there'll be twice as many firesticks. If they find us . . ."

"But what else can we do?" asked the *vóra*.

"The one thing they won't expect us to do. The river is close by. I say we swim it."

"Swim!" whimpered Sirva. "But the river's so swift, so wide."

"It's too far across even for the strongest of us," huffed Malik.

"And what about Sirva?" put in Selaks. "She's badly

injured—how can she possibly swim?"

"It'll be easier than running," said Timmax eagerly. "And we could help her—swim alongside her, I mean."

"I've followed this river for a time and know something of its ways," said Durnál. "It winds in broad curves instead of running straight. If it curves back beyond the bluff, we won't have to swim so hard to reach the other side." He stared up at Tok, perched on a branch overhead. "You've been in the air, raven. What did you see?"

"You're right," said Tok. "The river flows in a great loop around the bluff. I saw it."

Alkara's eyes lit up. "I see what you mean," she said to Durnál. "If we swim out to the main current, it will carry us most of the way toward the far shore."

"Yes. We'll have to swim hard away from this shore, and again to reach the far shore. But in between the current will do most of the work for us. It will carry us far downstream away from the Two-Legs. All we'll have to do is keep our heads above water."

"But they'll see us swimming," protested Malik. "It's sure death."

"Maybe," agreed Durnál. "But what waits for us here if we stay? And if we make our way downstream to the bluff and swim from there, the Two-Legs are less likely to see us."

"I think we must risk it," said Alkara. The rest of the wolves growled in agreement.

She led them down the slope to the river. At the bottom, Durnál slipped into the shallows. "The footing is firm," he told the others. "Stay close to the shore."

They moved cautiously downstream, keeping close under the bushes that overhung the riverbank. After a while they could hear the voices of the Two-Legs, and now and then the air-*grawl* passed overhead.

"That's the worst danger," Durnál muttered under his breath. "If that thing spots us . . ."

"At least these Two-Legs have no dogs—*they'd* scent us at once," said Malik. "These Two-Legs must have noses like stones."

"Shhh!" ordered Alkara.

Tok, riding on the back of Selaks, felt her shiver as the icy water rose higher and higher around her. Slowly they crept to the base of the bluff where no more bushes grew.

"Now," said Alkara. "Remember about the current!" Head held high, feet churning, she forged out into the river.

"I wish you'd lend me your wings, raven," muttered Selaks, as Tok lifted off her back and flapped out over the water.

Circling, he watched them go. Timmax swam close behind Alkara. Selaks came next, swimming downstream of Sirva. The little wolf paddled valiantly, but the current kept forcing her against Selaks's side. Next came Malik, and then the dark shape of Durnál. The wolves struck out strongly, but just as they reached the main current in the middle of the river, the air-*grawl* flew overhead. Tok saw the Two-Legs inside pointing downward and lifting their weapons. They had seen the wolves!

The *grawl* banked in a tight circle, and Tok saw the Two-Legs aim their firesticks. Two shots rang out, but the wolves swam on unharmed. A moment later, two more shots smacked harmlessly into the water. The current had carried the wolves far downstream now, and Tok saw them strike out for the other shore. Then he heard another shot, and Timmax's head vanished under the surface. Tok dived toward the water, pulling up above where the young wolf had disappeared. He saw the *vóra* trying to turn and swim back, but the current was too strong.

Selaks paddled on, supporting Sirva, her head turning downstream as she tried to catch a glimpse of Timmax.

Tok swooped low over her head. "Get Sirva to shore. I'll watch out for Timmax!" he cried above the rush of the river and the roar of the *grawl*. The dreadful thing had turned again and was heading back at them. Tok's wings pumped him higher into the air as it roared down on him. Two more shots whined past him. One hit the water near Malik, who swerved but kept on swimming. But Durnál vanished under the water.

Tok could hear shouts from the Two-Legs. A terrible spinning thing on the nose of the *grawl* churned out powerful air currents that threw him aside as it whizzed by, then left him tumbling in the vortex of air at its tail. Stunned, he plummeted toward the river, then, getting control of his wings again, he flapped heavily toward the far shore. He landed on a pine stub and folded his wings, trying to regain his senses, while the *grawl* roared away upstream.

Where were the wolves? He scanned the river downstream, but he could see nothing in the water. Timmax and Durnál were gone then, he thought. His heart was sore at the thought of the merry young wolf who had thought the journey would be an adventure. And of Durnál, who had fought so bravely. If it weren't for Tok, neither of them would be dead. He closed his eyes, hunching his shoulders in misery. He had promised Adanax that his children would have a better life. But he had really been thinking only of his own selfish glory if he brought the Grey Lords to the Raven Mountains. What did that matter now?

He gave his rumpled feathers a shake. His duty now was to the survivors. He must find them. Spreading his wings, he coasted along the shore of the river, croaking as he went. At last he heard a faint answering bark from below. Peering down, he glimpsed Selaks's light coat among the trees.

The four dripping wolves were gathered near the shore, under cover of the forest.

"For a moment there we thought the *grawl* had gotten you too," said Selaks, as he fluttered down beside her. Then she gave herself a shake from nose to tail, showering him with water.

"Could you see any sign of the others?" demanded Alkara.

"No," said Tok sadly.

The *vóra* bowed her head. "We were so close," she mourned. "Just a little farther and we would have been safe on shore."

"So much for following the outlander's plan," said Malik. "Timmax is dead because of him."

"We're all outlanders here," Alkara reminded him.

235

"And Durnál was right. If we had tried to hide they would have killed us all."

"At least the killer got what he deserved," said Malik. "He was the one who brought the hunt down on us."

The *vóra* gave him a long stare, but said nothing.

Then from downriver came a long deep howl. The wolves pricked up their ears and stared at each other.

"Not Timmax," said the *vóra*, jumping to her feet.

"It must be the stranger!" yelped Selaks.

Lifting her muzzle, Alkara howled back. A moment later there was a reply. The *vóra* bounded off through the trees with the rest of the pack on her heels.

Chapter 32

The scent of danger is stronger than skiffet.

—Wolf proverb

Some way downstream, a gravelly point overgrown with bushes jutted out into the river. As they ran up, Durnál stepped out of a thicket. Behind him, shivering, limped Timmax.

"Timmax!" cried Selaks, hurling herself on him. "Oh, Timmax, I thought I saw you shot!"

"Ouch, sister!" he complained, fending her off. "I *am* shot. And I nearly drowned too!"

"Luckily, he's not badly hurt," added Durnál, grinning. "The shot went clean through his shoulder. No bones broken, no real harm done."

"Well, it still hurts," muttered the young wolf, as the others gathered around to sniff his wound and lick it. Then, with a worshipful glance at Durnál, he went on, "But I owe my life to Durnál. He grabbed me by the scruff of my neck and hauled me to shore."

"But weren't you shot too?" asked Tok, from his perch on Selaks's back. "I saw you go down."

"I ducked," said Durnál. "When I bobbed up down-

237

stream, I saw Timmax floating by and grabbed him. Then I got us to shore and under cover as fast as I could."

"Two deeds you have done for us today," said Alkara. "Without you we'd be dead by now. Won't you change your mind and stay with us?"

The lone wolf looked at each of them one by one. But it seemed to Tok that his eyes rested longest on Selaks, who was busy licking Timmax's shoulder.

"At least stay with us until we reach the new lands," coaxed the *vóra*. "Then, if you still wish to leave us, you can."

"And what do *you* say?" Durnál asked, fixing his gaze on Malik.

The grey wolf bristled. "Who am I to say anything?" he replied. "The *vóra* has spoken. If she wishes to bring an outlander among us, it's her affair." Turning his back, he trotted down to the shore and began to lap water. With a cold glance at Durnál, Selaks followed her brother.

"I agree, *vóra*," said Durnál, turning back to Alkara. "I'll go with you to the new lands. After that I'll follow my *numon*."

The sounds of the hunt had died away on the far shore, and the *grawl* had gone. Wearily, the wolves moved deeper into the woods, seeking rest and shelter. Tok flew over to Alkara as she curled up in the wet snow under the trees.

"You're pleased about Durnál, aren't you?" he asked.

She gazed at him with calm yellow eyes. "It comforts me to have someone like him among us," she said. "He's a *vór*."

"A *vór*! But where's his pack, then?"

"That is something he may never tell us," said Alkara. "But a *vór* he is all the same."

"What about the killings?" asked Tok. "Do you think he did them?"

The *vóra* sighed. "I wish I thought so. A lone wolf can kill as it chooses. It doesn't endanger anyone but itself. But if Malik has killed, against my direct orders . . ." She said no more, but covered her nose with her brushy tail and closed her eyes.

Tok looked around for Selaks and flapped onto a branch over her head. Maybe Durnál had killed the beasts in the field near the river, he thought. But what about the killing near the ravine long before they met the lone wolf?

"You don't seem to think much of Durnál," he said to Selaks. "Despite all he's done for us."

She stared up at him with angry eyes. "I can't stand him!" she snapped. "He's so grim and ugly. And Malik's right. It's *his* fault that the Two-Legs hunted us in the first place."

Tok noticed that Durnál's ears were pricked up. At Selaks's words, the black wolf lay his head down on his paws.

The pack woke before dawn and moved on, not pausing to hunt. Tok went for a quick flight downriver. "There's no sign of the Two-Legs," he told Alkara. "And the air-*grawl*'s nowhere in sight."

"Good. But the farther we are from where they hunted us, the safer I'll feel," said Alkara. "At least the woods allow us to travel by day."

The wolves had sorted themselves into line with much snapping and snarling. Durnál took his place at the end,

with Timmax and Sirva and Selaks ahead of him. Malik
ran behind the *vóra*.

"What's wrong with all of you?" Tok asked Selaks,
catching up to her and hopping onto her back.

"Wrong?"

"You're all so cranky. I would have thought you'd be
glad to be alive."

She flicked her ears. "I suppose we are. But we're hungry too, and weary of small game. And there's a stranger
among us." She thought for a moment, then added,
"And . . . I suppose we're restless because it's the Season."

"The Season?"

"The time when *vór* and *vóra* mate, so new pups will be
born in the spring. But here we are with a *vóra* who's past
rearing young, and no *vór*, and no lands marked with our
own *skiffet*. It's worrisome. Don't ravens have a Season,
Tok?"

"Of course we do. About the same as yours," he replied.
She was right. Here in the soft lowlands, winter was growing old. The signs were all around them now that he came
to think about it. The cold was less biting, and the snow
softer. Tiny icicles formed on the black boughs of the evergreens now as melting snow trickled during the day, only
to freeze again at night. He cocked his head, listening.
Over the panting of the wolves as they ran, he could hear
a chickadee singing its spring song.

Spring . . . He glanced up at the new moon, pale and
slender. The Moon of Courtship. Already ravens would be
feeling the changing season, long before the mountain
snows melted. There would be matings and nest buildings

240

among the lords and ladies, while the rest of the raven-horde, the ones with no territories, watched and waited. Would Tarkah be one of those? he wondered. Or had she already accepted a lord? He snapped his beak, annoyed with himself. It was *unkora* to mope like this.

They traveled along the north side of the river for many days, grateful for the shelter of the woods. The hunting wasn't good, but they found enough to keep them from starving. Tok kept a close eye on Malik's rabbit stalking and mouse hunting. He seemed as eager as the rest of them now, and Tok hoped he had put thoughts of killing the animals of the Two-Legs behind him.

In his scouting flights, Tok watched for nearby roosts of the Two-Legs that might have animals, but most lay far from the river. Just as well, he told himself. Even the keen noses of the wolves couldn't scent prey at that distance. From the air he could see that the river was leaving the open lands and entering a countryside of barren hills. Ahead, the river had carved a steep-walled canyon for itself through their slopes. The wolves would either have to go through the canyon or take their chances on the open hillsides where snow still lay deep.

"Let's stay with the river," said Alkara, when he told her. "Remember that air-*grawl*."

"Can we follow the river through the canyon, raven?" asked Durnál.

"There's a deep gorge with white-water rapids," replied Tok. "No path there. But I've found a trail that climbs above the gorge. There's no cover, though."

"Could we cross it at night?" asked the *vóra*. "That way

there's less chance of being seen by any Two-Legs."

"The trail will be slippery," warned Tok. "The snow is soft, and we can't travel as fast as we once did."

He thought of Timmax and Sirva, both limping badly, still lagging far behind the others. He noticed that they seemed very friendly now and spent much time licking each other's sore spots. Malik, too, had noticed. He began making small presents to Sirva—a rabbit leg, a mouse. She always thanked him, but her eyes rested more often on Timmax now.

"How far is it through the canyon?" asked the *vóra*.

"At least a day's journey. More if you travel at night," replied Tok.

Alkara hesitated. Then, "If the footing is treacherous, we must travel by day," she decided. "Because of Timmax and Sirva."

The next morning, the wolves left the shelter of the trees and began to climb the trail above the gorge. It was their first time under the open sky for many days, and they cast nervous glances upward as they went, afraid that an air-*grawl* might swoop down on them out of nowhere.

The trail climbed steeply at first among huge boulders that had sheared off the face of the cliff and tumbled into the gorge.

"Hoofs and hides!" muttered Timmax, struggling uphill. "This path was made for mountain goats!"

The footing was treacherous. The path had frozen hard during the night, but now the first rays of the sun were reaching it, making the snow slick under the pads of the wolves' paws.

"You're sure this trail leads somewhere, croaker?" growled Malik. "It will be worse going down if we have to turn back."

"I'm sure," replied Tok. "It gets a bit easier higher up. The trail levels off and follows a ledge across the face of the cliff."

"What made this trail?" asked Selaks. "Some animals must use it, but I can't smell a thing."

"Nor I," said Alkara over her shoulder. "This place is dead." She shuddered.

It was true, thought Tok, suddenly missing the small sounds of the woods. No birds sang here, no creatures scurried. A brooding silence hung over the canyon. All they could hear was the voice of the river far below them.

Higher and higher they climbed. At last they reached the ledge and started across it. The trail was narrow, with the sheer wall of the cliff on their left and a dizzying drop into the gorge on their right. Small pebbles lay on the path beneath the snow, and these shifted treacherously underfoot. Sirva whined uneasily as several she had dislodged clattered down into the canyon below.

Alkara paused to rest for a few moments as the wolves stood listening to the silence.

"There's something wrong with this place," muttered Selaks. "It feels as if everything is waiting for something to happen."

Suddenly Timmax threw back his head and howled. It made a shocking sound, echoing and re-echoing off the stony cliffs around them.

The other wolves turned and stared at him.

"What do you think you're doing?" demanded Alkara. "This is no time for a sing-song!"

"Sorry!" Timmax hung his head. "I just couldn't stand that awful silence anymore."

Suddenly a muffled boom echoed high above them. The wolves pricked up their ears, and Tok peered up at the heavy snow pack on the top of the cliffs. Then he croaked in alarm. The snow was moving!

"Run!" he screamed. An avalanche roared down on them, scouring rocks off the face of the cliff as it came.

Alkara and Malik darted ahead along the narrow ledge. The wounded wolves limped forward, with Selaks and Durnál close behind them.

"Timmax! Sirva! Hurry!" cried Selaks.

But it was too late. A moment later, Durnál disappeared under the mountain of moving snow. Tok shot into the air as Selaks made a mighty leap toward safety. But the edge of the cascading snow caught her hind legs. As the others watched in horror, she clung desperately to the edge of the path with her front paws for a moment. Then she too was swept over the brink, and vanished into the mass of snow thundering down into the gorge.

Chapter 33

Out of the jaws of sorrow, joy.
—Wolf proverb

The roar of the avalanche faded away into silence. Stunned, the wolves stared down into the depths below them.

Timmax began to tremble violently. "It's my fault! Mine!" he whimpered.

"Yes, it is!" snapped Malik, turning on him with bared fangs. "You put us all in danger with your foolishness. Now you've killed your own sister! Live with *that*, if you can!"

Tok swooped over the *vóra's* head. "They may still be alive!" he cried. "I'm going after them."

Alkara nodded gravely. "Our hearts go with you. But we must go on as we can," she said. "We can't help them from here, and may still be in danger ourselves. More snow may break loose at any moment." Turning, she led the way east, followed by Malik. Timmax limped miserably after them, and Sirva pressed close behind, as if trying to comfort him.

Tok dived down the face of the cliff. The cloud of flying snow had settled, and the bottom of the gorge was a tumble of white mixed with pieces of trees carried down from the heights and rocks dislodged from the face of the cliff. Could anything be alive under all that? Tok flapped here and there, looking and listening for any sign of life. Durnál had been struck by the leading edge of the snow slide, and Selaks a moment later. Perhaps he'd find some sign of them near the river.

The dark water of the river was already eating into the dam of snow that had fallen into it. Tok scanned the edge of the avalanche carefully. Then he remembered how keen wolf ears are. He began to croak loudly as he walked over the snow, at the same time keeping a wary eye on the heights above.

Croak, listen. *Croak,* listen. At last he thought he heard something that sounded more like a wheeze than an answering bark. It came again and he hopped toward the sound. Now he could see a tuft of something dark in the snow. It was the tip of a wolf's tail. He tweaked it, once, twice, then Durnál's muffled voice gasped, "Enough, raven! Help me get out of this!"

Following a line to where he thought the wolf's head might be, Tok scrabbled away at the snow with beak and claw, and managed to shift some of it. At last the tip of a black nose appeared. Durnál drew in his breath with a *whuff,* and worked his muzzle further out. Tok dashed snow left and right with his beak, until Durnál's front paws were free and he began to dig his way out.

"Thank you, raven," he said, shaking himself. "I thought I was done for until I heard your voice."

Tok had already flapped off over the snow. "Help me,"

he begged. "Selaks was swept away too. The very edge of the avalanche caught her."

"Selaks? No!" Durnál floundered after him.

"She might be near the edge—somewhere," said Tok. But the snow lay thick and deep and he was beginning to lose hope.

"You look, I'll listen," said Durnál. "My ears are keener than yours."

Step by step the two of them searched the snow at the edge of the slide.

"Nothing," Durnál muttered at last. "She must be deep-buried." His head drooped wearily. "She had her whole life yet to live," he said. Then, under his breath, "It should have been me."

Suddenly the snow shifted under their feet. With a frightened quork, Tok shot into the air, while Durnál slid down into the river. A whole chunk of the snow, undercut by the flowing water, had collapsed under them.

"The Lanna's curse on this river . . ." spluttered Durnál, struggling toward shore. Then, "Raven, come here!"

Tok fluttered down beside him. The collapsing snow had opened a kind of cave under the crust, and there, half hidden under a smashed treetop, lay Selaks.

"Has it crushed her?" gasped Tok, as Durnál seized her by the back of the neck and pulled her free. She lay still, but her chest was rising and falling.

"No," he grunted. "It may have saved her—made an open space that let her breathe." He dragged her clear of the overhanging snow just before it, too, fell into the river.

Towing her downstream, he pulled her out of the shallows. Then he licked her nostrils free of snow and blew his warm breath onto her face.

After a few moments, Selaks sneezed and opened her eyes. "The next time you're planning a journey, raven," she said, gazing balefully up at Tok, "remind me not to come along!"

"I'll tell the others you're safe," cried Tok, spreading his wings. "They're all grieving. Timmax is heartbroken."

"So he should be, the idiot!" snapped Selaks. "Go ahead. The outlander and I will wait for you here. You'll have to find us a way out of this mess."

When Tok returned, he found the two wolves splashing downstream through the shallows. The walls of the canyon were so steep that there was no shore to walk along.

"How long will it take to get out of here?" demanded Selaks.

"At least a full day's journey," said Tok. "The others will meet us downstream where the hills open out."

The wolves sloshed onward, their paws slipping on the icy rocks in the river. Their outer fur was soon soaked with water, and they stopped often to shake, trying to keep their underfur dry. Tok, clinging to Selaks's back, was soon as wet as they were.

"You could at least warn me when you're going to shake," he complained, spreading his wings to dry the feathers.

"Getting a bit wet, are you? Too bad. *You* don't have to flounder down this wretched river," she pointed out.

Ahead they could hear a growing roar of water, and Tok took off to investigate. "There are rapids ahead," he told them when he got back. "A mass of big rocks in the river. You'll have to either clamber over them or swim for it."

"Not again!" groaned Durnál.

The wolves tried to get around the rapids by climbing over the rocks at the base of the cliffs. But their claws slipped on the wet stone and soon both were swimming for their lives. It was hard for them to go forward, because the river formed eddies and deep pools among the rocks. Again and again, Selaks and Durnál were swept into these and had to paddle out again to reach the main current. Tok rock-hopped above them, croaking directions about how to get through.

Ahead loomed a kind of natural dam formed by two gigantic boulders. Between them the river plunged through a narrow channel in a spill of turbulent black water. Durnál tried the passage first, paddling toward the gap between the rocks. Suddenly he disappeared from sight. Flapping over the boulders, Tok saw him shoot down a waterfall and vanish into a pool below. Moments later he floated to the surface, half-dazed and coughing.

"Warn Selaks!" he gasped. "There's a strong undertow at the bottom."

But Selaks had already been swept over the falls and she, too, was plunged deep under the pool.

Battered and soaked, the two wolves paddled wearily for the shallows. "When will this be over?" wheezed Selaks.

"The shore widens a bit further downstream," Tok told her. "There are rocks and trees, you can rest there."

The wolves struggled on, both shivering now. The sun hung low over the canyon rim and the river lay in deep shadow. At last they came to the widening of the shore, where landslides had dumped rock and earth from the heights above. Bushes had sprung up there, and a few stunted pines had managed to take root among the rocks.

Wearily, the wolves crept under the trees and threw themselves down. They fell asleep at once.

Tok perched on a branch overhead and watched the line of sunlight creep higher and higher up the cliffs. Then it was gone, and darkness fell. He tucked his head under his wing.

He woke when the rising moon climbed over the canyon. Selaks roused too. Lifting her head, she gazed around. "At least this is better than being in the water," she said.

"Or under a mountain of snow. Which is where you'd be if Durnál hadn't pulled you out," Tok told her. "You didn't thank him for it."

"Why should I?" she yawned, stretching. "It's what any pack member does for another. Even though Durnál doesn't belong to our pack." Then she went on, "Anyway, seeing that we're wide awake, you might as well answer a question for me. What made you decide to go looking for the Grey Lords, Skydancer? Oh, you've told us about the hard winters in your Raven Mountains. But not many would dare to set off on such a long journey just for that."

A long moment passed. "You're right," Tok said at last.

"There was a reason why I had to leave the Raven Mountains." And so he told her all of it—about his father, and Grakk, and the sentence of the Kort. About his journey with Kaa, and his flight to the Hills of Plenty. "So at last I came to the Lost Hills," he finished. "And found you."

Her eyes gleamed up at him. "So that's why you need us so much," she said softly.

"He's even more of an outcast than I am," said Durnál out of the darkness. He looked like a wolf of shadow, his eyes reflecting ghostly silver under the moon.

Selaks turned her gaze on him. "Skydancer says you saved my life. He thinks I'm ungrateful because I didn't thank you."

"Aren't you?" rumbled Durnál. Tok saw his teeth gleam as he grinned at her.

She tossed her head. Then, "You come from far away, too?" she asked.

"From the Cold Forests on the fringe of the barren lands," he replied.

"And you're always alone?" She shuddered. "I couldn't live like that. Without a *vór* or a pack."

"It's not a life I'd choose, but it's all that's left to me."

"And . . . and will you stay with us when we reach the raven's new lands?"

"Malik wouldn't like it."

"No, he wouldn't," she agreed. "But . . ."

"Only one *vór* to a pack, Selaks."

She gave him a long look. Then, "Did you kill the Two-Legs' animals? The ones we were hunted for?"

"I did not."

She said no more, but put her head down on her paws and closed her eyes.

Tok woke early to the sound of splashing. He was astonished to see the dignified Durnál capering about in the shallows, as lively as a pup. As he watched, the wolf plunged his muzzle underwater and emerged with a large fish in his jaws.

Selaks trotted down to the shore, tail wagging.

"A meal for two," said Durnál, dropping the thrashing fish at her feet. "That is, you might leave the head for the raven," he added, turning back to the river.

"I *might,*" agreed Selaks, with a wicked grin.

Tok drooled. He hadn't had fresh fish for a long time.

Selaks ate the fish bite by slow bite, beginning at the tail. When she reached the head, she glanced teasingly at Tok, who was bouncing up and down on his branch. "Oh, well," she said, stepping away.

Tok zoomed down and seized the fish head before she could change her mind. Returning with it to the tree, he wedged it in a branch and pecked out the eyes with relish. Then he set about stripping every shred of flesh from the bones. By the time he was finished, Durnál had caught another fish and Tok got that head too.

With food in his belly, Tok's spirits rose. He snapped a twig off the tree he sat in and shuffled it between his claws. Then he swung upside down from the branch, first by one foot, then by the other, waving the twig about in his beak. Tiring of his game, he dropped the twig on Selaks's head.

Durnál snorted.

"What are you *doing?*" Selaks demanded, glaring up at Tok.

Tok gave a quork of laughter and stretched his wings. "Playing, why not? We're alive, aren't we? And there can't be much more of this canyon."

"Easy for you to say," growled Selaks, as the two wolves gloomily eyed the river. "Another day like yesterday and I'll be a fish myself!"

Durnál heaved himself into the shallows. "Lead on, raven," he said.

But they found that they could travel faster than the day before. There was often a strip of shore to walk on at the foot of the cliffs now, and they met with no more rapids.

By late afternoon, the canyon walls began to draw back from the river and they were able to run beside it freely. At nightfall they emerged at last into a valley and found the others there waiting for them.

"Selaks!" cried Timmax. Forgetting his sore shoulder, he jumped around her, nuzzling and licking.

"You're lucky you still have a sister," she complained. But she nuzzled him back all the same. Sirva greeted her gladly, then they all gathered around Alkara, play-biting and rubbing against her.

Only Durnál stood apart, watching the others' joy.

Tok flew over and landed on his back. Then he looked around. "And . . . Malik?" he asked.

Chapter 34

Where will we run, sisters?
To the far-off rim of the world
We will run, brothers!

—"Wolf Running Song" from
Songs of the Lanna

Alkara lifted her head. "Gone scouting, he said," she replied. She and Tok exchanged a long glance, then the *vóra's* eyes shifted away.

Malik must have defied her, thought Tok. And she didn't think she could force him to give in again. He gazed at her searchingly. She looked terribly weary, he thought. Her coat was dull and he could see the outlines of her ribs under it. None of them had been eating nearly enough, and Alkara was much older than the rest. Their perilous crossing was consuming her.

"Have you hunted?" asked Durnál.

"A little. There doesn't seem to be much game in these hills," the *vóra* replied.

Suddenly the wolves' heads swiveled around as a shadowy figure loped down the hillside toward them. Selaks bounded toward it.

"Well-met, sister!" said Malik, wrestling her to the

ground. "For a while we thought we'd lost you."

"Where have you been?" she asked, shaking snow out of her fur as she got up.

"I decided to have a look at the land ahead," he replied. "So the raven wouldn't be able to lead us into any more danger."

"*You* decided?" Selaks's eyes widened.

"After asking our *vóra*, of course," he said, with a sideways glance at Alkara.

The *vóra* said nothing. The rest of the wolves shifted uneasily, sensing tension between her and Malik.

"And what did you find out?" asked Tok.

"The river turns south beyond these hills," replied Malik. "I think we must leave it—at least if the mountains are in the east as you say, croaker. The land looks empty. I could see no more of the cursed Two-Legs."

"We'll stay here for tonight, then," said Alkara. "Timmax and Sirva can rest. We must try to move swiftly now if we'll be crossing open country."

After his restless night, Tok slept easily. But once again the moon roused him, spilling its bright light across the snow. Below him, the wolves seemed to sense it too. They sighed and shifted in their sleep below him. Five furry mounds . . . Tok's eyes snapped wide open. One wolf was missing! Was it Malik again? But no, he could make out the shape of the big grey wolf curled at the base of a tree.

The missing wolf was Selaks!

Tok spread his wings and flapped clear of the trees. By the light of the moon he could clearly see Malik's tracks coming down the hillside. There were no others, so she hadn't gone that way. Where had she gone then, he wondered. And why?

Perhaps she had followed the river. Angling his wings, he banked down close to the black water. She wouldn't have swum across—she'd surely had enough of the water. So she must still be on the north side. The ground was rough, and each mound and hummock cast shadows across the snow. But farther along, the ground became more even. At last he saw a set of tracks leading up another slope ahead. He swooped down and lit on the snow for a closer look.

One of the paw prints showed only three toes. Selaks.

What was she doing out here? he wondered, as he took to the air again. Was she hunting? Had the night wind brought her a trace of scent the others hadn't caught?

Cresting the hill, he found himself looking down on a bend in the river. As Malik had said, it turned away from the hills and wound off to the south. Had Selaks followed it, hoping to find game beside the water?

But no. The tracks bore north, cutting straight across the rolling ground. She wasn't roaming; she was heading confidently in one direction. Her keen nose must have caught a distant scent that she'd decided to go after, he told himself. Then over the next ridge he saw the lights of a Two-Legs' roost. Malik hadn't mentioned it. Had he missed it somehow? Selaks must have scented it, because her tracks went straight toward it. Was she going to disobey the *vóra* too? Tok remembered her glee after her raid with Malik, and his heart sank.

Then a terrible thought struck him. *Could Selaks have*

been the guilty one all along?

Tok was so shocked at the thought that his wings faltered in midair. She couldn't be, he told himself desperately. It was Malik who had gone missing in the ravine. Malik who had left them after they crossed the great path. Selaks had helped Sirva all the way to the wood, and then she'd been there all the time, he reassured himself.

But had she? whispered the voice of his doubt. She had disappeared long before he had flown off to retrace their trail to the great path. If she had gone straight across country, she could have reached the animals, killed, and gone back to the woods before he returned. Alkara might have thought she was just hunting in the woods. And back at the ravine he had seen Malik returning, but could Selaks not have gone and returned while he was still asleep?

On heavy wings, he followed the tracks toward the Two-Legs' roost. He came to one of their paths where the snow was scraped clear and the tracks disappeared. Halfway up it, he found the carcass of a dog. The snow at the edge of the path was churned up—the beast had put up a fight. But its throat was torn, and its blood had spilled out on the snow. It was stiff now, its shaggy fur ruffled by the cold night wind.

Tok flew toward the roost. The ground about it had been scraped too, making it hard to see tracks. In the big roost where the animals lived he could hear nothing but peaceful breathing and gentle movements. There was no way in that he could see. So the animals inside hadn't been harmed.

But in a drift of snow at the side of the structure he

found a single three-toed track. She had prowled about hoping to kill, then, but gone away disappointed. Tok flapped away down the hillside. It was worse than he had thought. Malik was openly a rebel. But Selaks too had broken her word to Alkara. The pack was falling apart as the *vóra* grew weaker. And if they couldn't control their killing until they reached safety, they might all be wiped out. He remembered the air-*grawl* and shivered.

Selaks was back with the rest when he returned. She gazed up at him as he alighted on a branch above her head.

"Good hunting, Skydancer?" she asked.

Tok was too heartsick to answer. He tried to tell himself that he shouldn't blame her. She was a wolf, after all. Wolves killed. Ravens did too, whenever they could. But in his heart he knew that it wasn't the killing that mattered. It was the dishonesty. Selaks had given her word to her *vóra*. To break it was to break her honor.

The next morning the wolves left the canyon far behind them. Where the river turned south they left that too and struck out across the hills. It had turned colder in the night, and there was a heavy crust on the snow. The wolves trotted over it easily, even uphill.

"How do you do it?" Tok asked Alkara when they stopped to rest.

She spread one of her big furry paws. "Good for swimming, good for running on snow," she told him. Then, "You seem glum, Tok. And you're riding with me, not Selaks. Is anything the matter?"

Tok cocked his head and peered up at her. "Malik— he's doing as he likes now, isn't he?"

She sighed. "Yes. And I can't stop him. I must save my strength for a day when I may need it most. The others feel it, of course. If only we could reach your new lands, raven," she added wistfully.

"We're still well to the north of the Raven Mountains," Tok told her. "What land we'll find when we leave these hills, I don't know. Please Skyah it won't be more lands of the Two-Legs."

Leaving her, he mounted high into the air, riding faint currents above the snowy hills. Behind him, the river looped away to the south. Ahead, beyond the hills, he could see a blackish smudge along the horizon. Eagerly he focused his far sight. The line was jagged, and its deep color meant just one thing—forests. He was looking at mountains!

Praise Skyah! he thought. With a cry of joy he rolled over and over in the air. He looped-the-loop, flew upside down, then tumbled toward the ground, shooting right over the heads of the astonished wolves.

"Fancy flying, Skydancer," said Selaks when at last he landed among them. "What was it all about?"

"Mountains!" he panted. "I can see mountains in the distance, covered with trees!"

The wolves whined in excitement. Even Malik pranced eagerly with his front paws.

"How far away?" he demanded.

"Yes, how soon can we reach them?" echoed Alkara.

"They are still far away—many days' journey," Tok answered. "But, *mountains!*"

"Run, my wolves," cried Alkara.

The wolves sprang away as if they were ready to run right to the horizon's edge. The good news lent speed to their paws, and they fairly flew over the snow. Sirva and Timmax managed to keep up now, though they lagged at the end of the line. On and on the pack went, while the sun swung by overhead. That evening they threw themselves down and slept briefly where they dropped, then got up and ran through the rest of the night. They rested the next day, then ran on that night and many nights after. No wandering, scant hunting, just a ground-eating lope that carried them on toward the mountains. Tok marveled at their endurance.

Each day the hills became steeper and steeper, true foothills now, with the range of mountains looming up beyond the foothills. At last they were among the mountains themselves, great rugged summits lost in cloud, thickly furred with dark evergreens loaded with snow. Tok led the wolves up toward a low pass between two mountains. They climbed into winter, leaving the first signs of spring behind them. Here it was very cold, and the snow was deeper. It was hard going now, even for wolves. But they struggled on, tongues lolling out of their mouths, their breaths steaming around their faces.

At last they reached the top of the pass. The snow was fresh and powdery, and the wolves threw themselves into it, biting great mouthfuls, rolling and playing. Below lay a broad valley with more mountains to the east and south. The sun, setting behind them, cast inky shadows across the snow.

"The new land!" exclaimed Malik, gazing down into

the valley.

Alkara glanced at him, puzzled. "But . . ." she began.

Malik raised his muzzle and howled, cutting her off. One by one the others joined him. The mountains echoed their voices as they sang the sun down.

Chapter 35

I am the pack
Karlán's *keeper*
Still center of the running world.

—"Vór's Song"
from Songs of the Lanna

The wolves spent the night below the pass, sheltering from the wind amid a dense grove of evergreens. In the morning they moved down toward the valley like famished shadows. Tok noticed that Alkara let Malik take the lead, breaking trail through the fresh snow. The old she-wolf stumbled sometimes now, as though at the end of her strength.

Near the bottom of the pass, Malik stopped and turned his nose into the wind. "I smell game. Big game. But I don't know what it is," he muttered.

The rest of the pack tested the wind eagerly.

"Meat!" muttered Timmax, licking his chops. "I've almost forgotten what it's like to make a real kill."

"Yes! Rabbits are a lot better than nothing, but if I eat many more I'll be hopping," said Sirva.

"Can you see any game ahead, Skydancer?" asked Alkara.

Tok spread his wings and flapped his way up to a tree-top. On the floor of the valley below he could make out a series of dots moving slowly across the snow. He brought them into focus. They were large brown animals with high shoulders and big ears. They were grazing, kicking away the snow to get at the grasses beneath.

"Elk," he reported to the wolves. "I've seen them in the Raven Mountains. They're a bit like deer, but much larger."

"Good to eat?" Timmax wanted to know.

"Very!" Tok clacked his beak, thinking of meaty bones for the picking.

The wolves' tails began to wag, and their eyes blazed with excitement.

"What are we waiting for?" growled Malik, picking up the pace.

"Let's go!" cried Timmax. He and Sirva dashed after Malik with eager little yelps.

"Not so fast!" ordered Alkara, as she and Selaks caught up with them. "Timmax and Sirva must stay toward the rear to keep the herd from running back. There's no cover, so the rest of us can only stalk them from downwind and watch for a straggler."

Tok lifted into the air and watched the wolves fan out across the floor of the valley. Malik and Selaks trotted to one side, Alkara and Durnál to the other, moving to flank the herd. Whenever the elk raised their heads, the wolves would freeze. To Tok, their dappled coats seemed to melt into patches of shadow on the snow.

Suddenly one of the elk caught their scent. It lifted its

head and uttered a snort of alarm. In a moment the whole herd was running. Heads up, stepping high, the elk plunged through the fresh snow. The wolves coursed at their heels, tongues lolling. Tok could tell that they weren't running flat out yet. Instead they seemed to be testing the herd, drawing a bit closer so the animals became more frantic, then dropping back to an easier pace.

The elk began to spread out as the strongest animals gained more ground, leaving the weaker ones behind. One animal kept breaking pace as it labored along. At once the wolves turned toward it. Pacing their quarry now, the wolves ran the elk harder and harder. It plunged on, panting. Then Malik and Selaks put on a burst of speed. Malik sprang for the elk's throat, while Selaks sank her teeth into its shoulder. The three crashed to the ground in a cloud of flying snow. But the elk was bigger and stronger than the deer they were used to, and it shook them off and plunged onward.

Then Durnál and Alkara caught up and seized its rump in their fangs. The elk turned and struck at them with its razor-sharp front hooves, just missing Durnál. But Malik and Selaks threw themselves at its neck and shoulders again, dragging it down once more. Malik's fangs met in the elk's neck. It kicked twice, trembled and lay still.

The wolves threw themselves on the carcass and began to feed, while Timmax and Sirva trotted up to claim their share. Tok landed nearby. Quorking eagerly, he walked around the carcass, snatching bits where he could and biting beakfuls of blood-spattered snow.

"Beware, croaker!" Malik's tone was joking, but he showed all his teeth. "I might still fancy a bite of raven if you try to steal my meat."

Tok snatched a bone and took off with it. Only a fool would try to get between a half-starved wolf pack and its dinner.

At last, hunger satisfied, the wolves returned to the shelter of the trees. Tok flew over to the carcass and gorged himself on their leftovers. Then he flapped heavily after the wolves.

Timmax was lying on his back, his belly bulging. "What a meal!" he groaned.

Selaks licked blood off her face. "About time," she muttered. Then, "This is a rich and beautiful land, Skydancer," she added, looking up at Tok.

Tok froze on his perch. "But this isn't the new land I told you about!" he protested. "The Raven Mountains are farther south. You said you'd go there with me!"

"This valley is good enough for me," yawned Malik. "In fact . . ." He got to his feet and strolled over to a large pine tree. Lifting his leg, he marked it. "First *skiffet*," he added, staring challengingly at the others. "I say we go no farther."

The other wolves glanced doubtfully at the *vóra*.

"Tell them this isn't their new land, Alkara," pleaded Tok.

"Skydancer is right," she said slowly. "This isn't the land of my Seeing. My heart tells me we should go on." She looked from one disappointed wolf face to another. "But what do the rest of you say?"

"I think it's wonderful here," ventured Sirva, with a sideways glance at Timmax.

"Yes. How do we know we'll find anywhere else as good?" he asked.

"The Raven Mountains are even better," said Tok. "Plenty of elk. Deer too. And moose—they're even bigger than elk."

"Bigger than elk?" Malik narrowed his eyes. "I don't believe it. Don't listen to the croaker. He's trying to fool you to get his own way."

"I believe him," said Selaks. "Skydancer has never lied to us. But we've journeyed too long." Getting to her feet, she walked to the tree and marked *skiffet*. One by one the others did too, except for Durnál.

"I'm sorry, Tok," said Selaks when the marking was done. "I know why you want us to go on. It's just that it's too far. You've more than kept your promise to Adanax. You've found us a fine new home. Maybe someday . . . "

Angrily, Tok flapped higher in his tree and turned his back on all of them.

Below him, the wolves curled up on the ground and went to sleep.

Tok clung to his perch, his heart now as heavy as his stomach. He had never thought that the wolves might not want to go on with him to the end. Even Selaks had deserted him, he thought bitterly. His long journey had been for nothing. Without the wolves he had no way to prove to the Kort that he was *kora*.

He had to stretch his wings and think it through. Despite his heavy meal, he lifted himself easily above the treetops. The afternoon sun was building thermals over the mountains, and he rode them upward, feeling the warmth on the feathers of his back. The air was less cold than it had been up on the pass. Soon it would be spring here too. But he had no heart for dancing alone. If only there were other ravens . . .

He banked south over a great ridge of mountains, feeling the lift of rising air currents under his wings. He let them carry him higher over the black summits. The whole valley spread out below him now. Gazing down he could see the notched pass through the mountains, the woods below where the wolves were resting, the tiny dot of the carcass on the field of snow. From this height he could now see that the valley was much longer than he had thought it was. It didn't stop at the near range of mountains but curved around them, angling away to the south. And near the far end of it . . . Roosts of the Two-Legs—three or four big ones! And dotted around the fields nearby, large herds of animals.

Tok was so startled that he tumbled in midair. He dived down for a closer look, but he was already sure the beasts were not elk or deer. They were like the ones that had been killed in the field near the river—squat brown creatures with white faces. But there were more of them here. Many more.

Tok flew swiftly back to the wolves, who were beginning to stir again after resting. He lit on a branch above Alkara. "You can't let them stay here," he told her. "You mustn't. There are Two-Legs at the far end of the valley. And many of their animals."

"Two-Legs? Here?" The *vóra* stared up at him in alarm.

Malik overheard. He raised his head, and for a moment a green light flickered in the depths of his eyes. Then, before Alkara could speak again, he said, "Two-Legs and their animals? Well, so what? Why should that drive us away from a good place? They're not at this end of the valley. There's room for all of us."

"Not if any of their animals get killed," warned Tok, staring down at him. "They'll hunt you down and kill you, as the Two-Legs tried to do back at the river."

The others were wide awake now. They exchanged worried glances, and a low mutter went around the pack.

"Skydancer is right," Alkara said firmly. "We can't live where there are Two-Legs. In the end it would be no better than our own hills. We must leave this valley!"

Malik jumped to his feet. "No!" he snarled. Raising his hackles, he glared at Alkara. Then he turned his angry gaze on the others. All of them, even Selaks, dropped their eyes and laid their ears back. "Alkara is old," the big grey wolf went on. "She frets too much. I say that this is our new land—and that *I* am *vór* now. Does anyone dare deny me?"

Alkara got slowly to her feet. For a moment she locked eyes with Malik, mane bristling.

Tok held his breath. Would she try to stop him? Was she strong enough?

But after a moment, Alkara lowered her hackles. "No," she said. "I won't fight you, Malik. A pack should have a *vór*. And there are no challengers. Unless . . ." She glanced at Durnál. The black wolf held her gaze but said nothing. "So be it, then," she finished. "I have brought you safe to a new land, my wolves, and now my task is done. The rest is up to Malik."

"But your Seeing, *vóra!*" cried Tok. "You know this is not the land you Saw."

The old she-wolf looked up at him. "No, it is not," she said wearily. "But Malik is right about one thing. I grow old and my strength fails me. Perhaps my *numon* fails me too." Walking over to Malik, she flattened her ears and mouthed his muzzle. Ears pricked, tail high, he accepted her homage. Now the others jumped up and crowded around, doing him honor. The big wolf's eyes glowed with pride and joy.

Tok's heart was like a stone. Malik was *vór.*

Chapter 36

No wolf can escape its numon.

—Lore of the Lanna

Only Durnál stood apart from the rest of the pack.

Malik stared at him with cold eyes. "I admit that you've helped us on our way here, outlander, but there is no place for you in *my* pack. Follow your *numon* somewhere else."

Durnál met his gaze. "You are right, *vór,*" he said. But he made no move to go.

After a moment, Malik turned away.

One by one the wolves began moving back to the carcass to feed again. Tok didn't join them. And later, when Malik led them off across the valley at an easy trot, he didn't try to follow them. Why bother? Game was plentiful here—they could easily find it for themselves. They wouldn't need him anymore, he told himself. He sat brooding alone until dusk. Then he saw a solitary figure loping back toward him.

Selaks.

"Come, Skydancer, don't sulk," she said, staring up at him. "I know you're disappointed. But you belong with us.

Even Malik admits you can be useful. And I scarcely know how to run now without a great lump of raven on my back."

Moodily, Tok ruffled his feathers. "How can I live here?" he muttered. "There aren't any other ravens."

She considered. "Couldn't you fly off and find yourself a mate somewhere? Then you could bring her back here."

But even with other ravens for company he'd still be *unkora*, thought Tok. Could he live with that? Without the wolves to prove his deed, the Kort would never change its sentence.

"It's not just me," he said. "There's going to be trouble here if any of you kill the Two-Legs' animals." He stared down at her, trying to read her expression. If she wanted to kill tame animals she would have plenty of chances now.

She flicked her ears. "We won't have to. There's much game. And Malik says it's different here from in our own hills. The forests are thick—there's lots of cover. We can do as we please. If the Two-Legs come after us we can hide in the mountains."

"Malik!" Tok said bitterly. "He can always find a reason to do as he wants."

"He's young, you know," she pleaded. "Even though he's my brother, I know he's not perfect. But he'll grow wiser. Now that he has what he wants he'll settle down. He'll be a fine *vór* someday. You'll see!"

Then, when Tok made no reply, she stamped impatiently with her front paws. "Oh, come along, you old greedy-guts," she coaxed. "You know you'll always eat well when we have good hunting!"

With a sigh, he dropped off his branch and thumped down on her back.

It was long after nightfall before Selaks caught up with the rest of the pack. Their trail had led far down the valley. In the distance, Tok could see the lights in the roosts of the Two-Legs.

Selaks noticed too. "The pack here? This close to the Two-Legs? What's Malik doing?" she muttered. She followed the tracks of the others into a tangle of bushes at the foot of a cliff. "Where's the *vór?*" she demanded, staring at Alkara.

"Scouting," Alkara replied.

"Alone?" Selaks's voice was suddenly sharp. "Why did you let him go?"

"How could I stop him?" countered Alkara. "He's *vór* now. We all agreed. We have to trust him to do what's best for his pack." She lay her head on her paws.

Tok looked around for Durnál, but couldn't see him. Perhaps he had gone away, now that Malik was *vór.* The thought made him feel even gloomier. He'd come to depend on the steadiness of the big black wolf.

Selaks turned and bounded back along the trail. "Come on, Skydancer," she barked over her shoulder.

Tok flapped after her. "Where are you going?" he asked.

"To find Malik," she replied, lengthening her stride.

Was she really worried about Malik? wondered Tok. Or just looking for a chance to go after the Two-Legs' beasts herself? But then why bring him along as a witness?

Hunched on her shoulders, he listened to the huff of her breathing and the crunch of her paws on the snow. She

272

ran with her nose to the trail, sifting the scent of Malik from that of all the others. Soon a lone set of tracks veered away, heading south toward the roosts of the Two-Legs. Selaks followed them, placing her own feet in the paw prints as she ran.

Suddenly Tok's feathers bristled. He'd seen the wolves do that very thing before in deep snow! So the tracks he'd seen back in the hills near the Two-Legs' roost *had* been hers, but . . .

"Did you run in Malik's tracks back in the hills?" he demanded. "After he returned from scouting?"

"Yes," she panted. "At first I believed Durnál had killed those animals back near the river. But later I didn't. So I followed Malik's tracks. I had to find out!"

Tok felt the ice in his heart melt a little. Selaks wasn't the killer. She had run up to the Two-Legs' roost in the hills, leaving her own three-toed prints over Malik's. She'd found where he had killed the dog, and circled the animal roost.

"I thought it was *you* raiding that night," he confessed.

"So that's why you've been cross with me!" she said, shaking her ears. "No. I followed Malik's trail and saw where it went. Later I told him I'd found him out, and tried to convince him to stay away from the Two-Legs and their creatures. He promised he would. That once he was *vór* he'd be careful. But now . . ."

The trail circled far around the roosts of the Two-Legs, heading past them into the fields where the animals were herded together. Ahead they could hear the frightened bawling of beasts and the stamping of hooves. Selaks lifted her head, sniffing. After a few moments, Tok's duller sense of smell registered it too. A thick, hot, heady scent. Blood. Suddenly a dark shape loomed ahead, and Selaks nearly stumbled over a carcass lying in the snow. Then another. Under the moonlight the snow was black where blood had spilled from the beasts' torn throats. They came upon a third, and then ahead Tok heard snarling and an anguished bellow.

"Malik! Stop!" yelped Selaks.

Now they could make out a shadowy figure ahead of them. It was Malik. He was standing over a still-thrashing animal, fangs bared, his face masked with blood. A terrible green light blazed in his eyes as he turned on them, snarling.

"Stop!" Selaks yelled again. Then, "You're full-fed. There's no need to kill! Oh, Malik, you promised!"

Slowly the light died in Malik's eyes. His raised hackles went down. "Selaks!" he muttered. "Where did you come from?" Then he looked down at the dying beast at his feet. "How many?" he asked, after a long moment.

"Four!" she told him bitterly. "*Four*, Malik! Why? And why now, when you've got everything you've always wanted, when all of us are depending on you?"

Malik shuddered. "It's . . . it's like a madness," he faltered. "Ever since the first tame beast I killed." He blinked and licked blood from his muzzle. "I can't help it. The beasts are so easy, so stupid—they beg to be slaughtered. I even dream about it!"

"Malik, we've got to get out of this valley. Right now!" pleaded Selaks. "It's no good here. Not for you, not for us. Let's go with Skydancer to his Raven Mountains. He says there are no Two-Legs there."

"Leave? But why? The hunting is good here. I'm *vór* and I say we stay." Malik shook himself, and lifted his head. "What does the killing matter anyway? Since when has Selaks Three-toes become a friend of the Two-Legs and their creatures?"

"What matters is your word. To Alkara. And to me," Selaks said coldly. "I trusted you. Back at the river I blamed Durnál when you accused him. Then, after I followed you in the hills, and found you'd killed again, you promised to give this up. To put the pack first."

"I *am* putting the pack first," he insisted. "They will come to no harm. If the Two-Legs chase us we'll go up into the mountains. They will never catch us there."

"Don't you see that you've spoiled everything?" snapped Selaks. "You've broken your word. And the Two-Legs will never forget . . . *this*." She glanced at the bloody carcasses around them. "We'll always be in danger in this valley now, but you say you won't leave. You aren't fit to be *vór*."

Malik's eyes glinted dangerously. "Who is, then? Alkara can't lead anymore—she's worn out. Would you have Timmax for your *vór*?" he mocked. "Or that ragged outlander?"

"Durnál is more fit than you are," she told him, baring her teeth.

"Oh, ho!" he sneered. "I think I smell a plot. But you'll not take my pack away from me!" Curling back his lips he stalked forward and stood over her. "If you tell the others about this I'll drive you out," he snarled, showing every fang. "I might even kill you for your treachery, little sister. As for the outlander, I'll finish him now!"

He sprang past her and vanished into the darkness.

Chapter 37

O my playmate, o my brother!
Deer runner
Lapper of living blood
Song-singer
My heart cries out for you
O my playmate, o my brother!

—"Selaks's Lament"
from Songs of the Lanna

Turning in her tracks, Selaks sped after Malik. Moments later Tok, flying on ahead of her, saw a dark figure bounding toward them from the south.

"Durnál!" he croaked, wheeling over his head. "I thought you had left!"

Durnál skidded to a stop as Selaks ran up.

"I did leave," said Durnál. "I don't belong with the pack—with any pack. But then I heard the animals bawling."

"Malik killed four of them," Selaks said bitterly. "For nothing. He has been killing the Two-Legs' creatures all along."

Durnál's eyes narrowed. "Where is he?"

"Gone back to the others," said Tok. "Looking for you."

"He'll find me!"

Durnál turned and sped off toward the mountains with Selaks on his heels.

From the air, Tok could see lights moving back and forth at the Two-Legs' roosts, and hear voices shouting. They must have heard the animals too. Soon they would discover the killings, and then . . .

Clouds were riding across the moon and there was a raw edge to the wind. There would be snow, Tok thought. If only it would come soon the wolves could disappear into it and the snow would cover their tracks.

They found the pack gathered around Malik on a ridge some distance from the foot of the mountains.

"So!" he said, as the three of them came up. "I was right. My dear sister has been plotting treason with this outlander!"

Startled, the other wolves stared at Selaks.

"There's no plot—" she began.

Malik's lips drew back in a snarl. "Be quiet, or I'll quiet you," he threatened.

Timmax's eyes widened. "Selaks would *never*—"

"What I said is true. You have my word on it as *vór*."

"Your *word?*" mocked Selaks. "You're a word-breaker, Malik. You are not fit to be *vór!*" Then, to the others, "He has been killing the Two-Legs' animals. That's why they hunted us at the river. And he did it again later, in the hills. Now he has killed again, right in this valley— killed four of their beasts when he has no need."

Alkara's eyes flashed, and she raised her hackles.

"What a fool I was to let my weariness cloud my Seeing!" she growled. "This isn't our new land. And Malik's *numon* is clear to me now. We were wrong to choose him as our *vór*. A *vór* must not endanger his pack!"

"Bah!" said Malik. "No one is in danger. The Two-Legs can't catch us in the mountains."

"If what Selaks says is true, I won't follow you, Malik," said Timmax.

Malik took a step toward him. "Beware, little brother," he growled.

Sirva bounded forward and stood shoulder to shoulder with Timmax. "I won't follow a word-breaker either," she said.

"You're no loss, little skulker," snapped Malik.

Alkara turned to Durnál. "Will you accept the *vór*-ship?" she challenged.

Malik took a menacing step toward the lone wolf. But the others fixed their gazes on him, tails waving.

"No!" growled Durnál. "I am not fit to be *vór*."

"Not fit? But you've saved us again and again!" yelped Timmax.

"What nonsense is this, Durnál?" Alkara demanded. "You're already a *vór*. It's written all over you."

"Was," said Durnál in a low voice. "I *was* a *vór*. And my pack died because of me. All of them."

The wolves stared at him, horrified.

"Like Malik, here, I thought it was safe to kill the beasts of the Two-Legs," Durnál went on. "Easy meat, I thought they were. A gift to my wolves from the Lanna. I didn't understand how terrible the vengeance of the Two-

Legs would be. They wiped out my pack—by trapping, by poison. When the last of us tried to flee, my mate and my pups were shot down by an air-*grawl*."

Selaks whined and laid her ears back against her head.

Durnál locked eyes with Malik. "So I don't deserve the *vór*-ship. But even though I was a fool, I killed only for food. Never for the pleasure of it, as you do."

With a growl, Malik sprang on him, and the two of them rolled snarling in the snow.

The others stood frozen, eyes fixed on the battle, as the two huge wolves slashed and clawed at each other, neither gaining the advantage.

But Tok was listening to a dull roar that was growing in the distance. He stared back toward the roosts of the Two-Legs. Bright lights were moving there, heading in their direction. "Listen!" he shouted. "The Two-Legs are coming. Can't you hear them?"

Selaks whirled around. Durnál and Malik broke apart and turned into the wind, their ears pricked forward, listening.

"What can you see, croaker?" demanded Malik.

"*Grawls* with lights. The Two-Legs are tracking us!"

"Follow me!" ordered Malik, shouldering Durnál aside. "We'll outrun them easily."

The wolves fled after him toward the mountainside. Tok shot into the air, gaining height to get a better look. The Two-Legs were riding on the strangest things he had ever seen. Much smaller than their other *grawls*, these sped across the snowy fields with a snarling whine. On the front of each of them blazed a single shining eye.

The wolves were running flat out, streaking across the snow. But the *grawls* were faster. Two of them headed straight for the mountain, then turned south, cutting off the wolves' retreat. Shots rang out and the wolves veered away from the mountainside. From the west three more *grawls* sped after them.

The Two-Legs were running them as the wolves had run the elk, thought Tok. Except that this wasn't a race between two creatures of flesh and blood. The snow-*grawls* didn't tire. No matter how far and fast the wolves fled, the *grawls* kept pace.

More shots rang out and the wolves swerved again. Tok beat his way into the cold wind blowing down from the mountains, peering at the dark slopes below. The Two-Legs were running the wolves in a certain direction, rather than trying to pick them off one by one, he told himself. Why?

The main valley was rimmed by steep mountains. But near the south end of it side-valleys opened to the east. At the end of the farthest one, two snow-covered peaks reared up, with a high pass between them. If the wolves could reach it, they might escape that way.

But the snow-*grawls* were driving the wolves toward the head of a closer valley. Tok dived down into it. Its walls were steep, without many trees, and it ended in a sheer wall of rock. There was no way out. If the wolves ran into it, the Two-Legs would corner them and shoot them down.

Riding the gale, Tok shot back down the canyon. The wolves were near the entrance now, the snow-*grawls* closing in on both sides driving them toward it. Tongues lolling, eyes glazed, the wolves followed Malik blindly, trying to escape the blazing lights, the terrible roar.

Tok swooped low over the big wolf's head. "Not this valley!" he screamed over the roar of the *grawls*. "It's a trap—you'll all be killed!"

Malik's eyes rolled wildly up at him. "My pack!" he panted. "Mustn't die . . . My fault!" Then, to Selaks, who was running on his right flank, "Break through! Run straight on, no matter what!" He put on a burst of speed. Veering left, he ran straight toward the nearest snow-*grawl*. Selaks and the others swerved after him.

With a hoarse scream, Tok swooped low over the *grawl*, trying to distract the riders. As he tumbled in the air to swoop again, a firestick exploded and he saw Malik falter, but the wolf charged on. At full speed he threw himself at the riders. The *grawl* swerved, then turned over in the snow, its light glaring upward into the black sky. Malik had landed on top of one of the riders and the two of them rolled over and over in the snow.

The rest of the pack streaked past the overturned *grawl*, vanishing into the darkness beyond.

"Run, Malik!" yelled Tok, as the other rider struggled to his feet and aimed his firestick. Malik sprang away, but the blast of the weapon struck his side, spinning him around and flinging him to the ground in a crumpled heap.

The other *grawls* were roaring to a halt beside the fallen one. There was a babble of voices.

Malik lay in the shadows outside the circle of blazing light. Tok dropped down beside him. The big wolf's coat was black with blood, but he managed to open his eyes. "My pack," he gasped, "did they . . . ?"

"They broke free—*vór*," Tok said.

A light kindled in Malik's eyes for a moment, then died. He shuddered and lay still.

The Two-Legs righted the overturned *grawl*, muttering among themselves and glancing up at the sky. Then they turned their lights on Malik's body, and Tok flapped off hastily. He circled while they fastened it by the neck behind one of the *grawls*. Then the *grawls* snarled to life and sped off, towing the body behind them.

Tok wheeled away on heavy wings, as the concealing snow, too late, came down like a curtain on the valley.

Chapter 38

In the Dawn Time, First Vór and First Vóra
came to earth down the Wolf Trail in the sky.
Wolf spirits run home along it still, star by star.
                                        —Myths of the Lanna

Tok swooped back and forth through the flying snow, trying to locate the wolves. He found them waiting below the mountain wall at the south end of the valley.

"Where are the Two-Legs?" called Alkara. "I can't hear their *grawls*."

"They turned back," he told her.

"And Malik?" demanded Selaks as Tok landed on her shoulders.

"Dead," he replied. "The Two-Legs shot him after you escaped."

"Shot!" whined Selaks. "Oh, Malik!" Tok felt a shudder run through her body.

"Are you sure he's dead?" asked Alkara. "Not just wounded?"

"Yes." Tok shivered, trying to blot out the terrible image of Malik's body being towed away.

The wolves gazed at him in silence. Then, "He died like a *vór*," said Alkara. "He found his heart at last and saved the pack. We shall sing him on his way up the Wolf Trail."

Pointing their muzzles skyward, the wolves sang, sorrowing. When the song ended, Alkara led them along the side valley. She seemed to have shaken off her weariness and now set a fast pace.

Tok flew ahead to the *vóra*. "I saw high peaks beyond here before the storm closed in," he told her. "There must be a way between them, but I won't be able to find it in this snow."

Alkara seemed serene. "We will find the way. I'm sure now that our *numon* lies in your Raven Mountains. Malik would never accept that."

"No," agreed Tok.

"My brother was wrong about that and . . . all the rest," came Selaks's grieving voice from behind them. "But he was ever brave and strong. That's the way I will remember him now."

"What about Durnál?" Tok asked Alkara, glancing back at the big black wolf loping at the end of the line.

She snorted. "Some folk can't smell *skiffet* right under their noses."

Tok puzzled about that for a while, then gave it up.

At last a steep slope appeared out of the driving snow ahead of them. They had reached the end of the side valley, and began to climb its southern slope. Soon they were among the trees, and the storm became less fierce, the snow less deep. On and on they went, always upward.

At last they reached the tree line, where the forest gave way to rocky heights clad in snow.

"Rest here a while," said Alkara. "The going will be harder once we leave the shelter of the trees."

"Great guts!" muttered Timmax, curling up in a snowbank. "It's hard enough already. I wish this blizzard would stop." Sirva glanced shyly at him. Then she went over and curled up against him. He nuzzled her affectionately.

Selaks gave a huff of surprise. "Well!" she said. "It looks like you're growing up fast, little brother. As for the blizzard, at least it's covering our tracks."

She found herself a spot under an evergreen and Tok settled down on a branch above her. He noticed that her eyes lingered on Durnál for a moment, but the lone wolf curled up away from the others as he always did. Selaks swept her brushy tail over her nose and closed her eyes.

Only Alkara did not rest. She stood at the edge of the trees, snow sifting down on her grizzled coat, staring up at the invisible heights above.

Was she Seeing? Tok wondered.

At dawn they began to climb again. If their instinct had not told them where the sun was, they would not have known that it was day. They climbed through a twilight of flying snow, the mountain peaks invisible above them.

"If only I could get above this, take a look around," muttered Tok. But there was no way he could fly straight into this strong a gale. He was having trouble enough clinging to the thick fur of Selaks's mane.

"Alkara knows the way. Haven't you noticed?" replied Selaks.

"How can she? She has never been here before!"

"There's more than one way of knowing. She's Seeing her way. Watch her."

Tok did, and it was as Selaks had said. Alkara seemed to have found a strange new strength. Refusing to let Durnál break trail, she pushed forward through chest-high drifts. While the others slipped and slid on the ice underneath, she never put a foot wrong. When there was a choice between two ways to go, she never hesitated. She climbed eagerly, leaving even Selaks behind.

The wind whined among the rocks, blowing streamers of snow into their faces. Tok's eyes crusted over, and he kept blinking his whitelids to clear them. Ahead, Alkara vanished and reappeared among the drifts.

Suddenly Selaks stopped short, and stared intently ahead. "I thought I saw . . ." she began, then she bounded ahead again.

"What?" demanded Tok, peering through the whirling snow. "How can you see anything if I can't?"

"It's something only a wolf can see," panted Selaks. "A strange white beast running beside Alkara—a spirit wolf made of snow. The Lanna have granted her a guide!"

The wolves climbed all day into the teeth of the storm. Around them, avalanches thundered down into unseen depths, and the wind buffeted them fiercely. It was as though the mountains themselves were trying to hurl them back down the pass. But through it all Alkara pushed forward. Heads down, ears lowered, the other wolves plodded upward in her footsteps.

Night fell, and still she didn't stop, though the pack

whined in complaint. She turned on them fiercely. "Don't you understand?" she snapped. "I have no time to rest!" Her eyes seemed to gaze through and beyond them. With a nimble bound, she plunged onward. Awed, the others stumbled after her.

At last the ground began to level out. By dawn the snow tapered off to a cloud of icy crystals sparkling in the air. As they came out on the far side of the mountains, the wind stripped the last of the clouds from the heights.

Suddenly Tok and the wolves found themselves looking down from the top of the world. Jagged snowy peaks rose on either side of them. Below rolled wave upon wave of lesser mountains and ridges. And in the blue distance rose a familiar shape.

Mount Storm! A wave of pure joy seized Tok. He sprang into the air and banked away on the dying gale. "The Raven Mountains!" he shouted, swooping and tumbling over the heads of the wolves. "Your new land!"

Alkara stood drinking in the view. Then she gave a long shuddering sigh. "It is exactly as I Saw it," she murmured. She turned to the others. "Now my task is truly done," she told them. "The rest is up to you, my wolves. To you most of all, *vór*," she added, turning to Durnál. "A new land, a new life. Your *numon* is before you now, not behind you."

"But . . . aren't you coming with us?" Selaks asked her.

The old wolf shook herself. "No. My *numon* was to see the new land. It is enough," she said. "But you, Selaks, will See much farther."

"I?" Selaks's eyes widened.

Alkara walked over to a nook among the rocks at the crest of the pass. She curled up in the snow, and laid her muzzle on her paws, her eyes gazing out over the Raven Mountains. Moment by moment her breathing slowed. At last her eyes closed, and her breathing stopped.

"She has joined the Lanna," said Durnál, looking down at the still figure.

Timmax and Sirva whined as a gust of wind blew a veil of powdery snow around Alkara.

But Selaks's eyes were shining. "I See!" she cried. "I See two spirit wolves running on the Wolf Trail!"

Durnál threw back his head and began to sing. One by one the others chimed in, their voices weaving a chord of farewell. Above them, Tok danced his good-bye on the wind.

When the last echoes of the song died away among the peaks, the other wolves turned toward Durnál. He stood ears pricked, tail held high, to see what they would do. Only his green eyes moved, locking for a moment with the eyes of each of them in turn. Their tails began to wag, and they rushed forward, tumbling over each other like pups in their eagerness. They nibbled his muzzle and rubbed against his flanks. Durnál ran his tongue out, laughing, as he accepted their homage.

Overhead, Tok turned a somersault in the air.

Part 6

The Return
of the
Grey Lords

Chapter 39

To live is to dance; to dance is to live.
                                        —Raven proverb

Below the branch Tok sat on, the wolves drowsed contentedly, their bellies bulging with meat from a deer they had just killed. Still famished from their long journey, they had eaten all of it.

Timmax was looking puzzled. "Have you noticed something strange about the deer in these mountains?" he asked. "They run as if they don't expect to be chased!"

Selaks glanced up from licking her fur. "Maybe they don't. Tok says there haven't been wolves here for years beyond memory. The deer have gotten lazy."

"We'll soon get them in shape," promised Durnál, grinning.

There were barks of laughter from the others.

Tok shifted his claws on the branch. All around them was the drip and trickle of a sudden thaw. On the tree he sat in, the leaf buds were swelling, though they weren't nearly ready to burst. He turned his head this way and that, listening. A cardinal was singing in the next tree, and not far away, a woodpecker was hammering away on a hollow stub. Crows cawed in the distance. But he heard no raven voices.

When would he see them? When? Now that he was so close to home, he could hardly bear to wait any longer. Peering upward through the canopy of branches, he scanned the sky for circling black shapes. Days and days had gone by since the wolves had come down from the high pass, and still he had found no ravens. The need to see their shaggy forms and hear their rough voices was an ache inside him.

But when he did meet them, what then? Would they be strangers, or would they know who he was? If they did know, would they listen to him, or would they just try to kill him on sight, as the sentence of the Kort gave them the right to do?

Tok roused his feathers and settled them again. There was no use brooding about it. The only thing he could do now was go on looking for them.

He dropped off the branch and landed on Selaks's back.

"Oof!" she grunted. "You're heavier than ever when you're full of meat."

"We have to move on," he said. "My only hope is to get to the Kort Tree and claim justice. Then I can tell them about you. Otherwise, sooner or later I will be attacked, and I may never get a chance to explain."

She lifted her head and looked toward Durnál. "I'm ready to go. What do you say, *vór?*"

Durnál stood up and shook himself from nose to tail.

"Lead on, Tok," he said. "We owe you that much and more."

"Is there time for one last pick at the carcass?" asked Timmax, scrambling to his feet.

Selaks prodded his belly with her nose. "Carcass? What carcass? There's nothing left but gnawed bones. But don't worry. There seem to be more deer in these mountains than fleas on a hare. We'll eat well wherever we go."

Sirva sighed and got up too. "Is it far, raven?" she asked.

Tok hesitated. At least three mountain ridges lay between them and the lands around Mount Storm. He didn't know this part of the country well, or how hard or easy the going might be on the ground. "Two days' journey, maybe more," he guessed.

The wolves set off at a comfortable trot, but soon had to slow down because of heavy snowdrifts. Half crazy to help them move faster, Tok flew ahead, scouting the route.

"If we'd only got here sooner!" he fretted. "You could have run more easily on the streams and ponds. But now the ice has gone soft in the thaw."

On the higher slopes, though, it was very cold and the wolves made better progress over the crusted snow.

○

"Only two more ridges to cross after this," Tok promised them, when they threw themselves down to rest later that day.

"Do you really think bringing us here will make any difference?" Selaks asked. "To you, I mean, with the other ravens?"

"I don't know," Tok confessed. "They may kill me any-way."

Durnál's eyes narrowed. "It sounds risky. And we won't be able to help you against other birds. Are you sure you want to do this?"

"What choice do I have?" asked Tok. "If I want to clear my name I have to take the chance!"

"Ah, yes," Durnál sighed. "Your name. And that fierce *kora* of yours. But is it worth your life, Tok?" The *vór* gazed up at him questioningly.

Tok thought for a long moment before he answered. Then, "If that's the price I have to pay," he said.

Selaks gave an annoyed yip. "Why must you be so stub-born?" she demanded. "Why can't you just stay here, out of danger? Or... we could find another place without ravens."

"But I have to be with other ravens," said Tok. "It's not just my name that matters. It's the dancing—it's my life. And though it's wonderful to dance alone, Skyah meant ravens to dance together." He stropped his beak thought-fully on the branch he sat on. "It's taken me a long time to understand that," he admitted. "I used to think dancing was just showing off. But the skydance means more than that. Much more." Then he added, "There's something else, too. At the start of my journey all I thought about was my name and getting revenge against my enemies. Finding the Grey Lords would prove my *kora*. I still want that. But it's even more important to show other ravens how we and wolves belong together, can help each other. That's why I have to go back."

"I still don't like the chance you're taking," grumbled Selaks. "I've gotten used to having you about, you know."

The wolves questioned him no more. After a brief rest they moved on again. Then, toward dusk, Tok heard a familiar chorus coming closer. Every feather on his body prickled with excitement. Ravens! Ravens at last!

Moments later, a mob of ravenets tumbled by overhead, calling and chasing each other. They paid him no heed.

Wistfully, Tok watched them out of sight.

"And I thought we wolves were noisy folk!" said Selaks. "What were those crazy birds doing?"

"Going to roost," Tok told her, remembering. "They're young ones without territories. As I was, before I had to leave. They'll settle down for the night in some big tree, listen to stories, share news about food . . ." He blinked his whitelids, fighting back old memories.

The wolves trotted on through the night, stopping now and then to rest. Tok rode on Selaks. By now he was used to night journeys.

By late morning they were well down into the next valley. Now the peak of Mount Storm could be seen beyond the next ridge.

"That's it!" Tok told the wolves. "That's where we're going. The Kort Tree is in a glade at the foot of that mountain."

He broke off, staring upward. High overhead he could see a crowd of ravens—dancing! A wave of longing swept over him. He had to join them! They'd be strangers, ravenets from last year's fall flights. The lords and ladies would be nesting now, too busy to dance. These ravens wouldn't know about him. It should be safe enough.

"I'm going up!" he cried to Selaks, lifting away.

"Are you crazy?" she yelped, leaping up on her hind paws as if trying to catch him. "You said other ravens might kill you!"

Ignoring her, Tok powered himself upward with heavy beats of his wings. At last he would be among his own kind again, part of the Great Dance to Skyah! Eagerly he banked toward the nearest birds, tumbling in the air as he joined their flight pattern.

As he had guessed, they were strangers, and younger than he was. Two brownish ravenets curiously eyed his bigger size, his gleaming black adult feathers.

"Are you a lord, sir?" one asked respectfully.

"Just a stranger," Tok told him, settling in wingtip to wingtip with them. Lazily the three of them banked and rolled in the air.

"Not bad," croaked one of the young birds. "For an elder."

"Elder, am I? Well, I can still dance for Skyah. Try this!" challenged Tok. He somersaulted, then dropped like a falling leaf, spinning round and round as he fell through the air. Instantly, the others followed.

"You're no numb-wing!" the young bird admitted as they pulled up and flew level with the treetops. More birds joined them as they found a thermal and circled higher on it.

As he rose, Tok glanced down to check his position, then his wings stiffened for a moment in midair. He hadn't meant to come this far south. Mount Storm now loomed in the near distance. The wolves would be far behind him now, with no one to lead them!

Dropping out of formation, he banked toward the north. On his way he passed another bird riding the thermal up. This was no youngster. In fact, he looked faintly familiar. One of Grakk's followers!

The other raven recognized him at the same moment, and swerved in the air. "Tok!" he croaked in disbelief. "Tok the murderer! The outcast!" Then, at the top of his voice, "Mob him, kill him! He's doomed by the sentence of the Kort!" He banked toward Mount Storm, screaming as he went.

Instantly other voices picked up the chorus.

"Which one is Tok?" a bird shouted through the din.

"That big fellow there. He's an outcast, an exile under doom of death. And he dares to come back!" Grakk's follower yelled down the wind.

Croaking with excitement, the ravens began to gather around Tok, edging closer in the air, buffeting him with their wings.

"Don't let him get away!"

"Drive him down!"

Their harsh voices echoed over the valleys. Now more columns of birds began to rise like coils of black smoke from the woods below.

He'd never make it back to the wolves now, Tok thought desperately. Why, oh why had he been such a fool?

The ravenhorde was driving him downward. Suddenly

one bird struck at Tok, rolling away before he could strike back. More blows followed. Tok twisted and rolled in the air, trying to shake off his tormentors. They were forcing him to fly east now, away from the direction he wanted to go.

His only hope was the Kort Tree. Folding his wings, Tok dropped from the sky like a stone. His move caught his pursuers by surprise and he gained a few moments. Then, with shrieks of rage they plunged after him. Tok pulled out of his dive at the last possible moment and shot away between the treetops, doubling back west toward Mount Storm. The wind was rising, lashing the trees and awakening the deep roaring voice of the forest. Branches seemed to reach for him as he sped through. If he made a mistake now he'd break a wing and that would be the end, he told himself. He flew without thinking—there was no time for that. Drawing on deepest instinct he banked and rolled wildly as branches whipped past him. Beneath his fear a reckless excitement drove him on. They hadn't caught him yet. Let them try!

On and on he hurtled, scarcely seeing the branches now, except as a greenish blur around him. Ahead he glimpsed Mount Storm, its summit lost in clouds. The glade—where exactly was the glade? Tok thought desperately, hearing the growing clamor of raven voices above and behind him. If he guessed wrong, he'd get no second chance once he broke cover. Mobs of ravens were circling above the treetops. Would they suspect his purpose?

He changed course slightly, trusting the map of the forest he carried inside his head. At last he broke free of the trees. His instinct was right. There at the end of a long glade stood the Kort Tree. Above it circled the raven-horde, the mass of its bodies blotting out the sun, its harsh voices echoing in the air.

Tok sped for the Tree. A scream went up from hundreds of throats, and ravens hurled themselves at him from every direction. They struck at him, spinning him in the air, almost knocking him to the ground. With the last of his strength he managed to reach the Tree. Bruised, battered, he clung gasping to the Speaker's Branch.

Suddenly the chorus of raven voices stilled.

"Justice! I claim the justice of the Kort!" Tok shouted into the angry silence.

Chapter 40

The last of the night before dawn
is the test of heroes.

—Sayings of the Tellers

The ravenhorde settled into the trees around the glade. An ominous sound was heard as they karked and quorked among themselves, clattering their beaks in rage. Not daring to attack him in the Kort Tree, they could only wait to see what would happen next.

The wait was short. The lords and ladies of the nearest territories were the first to arrive. Lord and Lady Korak wheeled in on silent wings and landed in the Tree. They were followed by another lord and lady Tok didn't know. Then Groh and Tok's mother swept in.

"Tok!" cried Karah. "Why did you come back? You know anyone can take your life now!"

"I'm looking forward to it," growled Lord Groh, raising his feather ears and glaring at Tok.

Tok stared up at the pair of them. His mother looked worn, he thought, her feathers less glossy than last year and her amber eyes dull. Groh looked bigger and more menacing than ever.

"I came back because I had to," he told Karah. "I've found something—something important."

"A likely story," sneered Groh. "He has probably committed a murder somewhere else and is trying to hide here."

"Landing on the Kort Tree yelling for justice doesn't look much like hiding to me," said a calm voice. Lady Korak dropped down onto the Speaker's Branch beside Tok. "You may be a fool but you are not a coward," she told him. Then she roused her feathers. "I am still Speaker for this Kort. What do you want? Why have you dared to return?"

Tok opened his beak to reply, then stopped. Grakk had just landed in the Tree. He sat, feathers puffed up, staring down at Tok. He was a lord, then, Tok thought bitterly. The lying murderer had been rewarded well.

Two more ravens now swooped down over the glade. Tarkah! thought Tok, staring at the larger one. He'd know her anywhere, though like him she was an adult now, her shining black feathers shot with blues and greens. Was she Grakk's lady?

"Tok!" she cried, wheeling past him. "I always feared you would come back, throw your life away!"

"Keep away from the Kort Tree," warned the Speaker, and Tarkah flapped away to land in a nearby evergreen.

Meanwhile, the other raven flew straight to Grakk and lit beside him. It was Laka. *She* was Lady Grakk! Tok's heart swelled with relief.

"I asked you, what do you want?" snapped the Speaker.

"If you have nothing to say, you are wasting our time. The sentence on you will be carried out at once."

"Lords and ladies of the Kort!" cried Tok. "Last year you condemned me for nest-breaking and murder. I told you then that I was innocent and I tell you the same now!"

"He can't prove it!" yelled Grakk. "We all saw the dead nestling he cached!"

With a papery rustle the lords and ladies shifted their feathers, and clacked their beaks angrily.

"The decision of the Kort was wrong," said Tok. "I have come to demand justice. If I can prove I have done a deed of valor, one that benefits ravenkind, will you declare me *kora*?"

"What deed could be worth that?" shouted Groh. "He murdered my nestlings!"

"I am no murderer," retorted Tok. "Lady Groh herself knows that. She told me so. Didn't you, Mother?" he added, gazing up at her.

"I did," said Karah. Groh glared at her, and gave her a buffet with his wing. But Karah held her head high. Stepping away from him on the branch, she went on, "The evidence against Tok must be false. I know in my heart my son would not kill my nestlings." Her wings drooped. "I should have said so at Tok's trial. But I had no proof of his innocence. I was half-crazed with grief, too, and did not want to contest with my lord."

A murmur went around the Kort. Lady Korak gazed at the others, trying to sense their mood. "It means much that Lady Groh speaks for you now," she said, turning back to Tok. "But you are still under sentence. Yet I think we should at least hear of this deed of yours."

"Thank you, my lady," said Tok. "After you hear me, if you do not find me *kora* you can kill me as you please. I will not try to flee or resist."

The Speaker's eyes flashed. "You gamble your life against your deed? We ravens like such risks!" Her eyes swept the Kort, where many birds nodded approvingly. "Very well," she went on. "The Kort accepts your bargain. What deed have you done to prove your *kora?*"

"I have found the Grey Lords, and brought them back with me."

A muttering went around the glade.

"Grey Lords?"

"They're nothing but a legend of the Tellers. A winter's tale for ravenets!"

"You are wrong!" cried Tok. "The Grey Lords are real. They still live in far lands, just as they once did here before the Two-Legs killed them. And our Tellers are right—they are our natural partners, fierce hunters who open prey so we ravens can feed. Think what that means, lords and ladies. No more hungry winters, no starving nestlings in spring . . ."

"Nonsense!" shouted Groh.

"Even if the Grey Lords do exist, why would they help us?" asked the Speaker.

"Because Skyah made it so," said Tok. "You will see."

"Where are these mighty birds, then?" sneered Groh. Yet he cast a nervous eye skyward as he spoke.

"They are not birds at all. We have been wrong about that. They are swift, yes. Grey, yes—or at least, some of them are. And they sing. But the Grey Lords are four-footed animals, wolves. They call themselves the Lanna."

There was an uproar in the Kort Tree and around the glade. The Speaker waited for it to die down, then she said, "You say you have found these amazing creatures, brought them here. Where are they, then?"

Groh laughed harshly. "They are nowhere, my lady. Because they do not exist. He is lying!"

"Of course he is!" Grakk dropped down closer to the Speaker's Branch. "Just as he lied about killing Lord Groh's nestlings."

"The Grey Lords are a day's journey away," said Tok. "In my foolish haste to dance with my own kind again, I left them behind. They travel more slowly than we, on four paws, not on wings."

"Listen to him, lords and ladies!" protested Groh. "He claims he has found these creatures, but he has no proof. If we let him go we can be sure no Grey Lords will ever arrive. They are nothing more than an old tale."

"Be silent!" snapped Lady Korak, glaring at him. "*I* speak for the Kort, Lord Groh!" The Speaker turned back to Tok. "What you tell us is strange and wonderful indeed—if it is true."

"It *is* true, my lady."

"We have only your word for that. We must see these Grey Lords for ourselves. Then we will know if you have done the deed you claim. If not, your life is forfeit. You agreed to that."

"The Grey Lords will come. Let me go and bring them to you."

"Oh ho!" cried Grakk. "That would be the last anyone would see of this liar. He has defied the Kort by coming here. Don't let him sneak away now!"

The Speaker nodded. "In this, Lord Grakk is right. Tok has defied the Kort. He must stay here until the Grey Lords come."

"But they don't know the way!" protested Tok. "They are still far to the north, beyond the mountain ridge."

"A likely story!" taunted Grakk.

Rage seized Tok. "Liar! Murderer!" he yelled, bounding into the air.

"Stay where you are!" snapped the Speaker.

Tok dropped back onto the branch.

"You may not threaten members of this Kort, Tok," she went on. "And you must stay where you are until your Grey Lords arrive." She glanced up at the sun. "I give you until dawn tomorrow. If they still have not come by then, the sentence of the Kort will be carried out."

Dawn! Tok's heart sank. Fleet as his wolves were, the distance was great. He peered at the sun, which hung low over the mountains. Soon it would be dusk. How could the wolves find their way to him in the dark?

Wings blackened the sky as the ravenhorde dispersed. Tok watched Tarkah wing away with the others. She hadn't believed him either. The thought was like a stone in his heart.

"Till dawn," muttered Groh, sweeping past him. "Then I'll split your chest with my beak!"

Two guard ravens settled low in the branches of the Kort Tree.

306

"I won't try to get away," Tok told them.

They stared back at him grimly, but made no answer.

The trees around the glade stood empty now, and all was silent except for the distant hooting of an owl. The sound reminded him of Kaa. How impatient he had been when Kaa tried to be his friend, thought Tok. But Kaa was gone. And now Tarkah had turned against him. It would have meant much to have a friend beside him now, at the end of things.

A sudden thought struck him. "Where is Lord Pruk?" he asked one of the guards.

"Dead. He starved this last winter," came the gruff reply.

Starved! Poor Pruk, thought Tok. Another friend gone.

Dusk settled over the forest. Tok watched the last light fade from the peak of Mount Storm, while darkness filled the valley below to the brim. His last night, he thought, ruffling his feathers. He had gambled and lost. Selaks and the others would come, he knew they would. But by the time they got there it would be too late. If only he had stayed with them!

The rising moon was full now, the Moon of Nestlings set in a notch between two mountain peaks. The moon of his leaving the Raven Mountains . . . He stared up at the raven on it. Fool! he told it. You tried to do the impossible too. We both failed.

At least the Kort knew about the wolves now, he thought. The old partnership would live again. Some day his name would be *kora*.

The thought comforted him a little. But despite what

he had said to Durnál, he wasn't ready to die. He wanted to go on living. And dancing. But if he could not. . . . He drew himself up. If he had to die, he would remember Kaa's courage and the brave wolves who had followed him through so much. He must try to be worthy of them.

Slowly the night wore away. The moon sank below the western mountains and a pale cold light began to grow in the east. The guard ravens stirred and stretched. Then came a heavy swishing sound that grew until the air was astir with the beating of many wings. The ravenhorde was returning.

Chapter 41

Truth before vengeance.
                        —Wisdom of the Kort

Tok drew a deep breath and folded his wings tightly around his body. In the half light, the horde settled into the woods around him, while the lords and ladies of the Kort took their places in the Tree.

"Well, Tok?" challenged the Speaker. "Where are your Grey Lords?"

"They are coming, my lady. I know they are," said Tok.

Suddenly Tok's mother dropped down on the branch beside them. "I believe Tok," she said to the Speaker. "Can we not wait a little longer?"

"Very well," said Lady Korak.

The sky grew brighter and a rim of fire appeared on the horizon. Slowly the globe of the sun appeared, kindling the clouds. The snow turned pink against the blackness of the forest all around.

"It is past dawn, Speaker," shouted Groh. "What are we waiting for?" The Kort muttered among themselves and stirred restlessly on their branches.

"Tok—" began the Speaker.

Then from the depths of the forest rose a high keening wail. Another voice joined it. And another and another. On and on they sang, building on each other, braiding shimmering strands of sound. The song hung in the air for a long moment before it faded away.

The ravens stirred on the branches, peering into the woods.

"What was *that?*" demanded the Speaker.

"The Grey Lords, the Singers," cried Tok. "They are here!"

Out of the shadowy woods the wolves came bounding, black and white, grey and tawny. And riding on the black wolf's back . . .

"Tarkah!" cried Tok. "How did you find them?"

"You said they were to the north, beyond the mountain ridge," she said. "I flew low in circles and called and called. Then at last I heard strange singing."

"She's a good guide," said Durnál. "We would not have found you without her." He stared up at the assembled ravens, who gazed back, beaks agape.

"You really are the Grey Lords?" demanded the Speaker.

"Ravens call us so," replied Durnál.

"You hunt? You open prey and share with ravens?"

Selaks gave a bark of laughter. "Let's just say ravens *take* a share," she said.

"And torment us and pull our tails when they're in the mood," Sirva put in, with a sly glance at Tok.

"*That's* true!" agreed Timmax. He glanced around the

310

clearing, his eyes widening at the boughs weighted down with ravens. "Gristle and gore!" he muttered. "It's going to take a lot of deer to feed this bunch!"

"I think it is time for the Kort to vote," said the Speaker. Snipping a twig from the branch with her beak, she held it in one claw. "Lords and ladies, if you believe Tok's deed proves his *kora*, drop your twigs." Her own was the first to fall.

There was a rapid patter of twigs on snow. When the voting was over, only three birds still held their twigs. Grakk and Laka and Groh. The ravens around them drew away a little, shuffling sideways on the branches.

"You three disagree with the rest of us, as is your right," the Speaker said coolly. "But all of us know one thing, and that is that *kora* cannot change. A raven who is *kora* has always been *kora* and always will be." She stared at Grakk. "Tok has proved himself. He is *kora*. So he was also *kora* when you accused him of nest-breaking and murder. Your evidence must have been false."

Grakk shifted on his branch, his eyes darting from one pair of accusing eyes to the next.

"We cannot prove that," the Speaker went on. "So you remain a lord, free to nest and raise young on your territory. But from this day your *kora* is suspect. You will never have honor among us again. You are no longer a member of this Kort!"

The other ravens clattered their beaks and muttered their approval of her words.

"Shame on him!"

"*Unkora, unkora!*"

Amid a storm of hisses, Grakk took wing and slipped away into the forest. With a frightened glance around the Kort, Laka followed him.

Next the Speaker turned to Groh. "Perhaps you were too ready, as we all were, to believe false evidence, Lord Groh," she told him. "But that is not a crime. The Kort has no quarrel with you."

Groh roused his feathers and lifted his ears. "But I have a quarrel with *him!*" he shouted, glaring down at Tok. "If the Kort gives me no justice, I'll take it myself!" He launched himself at Tok and knocked him from the Speaker's Branch with a blow of his heavy beak.

Tok seized him as he fell, and the two birds tumbled to the snow, clawing each other.

"No!" screamed Tok's mother.

"Stop, Groh!" ordered the Speaker.

The two of them drew apart for a moment. "Let me fight him, my lady!" yelled Tok. "For my dead father's sake. *He* is the one Groh harmed most. First Groh lied about him, then murdered him and stole his *kora!*"

"You are the liar!" sneered Groh. "And your mother cannot save you this time." He struck at Tok, and his beak opened a gash on Tok's head.

Selaks gave a bark of rage and bounded forward.

"No!" snapped Tok, shaking blood from his eyes. "I must finish this!"

The wolves whined, but drew back to allow space for the duel.

Spreading his wings, Tok struck back at Groh, grappling with his claws. The two rolled over and over.

A whirlwind of rage drove Tok, yet at the center of it he felt cold calmness. They were better matched now than last year, he thought grimly. Groh was still bigger, but Tok sensed that he himself was faster. It would have to be enough.

He slashed at his enemy, but Groh jumped out of reach. The two glared at each other, wings half spread, beaks agape. Then they sprang together again. Groh's beak landed a blow on Tok's chest where his old wound had healed. The burning pain took Tok's breath away, and before he could recover, the bigger bird had him down and pinned by one wing.

"Now you die," gloated Groh, his cold eyes staring into Tok's. Again his beak punched into Tok's chest.

Gasping, Tok scooped air with his free wing, flipping himself over Groh's back, striking down with his claws.

With a yell, Groh twisted away, and Tok's other wing came free. Now he was over Groh, battering Groh's head with his beak and striking with his claws. Black feathers showered onto the snow. He could feel the older bird beginning to weaken. Turning, he buffeted him with his wings, forcing him backward. At last he had him down.

"How do you like death now, my lord?" Tok growled. "Now that it has come for you!"

"Go ahead!" croaked Groh. "What are you waiting for?"

Panting, Tok held himself in check. If you kill him, he told himself, you'll never know . . .

"Tell me the truth and I will let you live," he hissed, glaring into Groh's eyes. "You lied to my mother about my father, didn't you!"

Groh made a sudden lunge, trying to escape. Tok shifted his grip, pinning Groh with one claw across his throat. "Did you lie?" he demanded.

"Yes," gasped Groh.

"Louder!" Tok moved his claw enough to let his enemy draw breath.

"Yes! I wanted a territory. There was none free. So I told Karah I had seen Rokan feeding on stolen caches while she and her nestlings starved."

"*You* stole the caches. *You* ate the food," said Tok contemptuously. "And after my father had grown weak enough you killed him. And even that wasn't enough. You destroyed his *kora* with your lies."

From every bough and branch, raven eyes stared down coldly at Groh.

"You are not worth killing," said Tok, stepping back.

Selaks bounded forward, and Tok managed to flutter onto her shoulder. Turning her head, she tried to lick the blood from his feathers.

Groh struggled to his feet, shaking snow from his wings.

"After what you have just admitted before us all, you are a lord no longer," the Speaker said sternly. "Karah may choose another mate if she will. Since Tok has spared you, I put it to the Kort that you should be exiled as he was, on pain of death if you ever come back."

The Kort muttered in agreement.

"That is not all," the Speaker went on. "Rokan's name must be restored to *kora*. We have done him a great wrong."

Once more twigs were snipped. Once more they fell to the ground. This time the vote of the Kort was unanimous.

"Go!" said the Speaker, glaring down at Groh. "Or we will hunt you down."

With a harsh cry, Groh struggled into the air, and beat away over the forest.

Now the Speaker turned to Tok's mother. "Have you anything to say, Karah?" she challenged.

"I want no new lord," said Karah, lifting her proud head. "Let someone else have the territory. I will become a Teller. And my first Telling will be the story of a noble raven betrayed." Gazing down at Tok where he sat on Selaks's back, she added, "Forgive me, son of Rokan. I should never have believed evil about your father."

Tok gazed up at her in joy. She had given him his father's name before them all, and he was whole at last.

Chapter 42

Four perfect circles made Skyah: bright sun, pale moon,
a raven's amber eye, and the shape of a story.
                                    —Myths of the Tellers

"You can't mean it! You can't!" Selaks glared up at Tok, who was perched on a pine branch over her head.

"I haven't seen you so angry since I found you in that trap," he teased.

"It isn't funny!" snapped Selaks. "You appear out of nowhere, tell us tales of far-off lands, drag us through a hundred dangers. And now you say you are going to leave us!"

The other wolves had been dozing after a hunt. Now they pricked up their ears.

"I *can't* stay here," Tok explained. "Ravens must leave their birthplace to find new homes. I only came back to bring you here."

"But your mother's territory—it's yours for the asking!"

"I can't take it. It would be *unkora.*"

"You and your precious *kora!*" said Selaks bitterly.

Tok said nothing. There was nothing he could say.

316

After a long moment, the angry light faded from Selaks's eyes. "Oh well," she sighed. "I suppose *numon* is *numon*."

"It's not as though you'll be short of ravens," Tok pointed out. For greedy quorks could be heard nearby where a mob of birds was picking the carcass of the deer the wolves had killed.

"But none of them is *my* raven," mourned Selaks.

"I know what you mean," said Durnál, getting to his feet and coming over. "I've grown fond of *my* raven these last few days. I suppose I'll be losing her now."

Tarkah flapped onto the *vór's* shoulder and tweaked one of his ears. "If our hero up there gets around to asking me," she said, with a sly glance at Tok.

"You mean you'd go with me?" Tok stared in amazement. "But my mother's territory is free now. You could choose any raven in these mountains for your lord!"

Tarkah fanned her wings. "Oh, they're such a dull lot. And I'm choosy." She fluttered up beside Tok. Raising her head feathers, she gave him a pert bow. Then she delicately began to preen him. Blissfully, he half closed his eyes.

Selaks watched them for a moment, head cocked. "Good," she said. "At least you'll have someone with sense to look after you. And speaking of choosing . . ." She turned her golden gaze on Durnál.

He stared back, puzzled.

Selaks stamped her forepaws. "May the Lanna grant me patience!" she barked.

Now Timmax and Sirva came over, tails wagging

slowly. Sirva gave Timmax a nudge with her shoulder.

"Bones, *vór*," the young wolf said. "Don't you think you need a *vóra?*"

Sirva gave a yip of agreement.

"A *vóra?* You mean . . . Selaks? But . . ." Durnál turned to the white wolf.

She met his eyes, tail waving. Her creamy coat glistened in the sun, and her eyes were dancing. Bounding forward, she nuzzled his neck and blew her warm breath into his face.

Durnál's deep eyes lit up. "Selaks! But I thought you . . ." The two of them touched noses, while Timmax and Sirva capered around them, paying homage.

"My *vór*, my *vóra*," said Tok, spreading his wings and bowing to them on his branch.

The wolves looked up at him.

"Where will you go, Tok?" asked Durnál.

"East," he said. "As far as the mountains go, as long as there are ravens."

"Well, wolves have big families, you know," said the *vór* with a glance at his *vóra*. "Soon there will be many wolves here. So when you are settled in your new home, send to us, and we will come."

"I will," said Tok. He dropped down onto Selaks's back.

Turning her head she ruffled his feathers with her nose. "Fair flight, Skydancer," she said.

"Good hunting, *vóra*."

Tok launched himself into the air. He heard the swish of Tarkah's wings behind him as she followed.

Below them the wolves began to sing, their voices rising in a haunting chorus of farewell.

Tok and Tarkah circled upward, wingtip to wingtip. High over the forest-black ridges they began to dance, diving and tumbling. Grasping each other's claws, they swung round and round as they fell, the wind whining through their flight feathers. Breaking off at the last possible moment, they zoomed over the treetops and rose again, soaring for pure joy. At last they climbed through a gap in the clouds above Mount Storm and vanished into the blue air.

About the Author

Sharon Stewart was inspired to write *Raven Quest* when the image of a black raven—riding on the back of a white wolf in a swirling snowstorm—flashed across her mind. The resulting story owes much of its resonance to actual research about ravens' long-standing relationships with wolves.

Ms. Stewart is also the author of *The Dark Tower, My Anastasia, Minstrel Boy,* and *The Darkside Stories.*